Beauty and the Baby
by Marie Ferrarella

'Would you like to hold the baby?'

Carson began to answer no, that the joy of being the first to hold this new life belonged to Lori. But one look at the tiny being and he knew he was a goner. He fell hard and instantly in love.

'Yes,' he murmured, and took the infant in his arms.

The baby was so light, she felt like nothing. And like everything. Carson had no idea that it could happen so fast, that love could strike like lightning and fill every part of him with its mysterious glow. But it could and it had.

Something stirred deep within him, struggling to rise to the surface. Self-preservation had him trying to keep it down, push it back to where it could exist without causing complications.

'She's beautiful,' he told Lori. 'But then, I guess that was a given.'

Social Graces
by Dixie Browning

Whether or not she was ready to admit it, she'd been as turned on by that hot, sweet-salty kiss as he was.

It occurred to him that he might have set his mission back a few days.

Or maybe not. Maybe now that he'd defused this crazy physical attraction, he could concentrate on doing what he'd come down here to do.

So there was some electricity sizzling between them. Roughly enough to light up Shea Stadium. It might help if he could take her to bed and make love until he was cross-eyed, but that wasn't going to happen.

It might also help if he could find whatever he was looking for and get the hell out—put a few hundred miles between them. But somewhere along the line, that idea had lost its appeal.

Available in August 2004 from Silhouette Desire

Beauty and the Baby
by Marie Ferrarella
(The Mum Squad)
and
Social Graces
by Dixie Browning

Tempting the Tycoon
by Cindy Gerard
and
Awakening Beauty
by Amy J Fetzer

Plain Jane & the Hot Shot
by Meagan McKinney
(Montana)
and
Charming the Prince
by Laura Wright

Beauty and the Baby
MARIE FERRARELLA

Social Graces
DIXIE BROWNING

All the characters in this book have no existence outside the imagination of the author, and have no relation whatsoever to anyone bearing the same name or names. They are not even distantly inspired by any individual known or unknown to the author, and all the incidents are pure invention.

First published in Great Britain 2004
Silhouette Books, Eton House, 18-24 Paradise Road, Richmond, Surrey TW9 1SR

ISBN 0 373 04992 7

51-0804

Printed and bound in Spain
by Litografia Rosés S.A., Barcelona

BEAUTY AND THE BABY

by

Marie Ferrarella

MARIE FERRARELLA

earned a master's degree in Shakespearean comedy and, perhaps as a result, her writing is distinguished by humour and natural dialogue. The RITA® Award winning author's goal is to entertain and to make people laugh and feel good. She has written a large number of books for Silhouette. Her romances are beloved by fans worldwide and have been translated into Spanish, Italian, German, Russian, Polish, Japanese and Korean.

To single mothers everywhere,
struggling to make a difference in their children's lives.
I wish you strength and love.

Chapter One

"You look tired," Carson O'Neill said.

Lifting her head, his sister-in-law smiled at him in response. Carson watched the dimples in both cheeks grow deeper. He wasn't a man who ordinarily noticed dimples. Involved in his work, he noticed very little these days.

But, in almost an unconscious way, he had become aware of a great many things about Lori O'Neill ever since fate and his late brother, Kurt, had sent the woman his way.

Ever since Carson could remember, he'd been a caretaker. It wasn't something he just decided to do one day, wasn't even something he admitted wanting to do. It was just something that needed doing, a hard fact of life. Like the way he'd looked after his mother after his father had left. And the way he'd always looked out for his younger brother. Or tried to.

And the way he'd wound up here, the director of

St. Augustine's Teen Center, a place that had too many kids and too little money, but was somehow—thanks to his all but superhuman efforts—still beating the odds and staying open.

Carson picked up a basketball that had whacked him against the back of his calves a second ago and tossed it toward a boy whose head barely came up to his chest. The boy flashed a sudden grin and ran off with his retrieved prize. As always, there was a game in progress.

His responsibilities weren't something he'd sought out. They'd just been there, waiting for him to walk in and take over. On his father's departure, his mother had all but become a basket case, so, at fifteen, Carson had become the family's driving force.

It wasn't easy. Kurt had been a screwup, albeit an incredibly charming one, and he'd loved Kurt, so he had done his best to help him out, to set him straight. Done his best to be there with silent support and not so silent money whenever the occasion had called for it. Which, as time progressed, was often.

Despite all Carson's efforts to set his brother on the right road, Kurt had managed to kill himself in his search for speed. ''Death by motorcycle,'' the newspaper had glibly reported on the last page in the section that dealt with local news.

Kurt's death, a year after his mother's, should have freed him from the role of patriarch, but it hadn't. There was Lori to think of. Somehow, it seemed only natural that he should take Kurt's pregnant wife under his wing.

Not that Lori had asked.

She was an independent, spirited woman, which was what he'd liked about her. But she was also pregnant and, after Kurt's untimely death, faced with a mountain of Kurt's debts.

The old adage, "When it rained, it poured," was never truer than in Lori's case. Less than a month after Kurt's death, the company for which Lori worked as a graphic artist declared bankruptcy, leaving her jobless. Carson found himself stepping in with both feet.

He'd stepped in the same way when he'd heard that the youth center, where he and Kurt had spent their adolescent afternoons, was about to close its doors because there was no one to take over as director and precious little financing.

His ex-wife, Jaclyn, had called him a bleeding heart when he'd told her he was leaving his law firm and taking over the helm at St. Augustine's Teen Center. He had discovered that being a lawyer left him cold and gave him no sense of satisfaction. Very quickly it had become just a means to an end. An end that had pleased Jaclyn a great deal, but not him. He'd needed more. He'd needed meaning.

The abrupt change in his life's direction had left her far from pleased. She had screamed at him, calling him a fool. Calling him a great many other things as well. He hadn't realized that she'd known those kinds of words until she'd hurled them at him.

The last label had been a surprise, though. She'd called him a bleeding heart. It showed how little, after five years of marriage, she really knew about him. He was pragmatic, not emotional. Taking over at the center had been something that needed doing, for so many reasons.

Besides, his heart didn't bleed, it didn't feel anything at all. Especially not after Jaclyn had left, taking their two-year-old daughter with them. His heart only functioned. Just as he did.

Just as Lori did, he thought, looking at her now. Except that she did it with verve. He motioned her to his office just down the narrow hall beyond the gym. The girls, whose game Lori had been refereeing, watched her for a moment, then went on without her.

He closed the door behind Lori, then indicated the chair in front of his scarred desk, a desk that was a far cry from the expensive one he'd been sitting behind three years ago.

Ordinarily, Lori seemed tireless to him, almost undaunted by anything that life threw her way. The only time he'd ever seen her be anything other than upbeat was at Kurt's funeral.

But even then, she'd seemed more interested in comforting him. Not that he'd allowed that, of course. He was his own person, his own fortress. It was the way it had always been and the way it would always be. He was who he was. A loner. Carson knew he couldn't be any other way even if he wanted to. Which he didn't.

''What?'' Lori finally pressed.

She tried to read her brother-in-law's expression and failed. Nothing new there. Carson had always seemed inscrutable. Not like Kurt. She could always tell what Kurt was thinking if she looked into his eyes for more than a moment. Usually, he was trying to hide something.

"I've been watching you," Carson told her. "You seem tired today," he repeated.

Lori shook her head, denying the observation. She prided herself on being able to soldier on, no matter what. These days, however, the weight of her backpack was steadily increasing. Especially since she was carrying it in front of her.

"No, I'm not tired. Just a wee bit overwhelmed by all that energy out there." She nodded toward the area right outside the closetlike room that served as the youth center's general office. There were a few small rooms around the perimeter, but the center's main focus was the gym. It was there that the kids who frequented the center worked out their aggression and their tension.

Then, with a sigh, she slowly lowered herself into the chair in front of his desk, trying not to think about the daunting task of getting up again. She'd face that in a minute or so. Right now, it felt really good to be able to sit down.

Maybe she was tired at that, Lori thought. But she didn't like the idea that she showed it.

Just beyond the door were the sounds of kids letting off steam, channeling energy into something productive instead of destructive. Kids who, but for Carson's concentrated efforts, would have no place to go except into trouble.

She looked at her brother-in-law with affection. Carson had given up the promise of a lucrative life so that others could have a shot at having a decent one. Lori knew that these kids, every one of them, could have been Kurt or Carson all those years ago. Her late husband had told her all about his younger years on their second date, giving her details that had chilled her heart. Life had been hard here.

Both brothers had managed to come a long way from these mean streets, although it was easy enough for her to see that Kurt's soul had been anchored in the quick, the easy, the sleight of hand that arose from living the kinds of lives that were an everyday reality for the kids who came to St. Augustine's Youth Center. In a way, Kurt had never left that wild boy behind. It was that wild boy, she thought, that had eventually killed her husband.

Carson was another matter. Levelheaded, steadfast, Carson had chosen to walk on the straight and narrow safe side. He'd worked hard, put himself through school as he took care of his younger brother and mother. A football scholarship had helped. He'd believed his destiny lay with becoming a lawyer. He'd worked even harder once he'd graduated. A prestigious law firm had offered him a position and in exchange, he gave the firm his all.

Until three years ago. Thirty-eight months to be exact. That was when her brother-in-law had made the most selfless sacrifice she'd ever witnessed. He'd left the firm he'd been with to take on the headaches of the youth center that had been his salvation. But it hadn't been without a price.

Carson had taken on burdens and lost a wife.

Kurt had been against the move. He'd told his older brother that leaving the firm was the dumbest thing a grown man could do. All of his life, he'd struggled to get them both away from this very neighborhood and now he was returning to it. Embracing it at a great personal and financial cost.

It had made no sense to Kurt. But then, Kurt didn't understand what it meant to sacrifice. He'd never been that selfless. That had always been Carson's department.

And Carson was Carson, steadfast once he made a decision, unmoved by arguments, pleas or taunts, all of which had come from his wife before she'd packed up and left with their two-year-old daughter. Leaving him with divorce papers.

Lori knew losing his little girl had been what had hit Carson the hardest, although you'd never know it by anything that was ever said. But then, ever since she'd met him, Carson had always played everything close to the vest.

It was a wonder his chest wasn't crushed in by the weight, she mused now, looking at him. His desk was piled high with paperwork, which he hated. The man took a lot on himself. Would have taken her on as well if she'd allowed it. Again, that was just his way.

But she wasn't about to become another one of his burdens. She was a person, not a helpless rag doll. After Kurt's death, she'd squared her shoulders and forced herself to push on. To persevere. There were plenty of single mothers out there. She'd just joined the ranks, that was all. She'd taken this job only after Carson proved to her that it hadn't been offered out of charity, but because he really needed someone to help him out. It wasn't the kind of work she was used to, but it and the Lamaze classes she taught helped pay the bills. And they would do until something better came along.

Lori reasoned that as long as she kept good thoughts, eventually something better *had* to come along.

"You're also more than a little pregnant," Carson pointed out. The sun was shining into the room. There were telltale circles beneath her eyes. She wasn't getting enough sleep, he thought. "Maybe you should take it easier on yourself. Go home, Lori."

But she shook her head. "Can't. Rhonda didn't show up today, remember?"

He frowned. Rhonda Adams was one of the assistants who helped out at the center. Rhonda hadn't been showing up a lot lately. Something else he had to look into. Trouble was, finding someone to work long hours for little pay wasn't the easiest thing in the world.

"That's my concern," he told Lori, "not yours."

She hated the way he could turn a phrase and shut her out. She wondered if he did it intentionally, or if he was just oblivious to the effect of his words. "It is while you sign my paychecks."

"I don't sign your paychecks, the foundation does," he corrected. Foundation money and donations were what kept the teen center going, but times had gotten very tight.

Her eyes met his. He wasn't about to brush her off. "Figure of speech, Counselor."

"Don't call me that, I'm not a lawyer anymore."

Maybe he was getting a little too crabby these days. And he wasn't even sure why. Carson backed off.

She looked at him pointedly. ''Then stop sounding like one.''

''I'm serious, Lori. Don't tire yourself out. You are pregnant, even if you don't look it.'' His eyes swept over her form. Petite, the pert blue-eyed blonde was small-boned and if you looked quickly, her slightly rounded shape looked to be a trick played by some wayward breeze that had sneaked into the drafty gymnasium and had snuggled in beneath her blouse, billowing it out.

Lori looked down at her stomach. She'd felt pregnant from what she judged was the very first moment of conception. Somehow, she'd known, just known that there was something different that set this time apart from all the other times she and Kurt had made love.

Carson's words to the contrary, she felt huge. ''Thanks,'' she quipped. ''But right now, I feel as if I look like I'm smuggling a Thanksgiving turkey out of the building.''

His mouth curved ever so slightly. ''Looks to me like there's going to be a lot of people going hungry at that Thanksgiving dinner,'' he commented. He looked at her stomach again, trying to remember. ''You're what, seven months along?''

''Eight, but who's counting?'' she murmured.

She was, Lori added silently. Counting down every moment between now and her delivery date, fervently wishing that there was more time. More time in which to get ready for this colossal change that was coming into her life.

No one talking to her would have guessed at her true feelings. She was determined to keep up a brave front. She had to because of the Lamaze classes she taught at Blair Memorial Hospital twice a week. The women who attended them all looked to her as a calming influence, especially the three single moms-to-be with whom she'd bonded. She smiled to herself. If the women she was instructing only knew that her nerves were doing a frenzied dance inside of her every time she thought of the pending arrival, they wouldn't find her influence so calming.

She missed seeing the three women who had made up the group she'd whimsically dubbed The Mom Squad. But C.J., Joanna and Sherry's due dates were now in the past. The three all had beautiful, healthy babies now, and, by an odd turn of events, they also now had men at their sides who loved them. Men who wanted to spend the rest of their lives with them.

All she had were Kurt's pile of debts, which were dwindling thanks to her own tireless efforts, but none too quickly.

Stop feeling sorry for yourself, Lori upbraided herself. *You also have Carson.*

She glanced at the man who looked like a sterner, older version of her late husband. She wasn't about to minimize the effect of having him in her life. Having her brother-in-law's support went a long way toward helping her get her world in order.

Not that she leaned on him—well, not so that he really noticed. But just knowing he was around if she needed him meant a great deal to her. Carson had offered her a job helping at the center when her company had left her almost as high and dry as Kurt's death had. And he'd also been instrumental in pulling strings and getting her the job teaching the Lamaze classes at Blair.

That and the freelance work she found as a graphic designer helped her make ends meet. More importantly, it kept her sane. Kept her grief at bay. Kurt had never been a steady, dependable man, but in her own way, she'd loved him a great deal. Forgiven him a great deal, even his inability to grow up and take on responsibilities. Even the dalliances she'd discovered. It had taken her time, though, to forgive him his death.

She was still working on it.

Kurt had had no business racing like that, no business wanting to shake his fist at death just one more time because it made himself feel more powerful. Not when he had her and a baby on the way.

She sighed quietly. That had been Kurt—thoughtless, but engaging. At times, though, it had worn a little thin.

''Eight?'' Carson echoed.

She looked at him, her thoughts dissipating. Carson had forgotten, she thought. But then, there were a lot more important things on his mind than her pregnancy. Like constantly searching for funding.

''You're that far along?''

She tried not to laugh at his incredulous expression. ''You make it sound like a terminal disease.''

Broad shoulders rose and fell in a vague fashion.

''I guess I just didn't realize...'' An idea came to him suddenly. ''I can have you placed on disability—'' He didn't know where he'd find the money, but something could be arranged.

Lori knew what he was trying to do. Contrary to her ex-sister-in-law's beliefs, Carson's heart was in the right place, but in her book, what he was proposing was nothing short of charity.

''I'm not disabled,'' she countered.

He heard the stubborn tone in her voice. Admirable though her independence was, there were times when his sister-in-law could be a mule. Like now. ''Yeah, I know, but technically maternity leave doesn't start until after you give birth.''

It was her turn to shrug. ''So, I'll stick around until I give birth.''

''You should be home, Lori, taking care of yourself.''

Carson didn't see what the problem was, or why she had him fighting a war on two fronts, one to get her a paid leave and one to get her to actually leave. When Jaclyn had been pregnant, she'd insisted on having a woman come in and do all the chores that she didn't normally do anyway. After Sandy was born, Hannah had stayed on to care for the house and the baby.

Jaclyn had always maintained that she was too delicate to put up with the drudgery of routine. He'd indulged her because he'd loved her and because she was his wife, his responsibility.

And because he'd been crazy about their child.

In hindsight, Hannah had taken care of Sandy better than Jaclyn ever could. Carson didn't mind paying for that. There was nothing too good for Sandy.

"I am taking care of myself," Lori insisted. She was accustomed to looking after herself. She'd been on her own since she was twenty. Even after she'd met Kurt, she'd been the one to take care of him, not the other way around. "If I stayed at home with my feet up, I'd go crazy inside of a week. Three days, probably." She smiled at Carson, appreciating his concern but determined not to let him boss her around. "Haven't you heard, Counselor? Work is therapeutic. Speaking of which, I'd better be getting back. There's a basketball game I'm supposed to be refereeing."

Bracing herself, she placed a hand on either wooden armrest and pushed herself up. The movement was a little too sudden, a little too fast. Lori's head started to spin.

The walls darkened. The small room began to close in on her.

A tiny pinprick of panic scratched her skin.

Lori struggled against the encroaching darkness, struggled to push the walls back out again. The effort was futile. The walls turned all black as they raced toward her with a frightening speed.

Perspiration beaded along her forehead.

And then there was nothing.

The next thing Lori knew, she felt herself being jerked up. Someone's arms were closing around her. There was heat everywhere, swirling about her.

She realized her eyes were shut.

With a mighty effort, she pushed them open again

and found herself looking up into Carson's dark blue, solemn eyes. They were darker than Kurt's eyes had been. And far more serious.

Lori tried to smile. Even that took effort. He was holding her. Holding her very close. Was that why it felt so hot all of a sudden?

Because he looked so concerned, she forced herself to sound light. "Didn't your mother ever tell you that if you scowl so hard, your face'll freeze that way?"

"My mother told me very little," he told her, his voice monotone.

She'd given him one hell of a scare, fainting like that. He had no idea what to think, what to do, other than to feel utterly helpless. Somebody needed to hand out instruction booklets when it came to women. Maybe even an entire desk encyclopedia.

Carson carried her over to the sagging, rust-colored leather sofa and placed her down as gently as he could manage.

His brow furrowed as he looked at her. "You want me to call a doctor?"

She caught hold of Carson's hand in case he had any ideas about acting on his question. "No, I want you to stop looking as if I'm about to explode any second."

His eyes were drawn to the small bump in her abdomen that represented his future niece or nephew. It was easy to forget Lori was pregnant at times. She looked so small. How could there be another human being inside of her?

Still, eight months was eight months. "Well, aren't you?"

She placed her other hand protectively over her abdomen. She could feel her baby moving. It always created a feeling of awe within her. Three months of kicking and shifting and she still hadn't gotten used to the sensation.

"No," she assured him, using the same tranquil, patient voice she used in the Lamaze classes, "not at the moment. Pregnant women faint, Carson." She used his hand to draw herself up into a sitting position. And then slowly to her feet. He hovered protectively around her. "It's one of the few pleasures left to them." Her smile was meant to put him at ease. "Don't worry about it."

His arm was around her, just in case her knees failed again. "Why do you have to be so damn stubborn?"

She flashed a grin at him. "Maybe that's what keeps me going."

He knew her well enough to know there was no winning. "At least let me drive you home."

Lori shook her head. "I brought my car."

"So?" Carson didn't see the problem. "I'll drive that."

She cocked her head, looking at him. The man was a dear. "Then how will you get back?"

He bit back an oath. "Do you have to overthink everything?"

"Can't help it." Her eyes sparkled as she smiled more broadly at him. "Must be the company I keep." She took a deep cleansing breath, then released it slowly, just as she'd demonstrated countless times in class. "There, all better. Really." But as she tried to walk away, she found that he was still holding her. Still unwilling to allow her to leave on her own power.

She was standing less than an inch away from him. Feeling things she didn't think that women in her condition were capable of feeling. At least not about men who weren't responsible for getting them into this condition in the first place.

Chapter Two

Lori looked down at her brother-in-law's hands. Strong, capable, and right now they were on either side of her arms, anchoring her in place. She raised her eyes to meet his.

"Um, Carson."

"What?" Impatience laced with annoyance framed the single word.

She gave a slight tug. "I can't go anywhere if you're still holding on to me."

By all rights, he knew he should drop his hands to his sides. She was a grown woman, more than capable of making her own decisions. He'd always believed in live and let live. At least on paper. But there were times when he felt she was being unnecessarily stubborn on principle.

"Maybe that's the idea," he told her.

"Eventually, one of us is going to have to go to the bathroom," she deadpanned. She glanced at her belly before looking up at him again. ''Because of my condition, my guess is that it'll probably be me.'' A glimmer of a smile began to play on her lips. ''I'd rather not have to ask for permission.''

Carson felt a trace of embarrassment and wasn't sure if it was for her or himself. In either case, Carson dropped his hands in exasperation. But not before issuing a warning.

''First sign of you fading, I'm taking you home, no matter what you say.'' His eyes did almost as good a job as his hands at pinning her to the spot. ''I'll be watching you.''

''I never doubted it for a moment.'' The smile on her lips widened, reaching up to her eyes. He tried not to notice and failed miserably. There was something about Lori's eyes that always got to him. They had been the first thing he'd noticed about her when they'd met. The killer figure had been the second.

''What?'' he finally bit off.

Surly on the outside, mushy on the inside, she thought fondly. ''I just never envisioned my guardian angel would look like a football player, that's all.''

Carson laughed shortly, his expression never changing. He'd been accused of being a lot of things in his time, but never an angel. Not even by his mother. Certainly not by his ex-wife.

''Got a hell of a long way to go before I'm anyone's guardian angel.''

There was something in his eyes for a fleeting moment. Sadness? It was gone the next, but it succeeded in moving her. Carson didn't like being touched. Because she was a toucher and firmly believed in the benefits of human contact, she patted his cheek anyway. The man had been there for her, awkward, but ready to help right from the start. She wasn't about to forget that.

"Not nearly as far as you think, Carson." She turned on her heel with more ease than he thought possible for a woman in her condition. "Gotta get back to work."

But just as she stepped out the door, a dark-haired young woman swung open the door to the rear entrance and came rushing down the hall. In her haste, she narrowly avoided a collision with Lori.

Eyes the color of milk chocolate widened as the woman came to an abrupt halt less than an inch shy of impact. She sucked in her breath.

"Wow, sorry about that." She patted Lori's stomach. "Could have had an early delivery, huh?"

Carson's arm had closed protectively around Lori, pulling her back just in time. He glared at the other woman. Good help was hard to find. It was even harder to get it to come in on time. "There wouldn't have been any danger of that if you'd come in at ten the way you were supposed to, Rhonda."

The woman, barely three years out of her own teens and in Carson's opinion not yet fully entrenched in the adult world, gave him a high-wattage, apologetic grin. "Sorry, boss. Chuck decided to have a temper tantrum this morning."

Carson's frown deepened. His aide's current flame reminded him a lot of Kurt. "Either tell your boyfriend to grow up, or get another boyfriend."

His words rolled off her back like an inconsequential Southern California summer rain.

''Sorry,'' she repeated. ''You don't pay me enough for that.''

From what he knew, Rhonda was allowing her boyfriend to crash on her sofa. Chuck was currently ''in between jobs,'' a place the man had been residing in from the time Carson had hired Rhonda. ''Won't have to if the next boyfriend could hang onto a job.''

The familiar words made him stop abruptly. He slanted a look at Lori, wondering if his exchange with Rhonda had scraped over any old wounds. He'd lectured Kurt about hanging on to a job more times than he could remember, especially after he'd married Lori. Kurt's response had always been to laugh off his words, as if he thought his older brother was joking. Kurt had maintained that he was still looking for his niche. As far as Carson knew, Kurt never found it.

''So he could be an old grump like you, boss man? Don't think so.'' Rhonda winked broadly at Carson, shoving her hands into the back pockets of her worn jeans. ''I'd love to stand around and talk like this, but some of us have work to do.'' She waved to one of the young teens and hurried across the gym.

Carson turned his attention back to Lori. ''There goes your excuse.''

Lori looked at him. ''You've lost me.''

Interesting choice of words, he thought. And very appropriate.

''Just what I'm trying to do. At least for the rest of the afternoon. Rhonda can handle the kids.'' He nodded in the direction of the front entrance. ''Go home and take a nap before class tonight.''

It surprised her that he remembered her schedule, but then, she supposed it shouldn't. Carson liked to keep tabs on everything. It felt confining to her at times, but he never realized it. She knew he meant no harm.

She pressed her lips together, debating. It wouldn't hurt to grab a few minutes of her own, she thought. She'd been up half the night working on a new Web design project that had come in. When opportunity knocked, she couldn't afford not to be home. ''You're not going to be satisfied until I go, are you?''

''Nope.''

''Okay, you win.'' She sighed, surrendering. ''Always like to keep the boss happy.''

Carson crossed his arms before his rock-solid chest. ''Right, and I'm the bluebird of happiness.''

Her eyes swept over him. He was still every inch the football player who'd made the winning touchdown in the last game he ever played. ''I wouldn't perch on any branches if I were you.''

He grumbled something not entirely under his breath. Laughing, Lori walked away, heading for the lockers on the other end of the first floor. She was very conscious of his watching her and tried very hard not to move from side to side the way she felt inclined to these days. Or to place a hand to the small of her back in order to ease the ache there. Pregnant women did that and Carson seemed to equate pregnancy with weakness. The more she fit his stereotype, the more determined he would be to try to convince her to stay home.

She wasn't the stay-at-home type.

Lori made her way to the shadowy row of lockers where the kids stashed their backpacks, books and various paraphernalia while they used the facilities. Once out of eye range, she pressed her hand to the small of her back and massaged for a moment. For a peanut, this baby was giving her some backache.

After stretching, she went to her locker. Wanting to seem more like one of the teens, Lori had taken a locker to store her own belongings there. Usually, she only had her purse.

She paused in front of the upper locker, trying to remember her combination. It was nestled in overcrowded memory banks that retained every number that had any bearing on her life. She seemed to retain all manner of numbers, not just her own social security number, but her late husband's as well. It was in there with her license plate and the phone numbers and birthdays of several dozen people who currently figured prominently in her life.

She smiled as the combination came to her. Turning the dial on the old lock three revolutions to the left, a muffled sound caught her attention. Lori stopped and listened.

The sound came again.

It was a sob, she was sure of it. The kind that was muted by hands being pressed helplessly over a mouth too distressed to seal away the noise.

Concerned, curious, Lori set the lock back against

the metal door and moved around to the other side of the bank of battered lockers.

Huddled in the corner, her long tanned legs pulled in tightly against her chest, was one of the girls she'd missed seeing today. The young girl sounded as if her heart was breaking. Boy trouble?

"Angela?"

The girl only pulled herself in tighter. Someone else might have felt as if they were intruding and left. Lori's mind had never worked that way. Anyone in pain needed to be soothed.

She took a few steps toward the girl. "Angela, what's wrong?"

"Nothin'." The girl jerked her head up, wiping away the tears from her cheeks with the heel of her hand. She tossed her head defiantly, looking away. Her silence told Lori that this was none of her business.

Lori chose not to hear.

For her, working at the center was a complete departure from life as she had known it. Here the word "deprived" didn't mean not having the latest video game as soon as it came out. "Doing without" had serious connotations here that involved ill-fitting hand-me-down clothing and hunger pangs that had nothing to do with dieting. Here, life was painted in bleaker colors.

But then, that was what the center was for, painting rainbows over the shades of gray.

"Sorry, but I think it's something." Angela kept her face averted. "The tears were a dead giveaway." Still nothing. "You know, for a pregnant woman, I can be very patient.'' Lori planted herself in front of the teenager. ''I'm not going away until you level with me and tell me why you're sitting here by yourself, watering your knees.''

Normally, her banter could evoke a smile out of the girl. But not today.

This was worse than she thought. With effort, Lori lowered herself to the girl's level. Her voice lost its teasing banter. ''C'mon, Angela. Talk to me. Maybe I can help.''

Angela shook her head. Fresh tears formed in the corners of her eyes. ''Nobody can help me.'' She sighed with a hopelessness that was far too old for her to be feeling. ''Except maybe a doctor.''

In that moment, Lori understood. She knew what had reduced the fifteen-year-old to this kind of despair and tears.

Lori placed her hand on the girl's shoulder. She was so thin, so small. And living a nightmare shared by so many.

''Are you in trouble, Angela?''

It was an old-fashioned term, Lori knew, but in its own way as appropriate today as it had been when it was first coined. Because a pregnant girl just barely in high school was most assuredly in trouble.

The sigh was bottomless. ''Yeah, I'll say.'' She sniffled. Lori dug into her pocket and pulled out a tissue, offering it to her. Angela took it and dried the fresh tears. Her voice quavered as she spoke. ''A hell of a lot of trouble.''

There were no indications that the girl was pregnant, but then, she hadn't looked it herself until just recently, Lori thought. "How far along are you?"

"I don't know." Angela shrugged restlessly. She looked down at the tissue. It was shredding. "It's been over two months, I think."

"You need to see a doctor."

Lori could see the beginning of a new thought entering the girl's eyes. "Yeah, somebody who can make this go away."

Lori shook her head. She didn't want Angela thinking that she was cavalierly suggesting she have an abortion. Decisions like that couldn't be made quickly.

"No. Somebody who can tell you what's going on with your body." She took the girl's hands into her own, forming a bond. "You might not be pregnant, it might be something else." Although, Lori thought, other possibilities could be equally as frightening to a fifteen-year-old as having a baby.

Thin, dark brown brows furrowed in confusion as Angela looked at her. "Like what?"

She didn't know enough about medicine to hypothesize. "That's what you need to find out. Do you have a doctor?"

Again the thin shoulders rose and fell, half vague, half defiant. "There's this doctor on Figueroa Street. I hear she's pretty decent."

Lori thought of her own doctor, a woman she'd been going to and trusted since she'd gotten out of college. Dr. Sheila Pollack had become more like a friend than just a physician. Angela needed someone like that right now, a professional who could clear up the mysteries for her and keep her healthy. Someone who could make her feel at ease rather than afraid.

''All right, go to her.''

Angela frowned. ''Word on the street is she don't do no abortions.''

The girl's mind was stuck in a groove that might not be the answer she needed, or would even want a few months down the line. ''Don't do anything hasty,'' Lori counseled. ''If you're pregnant, talk to your mother.''

Angela looked at her as if she'd just suggested she cover herself with honey and walk into cave full of bears. ''Yeah, right and have her kill me? No thanks.'' There was disdain in the teen's voice, as if she'd just lost all credibility in the young girl's eyes.

When she moved to put her arm around the girl's shoulders, Angela jerked away. Lori wasn't put off. She tried again, more firmly this time. Angela needed to get a few barriers down. ''She might surprise you.''

Angela blew out a mocking breath. ''Only surprises my mother gives me are the boyfriends she brings home.'' She shivered.

Had one of them put the moves on Angela? It wouldn't have been the first time in history something like that had happened. Lori tread carefully, determined to do the right thing and not fail this girl she hadn't known six months ago.

''If you want, I can talk to your mother for you.''

Angela buried her face in her hands. Lori sat beside her on the floor, stroking her hair. ''What I want is not to be pregnant.''

''First find out if you are pregnant.''

Angela slowly raised her head and looked at her. ''And then?''

''And then—'' With effort, Lori raised herself to her feet, ''—we'll go from there. One step at a time. When I see you tomorrow, Angela, I want you to tell me you have an appointment with the doctor.''

The girl nodded, scrambled up to her feet and wiped away the last of the telltale streaks from her face. She looked at her for a long moment. And then, slowly, just the barest of smiles emerged. ''You know, you're pretty pushy for a pregnant woman.''

''You're not the first one to tell me that.'' Lori slipped her arm around the girl's shoulder and gave her a quick hug.

She couldn't get Angela's face out of her mind. All through her instructions at the Lamaze class, Lori kept visualizing Angela in her mind's eye. She could almost see her here at Blair, taking classes to prepare for the monumental change that lay ahead of her.

The classes weren't enough, Lori thought. Not for her and certainly not for a fifteen-year-old.

The classes Lori gave with such authority taught woman how to give birth, but not what to do after that. Not really, not if she was being honest with herself. There was more to being a parent than knowing how to give a sponge bath to a newborn and that you should support their heads above all else. So much more.

Lori walked down the long, brightly lit corridor of the first floor of one of Blair Memorial's annex buildings. She'd waited until the last couple had left before locking up. The building felt lonely to her despite the bright lights. Seeing Angela huddled in a corner like that today had brought out all her own insecurities and fears. She had no mother to cower before, but there wasn't a mother to turn to for guidance, either.

She missed her mother, Lori thought not for the first time as she unlocked the door of her 1995 Honda Civic. Missed her something awful. For once, she lowered her defenses and allowed the sadness to come.

With a sigh, she started up her car. Leukemia had robbed her of her mother more than a dozen years ago. A heart attack had claimed her father just as she was in the middle of college. By twenty, she was all alone and struggling to make the best of it. And then Kurt had entered her life and she felt as if the sun had finally come out in her world.

Now here she was, eight years later, struggling all over again. The upbeat, feisty manner that the rest of the world saw was not always a hundred percent authentic. There were times which she really ached to have someone in her corner.

She had someone in her corner, Lori reminded herself as she turned down the hospital's winding path. She had Carson.

Leaving the hospital grounds, she fleetingly debated stopping by the old-fashioned Ice Cream Parlor where she and the other three single mothers had so often gone after classes, eager to temporarily drown their problems in creamy confections sinfully overloaded with whipped cream and empty, sumptuous calories.

It wasn't nearly as much fun alone.

Lori drove by the establishment. It was still open and doing a brisk business. The tables beside the bay windows were all filled. She wavered only for a moment before she pressed down on the gas pedal. The Ice Cream Parlor became a reflection in her rearview mirror.

She couldn't help wondering what the other women were doing tonight and if they still found motherhood as exciting as they had in the beginning.

Would she? Or was her only certainty these days the fact that she found the prospect of giving birth and motherhood scary as hell?

She came to a stop at a red light. Her hands felt slippery on the steering wheel.

Opening night jitters, she told herself.

Her due date was breathing down her neck and although part of her felt as if she had been pregnant since the beginning of time, another part of her did not want to race to the finish line, did not want the awesome weight of being responsible for the welfare of someone else other than herself.

"I know what you're going through, Angela," she whispered into the darkness as she eased onto the gas pedal again.

Right now, Angela probably felt isolated and alone. Maybe if she gave the girl a call, to see how she was doing and if she'd called to make an appointment with the doctor, Angela wouldn't feel so alone.

The next moment, the thought was shot down in flames. She didn't have Angela's number. On top of that, she wasn't even sure where the girl lived or what her mother's name was, so surfing through the Internet's numerous helpful sites wouldn't be productive.

The number, she realized, was probably on Carson's computer.

Lori made a U-turn at the end of the next block and pointed her vehicle back toward the center.

By car, St. Augustine's Teen Center was only fifteen minutes away from Bedford and home, but it might as well have resided in a completely different world. Here, the streets were narrow rather than wide, and the neighborhoods had not grown old gracefully. The windows of the buildings seemed to be staring out hopelessly at cars as they drove by. The street lights cast shadows rather than illumination. It made Lori sad just to be here.

This was the kind of neighborhood Kurt and Carson had grown up in, she thought. The kind they had both tried to leave behind.

Except that Carson had come back. By choice.

Lori saw St. Augustine's Teen Center up ahead. Lights came from the rear of the building where Carson kept his office. She glanced at her watch. It was past eight.

What was Carson still doing here?

Chapter Three

The parking lot was deserted, except for Carson's beat-up pickup truck. His other car, a sedan, was housed in his garage at home. Right beside the classic Buick Skylark he had been lovingly restoring for the past three years. Lori had a hunch that working on the car was what kept him sane.

Everyone needed something, she mused.

Parking beside the truck, Lori got out and crossed to the rear entrance. Curiosity piqued, she let herself into the building and walked down the short hallway to the back office. Light was pooling out into the room onto the floor outside, beckoning to her.

For a moment, she stood in the doorway, watching him, trying to be impartial. Carson was really a very good-looking man, she thought. Handsomer, actually, than Kurt had been. There was a maturity about him, a steadfastness that marked his features. It was a plateau that Kurt hadn't reached yet.

What Carson needed, she decided, was a life. A life that went beyond these trouble-filled walls. Contrast was always a good thing.

Right now, he looked like a man with the weight of the world on his shoulders. A weight he guarded jealously. Carson O'Neill wasn't a man who shared responsibility or had ever learned how to delegate. He thought he had to do it all in order for it to be done right.

Carson glanced up. He'd thought he felt someone looking at him, but he hadn't expected it to be Lori. If he was surprised to see her standing there, he made sure he didn't show it. He let the papers he was shuffling through sit quietly on the desk.

"Can't seem to get rid of you, can I?" And then he realized how late it was. How did she get in after hours? It was late. "I thought I locked up."

"You did. I have keys, remember?" She held them up and jingled the set for his benefit before slipping them back into her purse.

He laughed shortly. "That'll teach me to hand out keys indiscriminately."

"You really are in a mood tonight, aren't you?" She noted that he wasn't smiling and there was an edge to his words.

Carson laced his fingers together as he leaned back in his chair and rocked, looking at the stack of bills that never seemed to go away, never seemed to get smaller. It felt as if he had come full circle in his life, except that this time, he was hunting for funds at work instead of in his private life.

"Looking for money that isn't there always does that to me."

She crossed to his desk and picked up the last paper in his in-box. It was from the electric company. The one beneath it was for the phones. Both were past due. She had a feeling they weren't the only ones.

Dropping the papers, Lori raised her eyes to his. "Trouble keeping the wolf away from the door?"

He shook his head. Times were tight. People picked and chose their charities carefully. St. Augustine's had no name and wasn't at the top of anyone's list. If it closed its doors, no one would notice. No one except the kids who needed it most.

Carson sighed. "It's beyond trouble. More like a major disaster." He glanced at the figures on the computer monitor again. They didn't get any better no matter how many times he looked at them. "I'm trying to meet 2003 prices with a 1950s budget."

Her heart went out to him. He was one of the good guys no matter what kind of face he tried to present to the world. But she was a firm believer in it always being darkest before the dawn. Somehow, he'd find the money to make it through one more month. And then another, and another. He had before.

Lori smiled at him. "I think this is the part where Mickey Rooney jumps up on a table and shouts, 'Hey kids, let's save the old place by putting on a show.'"

The funny thing was, Carson understood what she was talking about. She'd made him watch one of those old movies once. It was while Kurt was still alive. His brother was out of town on some get-rich-quick venture and he'd come down with the flu. This was right after he'd taken over at the center and Jaclyn had walked out on him. Lori had come by with chicken soup she'd made from scratch and a sack of videotapes to entertain him despite his protests to the contrary. It was around then that he'd begun to seriously envy his brother.

But he scowled now. He needed a miracle, not an old movie grounded in fantasy. "People really watched films like that in the old days?"

She nodded. "Ate them up."

He pushed himself away from the desk, wishing he could push himself away from the bills as easily. "Well, there's no one to put on a show here."

Lori had felt tired until she'd walked in. Now, one thought was forming into one hell of an idea. "No, but there could be a fund-raiser."

"What?" She was babbling, he thought. Fund-raisers were for fashionable causes backed by wealthy foundations and people blessed with too much money and too much time on their hands.

Lori's mind was racing. There was Sherry's fiancé, not to mention the man who had returned into Joanna's life. Both were well-connected billionaires in their own right. It could work.

Her grin was almost blinding. It matched the sparkle in her eyes as she turned them on him. He had trouble keeping his mind on the situation.

"I know a few people who know a few people who have more money than God." Maybe it was time she got together with the ladies of the Mom Squad again, Lori thought. She'd been the one who had baptized the group, the one who had been instrumental in bringing them all together for mutual support in the first place. Maybe it was time to spread some of that support around. ''From what I hear, they're always up for worthy causes.''

Even so, that did him no good. ''And probably get hit up by them every other minute of their lives.''

She looked at him fondly. No one would ever accuse Carson of being a rampaging optimist. ''Which is why having the inside track is a good thing.''

He looked at her skeptically. ''And you have the inside track.''

He didn't believe her. What else was new? She had a feeling that if he ever traced his family tree, he would find that his lineage went back to the original Doubting Thomas.

''Anymore 'inside,' she told him, ''and it might have to be surgically removed.''

''What the hell do they put in those prenatal vitamins of yours?'' She was dreaming, pure and simple. And wasting his time with pipe dreams. Miracles didn't happen to people like him.

She'd made up her mind about this and she wasn't about to allow him to rain on her parade. ''Energy.''

He laughed, shaking his head. Watching her as she moved about his broom closet of an office. ''Like you need some.''

Her eyes laughed at him. The man was never satisfied. She'd be satisfied just removing the furrow from between his brows. ''This afternoon you were complaining I looked tired.'' She grinned. ''There is just no pleasing you, is there?''

She had a way of lighting up a room, he thought,

even when he wanted nothing else than to stay in the dark. ''You don't have to please me, Lori—''

Lori came around to his side of the desk and then sat down on top of it. She looked down on Carson, her eyes teasing him. ''No, but I'd like to try. It's a dirty job but someone has to do it.''

''Why?''

His eyes looked so serious. Her grin softened into a smile. ''Because you deserve to be happy.''

He lifted his shoulders, shrugging carelessly. ''Not according to my ex-wife.''

''What does she know?'' Lori scoffed. She'd never really liked Jaclyn. The woman had turned out to be a self-serving gold digger, pushing Carson to get further along in his career not for his benefit, but for hers. ''If she knew anything, she wouldn't be your ex-wife, she'd still be your wife.''

The assertion embarrassed him. He didn't know how to handle compliments. He never had. ''What are you doing here, anyway?''

She'd almost forgotten. ''I came to see if I could find Angela's phone number.''

More than a hundred and seventy kids came to the center during the week. He was drawing a blank. ''Angela?''

''The tall, thin girl who's so good at basketball. Brunette, dark brown eyes. Laughs like a blue jay,'' she prompted.

The last struck a chord. ''Oh, right.'' And then he looked at her. He couldn't think of a more unlikely coupling. ''Why do you want her number?''

She debated just how much she should tell him. "I want to see how she's doing."

"Why? Can't find anyone your own age to play with?" Carson studied her face in the dim light. "You're serious."

"Yes."

He couldn't read her expression any more than he could read Japanese. "Why would you want to see how she's doing?" Instincts told him not to drop the matter. "Something wrong?"

Lori didn't want to break a confidence. "It could be."

The expression on Carson's face told her she'd lost all chance of leaving the building with the phone number without giving him some sort of an explanation. She hadn't promised Angela not to tell anyone, but it had been implied. Still, Carson had a good heart, despite his tough, blustery manner and he'd been running this center for a while now. He had a right to know what was going on. Besides, he might be able to offer some insight into how to handle the situation.

Lori bit her lower lip. "She thinks she might be pregnant."

The news stunned him. He stared at Lori blankly, wondering if he'd heard right. "She's only, what, thirteen?"

"Fifteen," Lori corrected, although she could see how he'd make the mistake. Angela had a baby face that made her look younger than she was.

Thirteen, fifteen, there hardly seemed a difference. "A baby."

She knew how Carson felt. But it was a sad fact of life. "Babies have been having babies for a long time now."

Carson scrubbed his hand over his face. Damn it, the center was supposed to prevent this kind of thing. The kids were supposed to use up their energy on sports, not sex. "How do you figure into this?"

"I found her crying in the back of the locker area today and got her to talk to me."

Lori had that kind of knack, he thought, the kind that made people open up to her, even hard cases. At times even he had trouble keeping his own counsel around her. "Does her mother know?"

She shook her head. "I think Angela's afraid of her mother."

"I'd be afraid of my mother if I was pregnant at fifteen."

She laughed. "If you were pregnant at fifteen, it would have made all the scientific journals." Her grin broadened and she was relieved to be able to have something to laugh at. "If you were pregnant at any age, it would have made the scientific journals."

Carson gave her a dry look. "Very funny." Maybe it would do Angela some good to talk to Lori, he reasoned. Girls in trouble tended to do drastic things. Minimizing his current program, Carson typed in something on his keyboard and brought up a directory. He scrolled down the screen. "Here it is, Angela Coleman." Taking an index card, he jotted down the phone number for Lori, then handed it to her.

She looked at the single line, then held the card out to him. "How about the address?"

"Oh no, I don't want you driving there in your condition." When she turned to look at the screen, he shut the program.

She frowned at his screensaver. "The DMV have a ban on pregnant women?"

She was going to fight him on this, he just knew it. The woman didn't have the sense of a flea. "Lori, it's not the safest neighborhood." He shouldn't have to tell her that.

"Angela lives there."

There were times he just wanted to take Lori by the shoulders and shake her. Because there were times that her Pollyanna attitude could put her in serious jeopardy. It was bad enough that she traveled here to work. He didn't want her taking unnecessary chances by pressing her luck. "There's nothing I can do about that. There is something I can do about you, though."

She knew he meant well, but good intentions still didn't give him the right to order her around. "Slavery went out a hundred and thirty-seven years ago, Carson. You don't own me."

He rose from his chair and looked down at her. "No, but I'm bigger."

Lori wiggled off the desk. And met him toe to toe, raising her chin defiantly. "Plan to stuff me into a box?"

Damn but her chin did present a tempting target. So did her lips. The thought shook him and he blocked it almost immediately. But not soon enough to erase it or its effect on him.

"If I have to."

And then her expression softened. He couldn't tell

if she'd been putting him on or not. Or was doing so now. ''In your own twisted little way, you care about me, don't you?''

''Don't overanalyze everything.'' He didn't want this going any further. ''You're carrying around my niece or nephew in there, that gives me the right to tell you not to be an idiot.''

''You do have a way with words.'' Lori looked at him for a long moment. Others might buy into his gruff routine, but she didn't. She'd seen something else in his eyes. A man who didn't know how to connect. Even though he sorely needed to. ''You miss her a lot, don't you?''

Now what the hell was she talking about? It was getting late and he was in no mood for this. ''Who?'' he snapped.

''Sandy.''

The mention of his now five-year-old daughter took some of the fire out of him. He let his guard down an inch. There was no shame in admitting his feelings about the little girl. ''Don't get to see her nearly enough.''

That was because he spent nearly every waking minute here, she thought. ''Why don't you take tomorrow off? I'll cover for you. Go see your daughter.''

It wasn't nearly that simple. ''I've got limited visitation rights,'' he ground out.

She'd forgotten about that. He'd told her about it during the only time she had ever seen him intoxicated. The terms of the divorce had just been worked out. Jaclyn in her wrath had hit him where she knew it would hurt the most. She'd used their daughter as a tool to get back at him.

Lori felt badly about raising a sore point. "It's not fair, you know."

He shrugged. There was nothing he could do about that now. "Whoever said that life was fair?" Carson shut down the computer and closed the monitor. He nodded at the card she was still holding. "Well, you've got your phone number. C'mon, I'll walk you to your car."

Nodding, she turned toward the door. "Okay."

"What," he feigned surprise, "no argument?"

She stopped in the doorway. "I can muster up something if you really want me to."

Ushering her over the threshold, he locked the office door behind him. "Never mind."

"You leaving, too?" Even as she asked, she laced both her arms through his.

He tried not to notice how close she was. Or that he found it oddly comforting and unsettling at the same time. He told himself that he was too tired to think clearly about anything. "There's no squeezing blood out of a stone."

She waited as he first locked the rear entrance, then tested the door to make sure it wouldn't give. "You know, I meant what I said."

Turning from the door, he began to walk to the cars. He was careful to keep a little distance between them. The night air felt warm and balmy and for some reason, he didn't feel quite in control of the situation.

"About what? You said a lot of things. You always say a lot of things."

If he was trying to divert her attention, he wasn't succeeding, she thought. ''About the fund-raiser.''

It was against his grain to go begging with his hat in his hand. But this wasn't for him, it was for the center. Maybe that was the way to go. But he was too tired to think intelligently about it tonight. ''We'll talk about it tomorrow.''

She'd more than half expected him to turn her down flat. ''Really?''

Why did she have to question everything? ''I said it didn't I?''

Pleased at the victory and enthused about the possibilities that a true fund-raiser could open up, Lori threw her arms around his neck and kissed him.

It was only meant to be just a light little peck on the lips. That was the way it started.

But then the peck became something more.

The contact between their lips opened a door, allowing something to seep out that had been kept, unconsciously, tightly under wraps by both of them.

Something warm and volatile.

And demanding.

Surprised, Lori looked into his eyes as she pulled her mouth back. Exactly one second before she kissed him again, harder this time. And with a great deal more feeling.

He meant to stop her, he really did. This was his sister-in-law for heaven's sake. By no means was this kind of thing supposed to happen outside of the realm of the Old Testament where men were encouraged to marry their dead brothers' widows.

But the taste of her soft lips feverishly pressed

against his had aroused something within him. Had unearthed feelings that he would have sworn on a stack of Bibles had been all but ground out beneath the heel of his ex-wife's shoe as she'd walked out of his life.

Carson wasn't altogether certain about their demise anymore. Those feelings felt very much alive and well, beating their wings within his chest.

His hands slipped from Lori's shoulders to her back. For a mindless moment, he pressed her closer as the sweetness of her mouth filled him. Filled all the empty, gaping holes within his soul like water rushing into an abyss.

Carson could feel his blood pumping hard through his veins, reminding him that there was more to him than just someone who came in early, left late and spent the core of his day trying to make a difference in the lives of kids most of society didn't care about.

Reminding him that he was a man. A man with needs that had been long neglected.

She hadn't meant for her kiss to be anything but innocent. Maybe her exuberance had gone too far, taking her to a place she had no business being. But oh, it did feel good to kiss a man. To be kissed by a man as if she mattered.

She could feel her head spinning, could feel her pulse racing. Making her glad to be alive.

For a moment longer, Lori allowed herself to linger, to ride this wild, surprising wave that took her into regions which were at once thrilling and frightening. Frightening because she wasn't supposed to be feeling this way, wasn't supposed to be reacting this way.

She was more than eight months pregnant for heaven's sake.

It didn't matter. All that mattered was this kiss.

And this man.

And then she became aware of something else. The baby picked that moment to kick.

Carson felt the punt being delivered to his lower abdomen. Reality came flying back with it. What the hell was he doing? This was wrong, all wrong.

Lori felt his hands leaving the small of her back, felt them grip her shoulders again. Then felt the bittersweetness of separation. His eyes were dark when he looked into her face.

"I'm not Kurt."

She shouldn't have done that, she thought. Shouldn't have jeopardized their friendship this way.

"I know." She smiled at him, struggling for humor, for control. "He wasn't as tall as you." Lori rubbed the back of her neck. "You're giving me a crick in my neck, Carson."

Her words diminished the seriousness of the moment. Carson gravitated toward it like a drowning man to a lifeline.

What the hell was that, he silently demanded of himself. It was so out of the boundaries of their relationship that he could have easily sworn it hadn't happened.

Except that it had and he felt shaken down to his shoes.

"Sorry about that," he mumbled.

She didn't know if he was talking about the crick in her neck, or about the kiss that had overtaken both of them. She took a chance he meant the latter. ''Don't be. I'm not.''

The look in her eyes went clear down to the center of the soul he was certain he no longer possessed. ''It's late. I'll follow you in my car.''

She tried to read his expression. Even if the lighting was better, she had a feeling she'd fail. ''Are you coming over?''

He was surprised at the question. ''No, just to make sure you get home safely.''

''I know how to drive, Carson. Pregnancy doesn't affect my ability to navigate.''

If that was true, the last few seconds wouldn't have happened. ''I wouldn't be so sure about that.''

She shook her head. ''You know, Carson, you'd be a very sweet man if you didn't get in your own way all the time.''

He had no idea what that meant. He felt like a man scrambling for high ground. ''I don't want to be a sweet man.''

''Too late.'' She smiled up at him again, her expression doing strange things to his insides. ''You can huff and puff all you want, Carson. But you don't fool me. I know the inner you.''

''I thought your degree was in digital arts, not psychoanalysis.''

''This isn't a football field, you don't have to bob and weave to avoid getting tackled.'' Her voice softened into a whisper. ''I'm not trying to tackle you, Carson.''

Maybe, he thought, but he didn't know what the hell she *was* trying to do. Or what the hell was wrong with him. He shouldn't have kissed her.

But she had been the one who had kissed him, he reminded himself.

All right, then, he shouldn't have kissed her back.

At a complete loss, he looked down at her as she opened her door and slid in behind the steering wheel.

"Go home, Carson. I can drive myself home without any mishaps."

As far as he was concerned, she'd already had one this evening. They both had.

Like a man frozen to the spot, Carson stood and watched his sister-in-law drive away. It was better than trying to sift through the jumble that served as his emotions.

Chapter Four

Poor Carson.

Lori felt her mouth curving as she took the freeway off-ramp onto Bedford's main thoroughfare. He'd looked absolutely stunned when he'd pulled away from her in the parking lot. She supposed she must have, too, though at least she knew that was how she'd felt.

Talk about surprises. She had no idea the man could kiss that way.

Had to be the best-kept secret around, she mused, since as far as she knew, her brother-in-law had no social life to speak of. Kurt had tried to fix him up a few times after his divorce but Carson had made it clear in no uncertain terms that he wasn't interested in dating again. Ever. He'd mumbled something about women being more trouble than they were worth. She'd begun to think of him as a hermit.

She could feel her smile broaden. And she'd

thought that Kurt was a fabulous kisser. She doubted that it was time dimming her memory of him, but her late husband had to take a back seat to his big brother.

Must run in the family. Maybe it was a genetic thing.

She turned down a long, oak-lined street. If the women in Bedford only knew what she knew now, the man would never know another quiet moment, she speculated.

Not that she was all that experienced when it came to male-female relationships, or even kissing. She couldn't exactly be accused of being a party girl—ever.

But she knew a lackluster kisser when she ran into one. Until Kurt had come into her life, she'd actually thought that the closeness thing was highly overrated. Until Kurt, no man had ever sent her head spinning and her pulse spiking off the charts the way some of her girlfriends liked to claim that their boyfriends did.

Kurt had been a wonderful lover. Kind, attentive, tender. It was why she could forgive his transgressions and shortcomings. In bed and out, her husband had been utterly engaging.

Impatient to get home now, she shifted restlessly in her seat, her seat belt chafing her, as she just missed catching the light. With a heavy sigh, she pushed down on the brake and waited. Traffic was sparse.

She wouldn't have thought that was something Kurt and his brother had in common. At least, not the kissing part. God knew the brothers O'Neill were both good-looking, tall, broad-shouldered, slim-hipped, with chiseled features that could set an Egyptian mummy's pulse going at ten paces. But there'd always been a spark in Kurt's light blue eyes. Even without saying a word, he had a way of making you feel that you were the only one in the room.

With Carson, you knew you were in the room but you weren't sure if he was. The man brought new meaning to the term strong, silent type.

Except that now, he brought a new meaning to the word "wow."

Lori ran her tongue along her lips before she realized what she was doing. She could still taste him. She felt a flutter in her stomach. The baby was trying to get comfortable again.

Stop it. He's your brother-in-law, not to mention your boss. Don't make anything out of this. It was a kiss, a plain, ordinary kiss. Just something that happened, that's all.

Maybe so, but she couldn't help wondering if perhaps, just perhaps, the sensual similarities between the brothers didn't end with just their lips. She seemed to have less control over her mind than over the earth's rotation on its axis.

Could Carson set sheets on fire like Kurt had?

No reason to believe that, and no way you're ever going to find out.

The warning echoed in her brain, causing reality to rush in again.

She was perfectly willing to believe that her condition was affecting her thought processes. That, and the fact that she was lonely.

Despite juggling portions of three jobs, despite her friends and her work at the center, despite the fact that almost every minute of her day outside the house was filled with noise, people and activity, Lori was lonely. Lonely for the intimate touch of a man's hand. Lonely for that sweet sense of sharing that was the very best part of a marriage.

Pulling up into her driveway, she all but yanked the emergency bake out of its socket as she brought the vehicle to a dead stop.

Get a grip, Lori, she cautioned herself.

As best she could, she snaked her way out from behind the wheel. She'd pushed the seat back as far as she could and still be able to reach the pedals. The space between her and the steering wheel still felt as if it was shrinking at an alarming rate. With each day that past, she felt more and more like a cork being wedged into the opening of bottle every time she got into the car. God, but she couldn't wait until she was herself again.

But then you'll have the baby to take care of.

The prospect of what was ahead of her once she gave birth was even scarier in the dark. She hoped this was just a phase she was going through.

Coming in, she closed the door behind her and kicked off her shoes. Lori dropped her purse on the floor beside them. The purse tipped over and two pens came rolling out. Not up to bending down, she left them there.

Someday, she thought, she was going to have to put a table next to the front door. But not tonight.

She felt tired and edgy at the same time.

She tried to tell herself it had to do with the baby, but she knew better. What she needed, she decided, was to get her mind off what had happened in the center's parking lot and onto something else. Something productive.

Lori took the phone number Carson had written down for her out of her pocket. The debate about whether or not she should make a call lasted only as long as it took her to walk to her phone in the living room. Picking up the cordless receiver, she crossed to the sofa and sank into a corner.

It wasn't possible to make herself comfortable. Pregnancy had taken that option away from her, but she made herself the least uncomfortable she could. Looking at the number on her lap, Lori pressed the area code and then the rest of the numbers that would connect her to Angela's house.

The phone rang nine times on the other end before anyone picked up. When they did, they sounded far from happy.

''Hello?'' a woman's voice snapped.

She wondered if this was Angela's mother. She certainly didn't sound friendly. ''May I speak to Angela, please?''

''She's not here.''

There was no effort to take a message. Lori had a feeling the woman was going to hang up. She talked quickly. ''When do you expect her back?''

The irritation level of the woman's voice rose a notch. ''Who knows? Kid comes and goes.''

Lori glanced at her watch. It was after nine. ''But it's a school night.''

''So? You her teacher?'' the woman challenged.

''No.''

The woman shot another question at her before she could elaborate. "The police?"

"No."

The next thing Lori knew, there was a dial tone buzzing in her ear. She sighed, pressing the off button on the phone's receiver. She stared at it for a moment, empathizing. No wonder Angela didn't feel she could talk to her mother.

But the girl could talk to her. Anytime. She had to impress that on Angela. And if Angela was pregnant, then Lori would go with her when she went to face her mother with the news. That Angela's mother had to be informed of her condition was not up for debate. The woman had to be made to take an interest in her daughter. Both of them could benefit from that.

Lori dug herself out of the sofa. She couldn't imagine what it was like, not having parents who loved and cared about you. Hers had been taken from her all too soon, but she had nothing but warm memories of both her mother and her father.

The lack of good parenting had been one of the things that had drawn her to Kurt. His charm had only been enough to bring her in at the beginning. But there was this lost little boy beneath it all, a lost boy who'd never experienced parental warmth. Who'd grown up without it. From what he had told her, his father had left when he was still very young and his mother had found her way into a bottle for solace. It was Carson who had raised him. Who had taken care of both Kurt and their mother from the time he was fifteen.

She supposed that explained a lot about Carson.

That kind of responsibility was hard on kid. Carson had worked hard at his education and after school, he took any job he could to help out. And somehow, he'd still found a way to be there for Kurt.

She knew Carson blamed himself for what had happened to Kurt. But the fact that Kurt was always drawn to the wild side, to speed, wasn't Carson's fault. He'd done the best he could to make a responsible person out of him. A man could only do so much.

But first, she mused, looking at the receiver still in her hand, they had to try. There was no way she was about to give up on Angela. It looked as if too many people had done that already.

She placed the receiver back in its slot, then made her way to the kitchen.

The refrigerator was as user unfriendly now as it had been this morning when she'd take out the last of the orange juice. She'd made a mental note to go shopping, but the day had gotten away from her and she'd forgotten all about going to the supermarket.

Not enough hours in the day, she thought, shaking her head. She let the door shut again. Oh well, it wouldn't hurt to skip a meal now and then.

She glanced down at her middle. It wasn't as if she was in any danger of wasting away. She'd done enough eating for two lately.

The sound of the doorbell caught her by surprise. She wasn't expecting anyone. Because of her erratic hours, her friends weren't in the habit of dropping by without warning.

The doorbell rang a second time before she got to

the front door. She looked through the peephole, but the image on the other side of the door wasn't clear. She told herself she needed to get one of those surveillance cameras for outside the door. The list of things she needed was mounting. First and foremost, she needed a fairy godmother.

''Who is it?'' she asked.

Didn't she see that it was him? ''Open the door, Lori,'' he said impatiently.

Carson?

She'd just left him in the parking lot. What was he doing here?

She opened the door before the silent question was completely formed in her brain. The man on her doorstep was holding a large brown bag against his chest and looked rather uncertain for Carson.

She smiled at him. ''Hi.''

''Hi.''

Was it her imagination, or did he sound almost a little sheepish? Or was that awkward? She supposed, under the circumstances, that she felt a little awkward herself right now, given what had happened in the parking lot.

Carson cleared his throat. ''I, um, haven't had any dinner yet.''

She laughed, thinking of her refrigerator. Carson had been over a few times for dinner, but this wasn't going to be one of those evenings. ''I'm afraid you're out of luck here unless you happen to like baking soda or wilted celery, or broccoli that looks as if it's about to mutate into another life-form.''

He felt as if a Boy Scout jamboree had used his tongue to practice their knot-making.

"No. I mean, I picked up some." He hoisted the bag, using it as a visual aid. "Mexican food. Then I remembered that you liked Mexican food, too, so I got extra. I figured you hadn't eaten either." Why was she making this so hard for him? Eating should have been a simple matter.

She knew that he would probably tell her it was silly, but she was really touched by the gesture. "No, I haven't." He was still standing on her doorstep. All six foot two of him still looked miserably awkward. It wasn't like Carson. She gestured for him to come in. "That was very nice of you."

He snorted, pushing the compliment and her thanks away as if it was a bomb about to detonate right in front of him.

"Don't make a big deal out of this." Carson pushed the door closed behind him. "Can't have you neglecting to feed the baby."

She grinned, leading the way to the kitchen. Mexican food had been her main craving of choice. "At this rate, he or she'll probably be born wearing a sombrero and humming Mexican music."

Carson placed the bag down on the kitchen counter. He was surprised by her comment. "That's stereotyping."

"No disrespect intended." She carefully unpacked the foam boxes out of the bag. "Stereotypes are usually rooted in reality. Besides, I love Mexican music. And Mexican jewelry and don't even get me started about the food."

Though her pale coloring gave no indication to the casual observer, her mother had been part Mexican. The meals Lori remembered her mother preparing still made her mouth water every time she thought about them. Some of her best memories involved standing beside her mother in the kitchen, helping her make the dishes that were such a staple in their house when she was young.

Opening the cupboard, Lori stood on her toes in order to take down two dinner plates from the second shelf. Without thinking, Carson reached in and took them down for her. Surprised, Lori turned around, brushing her abdomen against him.

He stepped back as quickly as if he'd been brushed by a flaming torch instead of a pregnant woman. "You're shorter," he pointed out, mumbling his excuse for lending a hand.

She glanced down at her feet. She didn't usually walk around barefoot in front of him. "I'm not wearing my shoes."

He grasped at the topic with gratitude. Unlike most of the women in his acquaintance, Lori had worn high heels ever since he'd met her. Even through her pregnancy. "How you can wear those heels at a time like this—"

She shrugged. She was so used to wearing them she didn't even think about it.

"I can't remember a time when I didn't wear high heels. Besides," she confessed, "they make me feel pretty." Shoes had always been her weakness and she thought there was nothing more attractive than a nice pair of three- or four-inch heels.

He opened one of the containers. Splitting the enchiladas between them, he scooped out the sauce, spreading it evenly on the two plates. ''You don't need shoes for that.''

She set the two glasses she was holding on the table and looked at him, a smile playing across her lips. Would wonders never cease?

''Why, Carson, is that a compliment?''

''No,'' he retorted. Why did she have to make a big deal out of a conversation? ''I mean...it's just an observation, that's all.''

He used the excuse of getting napkins out of the pantry to turn away from her, afraid that he was going to trip over a tongue that had suddenly gotten too long and thick for him to manage properly.

What the hell was he doing here, anyway? He'd had every intention of going home after she'd left the center. But then his stomach began to growl, reminding him that he hadn't eaten for most of the day. Stopping at the Tex-Mex restaurant had reminded him of her. As if she had gotten very far out of his mind.

He wasn't in the mood to eat alone tonight. God only knew why. He usually preferred his own company to anyone else's. That way, there was no need to make idle conversation.

Except that with Lori, the conversation wasn't idle. It jumped around like an entity with a life of its own. Pretty much the way she did most of the time.

He shrugged carelessly, completely wrapped up in what he was doing. Or trying to look that way. ''Nobody's looking at your feet anyway.''

''I know.'' She patted her stomach. Was it her

imagination, or had it gotten bigger since this morning? She was beginning to feel like the incredible expanding woman. ''They're all looking at my stomach.'' She paused, fisting one hand at what had once been her waist. ''Why is it that when a woman's pregnant, people can't keep their eyes off her stomach?''

He looked at her. Her eyes always got to him. Her eyes and her smile. ''That's not true.''

She knew he was just saying that to be nice. ''Well, it feels like it's true.'' She placed two sets of silverware out. ''I feel like everyone's eyes are on my middle, waiting for something to happen.''

He threw out the empty container for her and opened another. This one contained nachos with a cheese sauce. ''Maybe you think they're expecting that because that's how you feel.''

She moved the nachos to the middle of the table. ''So now who's practicing psychoanalysis?''

He never lost a beat. ''I'm a lawyer. Comes with the territory,'' he reminded her.

Pulling her chair out, she sat down. He straddled a chair opposite her. Like a cowboy about to go running off to a trail drive.

''So it does, Counselor.'' She studied him for a moment, thinking of the way he'd looked when she'd walked in on him at the center. Wondering if he'd think that she was prying if she asked. ''Do you ever regret giving it up?''

He thought he would. When he'd gone for his degree, he'd been sure that was what he wanted to do with his life. But arguing in court, trying to get a man free on a technicality, never taking into account whether or not that man was actually innocent, was something that never felt quite right to him.

It wasn't until he'd turned his life in another direction that it finally felt as if he was doing the right thing.

''No,'' he said honestly, ''oddly enough, I don't. Maybe because I don't have time to.'' He laughed shortly. ''The one who regretted my giving it up was Jaclyn.'' The arguments had started in earnest then. And he got to see the darker side of the woman he'd fallen in love with. It was a rude awakening. ''My taking over at the center didn't jibe with the vision of life she had in mind.'' He didn't hurt talking about her anymore. He didn't feel anything. It was as if that had all happened to someone else in another lifetime. ''Guess she has it now.''

Lori wasn't about to let him just throw out the comment and not follow it up. ''Oh?''

He reached for a nacho. There was rabid interest on her face. ''Didn't I tell you?''

He wasn't exactly the male equivalent of Chatty Cathy and they both knew it. ''Carson, you never tell me anything without my jabbing you with a dose of Sodium Pentothal.''

It was old news anyway, more than six months in the past. ''She married some Beverly Hills plastic surgeon. Has a house in Bel Air, a housekeeper, everything she ever wanted.''

Lori could feel that wall rising up again. The one he kept himself barricaded behind. Lori reached across the small table and placed her hand over his. ''Except a good man.''

He shrugged. Conscious of the warmth of her hand, he withdrew his. ''I had him checked out. I still keep in touch with my old firm's P.I. Her new husband seems a decent enough guy.''

''Why'd you have him checked out?'' Unless, she thought, he still had feelings for his ex that he wasn't willing to admit to.

Carson thought that would have been self-evident. ''If he was going to be living with my daughter, he damn well better not have any skeletons in his closet.''

She should have realized that was it. She'd seen him with the kids at the center, gruff, but protective beneath all that. ''You know, you're full of surprises, Carson O'Neill, you really are.''

She was doing it again, making him feel like squirming. He nodded at her plate. ''Your enchilada's getting cold. I know it's nothing like what you make, but in a pinch—''

He was apologizing again. ''Don't knock it.'' She savored a bite. ''It tastes *so* much better when I don't have to make it myself.''

He'd sampled her cooking and this couldn't hold a candle to hers. ''Funny, I was just thinking how much better it tasted when you made it.''

The compliment pleased her. Whether he realized it or not, he was good for her. ''Then I'll have to have you over for dinner again some night.''

He frowned, lowering his eyes to his plate. ''I wasn't fishing for an invitation.''

She knew that. ''Well, guess what? You caught one anyway.''

"But—"

She wasn't about to let him wiggle out of it. He'd done a nice thing for her and she wanted to return the favor. End of discussion. "Shut up and pass the nachos, Carson."

There were times when he knew it was pointless to try to argue with her. He did as he was told.

Chapter Five

Restless, Lori tossed the magazine back on the square marble tabletop. Dr. Sheila Pollack, her OB-GYN, made a practice of keeping current with the reading material in the tastefully decorated waiting room, but since she'd already been here three times this month for herself, Lori'd read everything of interest to her. The rest of the magazines were devoted to how those with money to burn decorated their homes and that certainly didn't include her.

She glanced at her watch, wondering how much longer Angela's exam was going to take. The door leading to the four exam rooms remained closed no matter how many times she looked expectantly at it.

She'd been the one to bring Angela here today. Every time she'd asked the girl if she'd made an appointment with a doctor, Angela had put her off, procrastinating. After three days of verbal waltzing, Lori had called her own doctor. Lisa, Dr. Pollack's nurse, had been sympathetic and agreed to slip Angela in to see the doctor in between patients.

This state of limbo about Angela's condition was unacceptable.

"Why do you care?" Angela had demanded when she'd cornered her just as the girl had walked into the center this afternoon and told her that she'd made the arrangements for her to see a doctor.

Lori'd ushered her out of the building. They had to leave immediately.

"Because I do, that's all. You need to face this, one way or another." She'd pointed out her car. "Now let's go."

Braced for an argument, she didn't get one. Angela made no further protest about the pending exam. She also didn't talk very much on the trip to Dr. Pollack's office in Bedford.

Mercifully, because the traffic on the freeway was flowing, they reached the Bedford medical complex across the street from Blair Memorial in a little under twenty minutes.

The wait inside turned out to be longer. As Angela sat fidgeting beside her, it was almost forty-five minutes before there was a free exam room. Angela had wanted to leave twice and had actually gotten up once, but she allowed herself to be talked into remaining. Lori had a feeling the girl just wanted someone to force her to find out. Wanted someone to care enough to find out.

And now Angela was in exam room one, finding out if her life was going to be forever altered. Lori couldn't help feeling nervous for her.

Lori stared down at her nails. All Dr. Pollack had to do was give her a pelvic and she'd known immediately that she was pregnant. Why was it taking so long with Angela?

She knew she had absolutely no say in this matter one way or another, but if Angela was pregnant, she was going to try to talk the girl into having the baby and then considering her options after that. Maybe Angela's mother would finally find some maternal feelings and come through for her.

At the very least, Angela could give the baby up for adoption. Teaching the Lamaze classes had made her realize that there were so many people out there longing for a child of their own. If Angela had her baby and then gave it up for adoption, she'd be giving the gift of life to not only her child, but to the couple who would be adopting him or her.

The door leading back to the waiting room finally opened.

For one beat, Lori held her breath, mentally practicing her speech and crossing her fingers that Angela would be receptive.

There were tears on the girl's cheeks. She was pregnant. Lori was on her feet instantly. The next second, she was hugging the girl to her as the other three women in the waiting room looked on.

"Honey, it's okay. I'll be there for you," she promised.

But Angela drew away, shaking her head. "No."

Lori ignored the presence of the other women in the room. "I know you don't think so now, but—"

Angela was still shaking her head. "No, you don't

understand.'' And then she grabbed Lori's arms urgently. ''I'm not pregnant. All this stuff at home, all this tension with my mom and my boyfriend, it's made me late, that's all. I'm not pregnant,'' she repeated. Her voice vibrated with overwhelming relief.

Lori blew out a breath, vicariously sharing the teenager's relief. Okay, she thought, no speech necessary. Catastrophe averted. She slipped an arm around the girl's slim shoulders.

''C'mon, let's go back to the center.''

Suddenly too emotional to say another word, Angela just nodded. Lori opened the door and guided her out of the office.

She gave Angela some time to really absorb the situation and to calm down. She knew the girl must have been terrified as she waited for the pelvic exam to be over. Dr. Pollack had a wonderfully comforting bedside manner, but that still didn't take the edge off the fear Angela had gone in with. One look at her face when she'd followed the nurse into the inner office had said it all.

As she turned down the block to the teen center, Lori glanced at Angela. The girl had been incredibly quiet all the way back, not even attempting to change the radio station to find more contemporary music, the way she had on the way there.

Though the news was good, Lori couldn't help wondering if a part of Angela was somehow just a little disappointed just the same. This was a bittersweet situation that required delicate negotiation.

Lori knew all about emotions being all over the map. Hers had been doing that for a long while now.

"You dodged a bullet that time, Angela. There's a lesson to be learned here."

"Yeah, I'll say." Lori saw the girl's profile harden. "I thought Vinnie loved me. He said he'd always love me, no matter what. But once I told him I thought I was pregnant, the S.O.B. said he didn't want anything to do with me. He said if I was pregnant, it wasn't his. Like I'd ever slept with anyone else." Angela looked at her, her voice impassioned. "I'm not like that, Lori."

She reached for Angela's hand and gave it a quick squeeze. "I know that, honey. But there's a bigger lesson here than finding out the kind of guy Vinnie is. Sex isn't a game, Angela, it's a responsibility."

"Is that what you learned?"

She heard the defensiveness in the girl's voice. She didn't want Angela to think she was criticizing her or lecturing to her. "I was married."

Angela flushed. "Sorry, I didn't mean that." She bit one of her fingernails. "I kinda mouth-off when I get mad."

Lori smiled at her. "I noticed." And then she thought about her own life. "But, in a way, I suppose I'm a pretty good example of all the things that a woman has to think about before she does decide to get pregnant. You have to finish your education before you start a family so that you're better equipped to provide for your baby in case something happens. All sorts of things happen in life that you're not ready for. My husband died, my company went bankrupt and I had to scramble to make a living so that when this baby comes, I can provide for it. I've got a college degree and I'm a lot older than you are, Angela.''

Angela's head bobbed up and down vigorously. ''I'll say.''

Lori got out of the car and looked at the girl over the hood of her car. Nothing like a teenager to make you feel old, she thought.

''Hey, not *that* much older. But what I'm saying here is that you've got all the time in the world for this when you get older, Angela. Don't rush out of your teens. Don't rush to take on responsibilities that shouldn't be there for you until you've had time to be fifteen and eighteen and twenty. And carefree.''

Angela bit down on her lower lip, as if she was actually mulling over the advise instead of blocking it out. ''I guess that makes sense.''

And then she flashed a smile that warmed Lori's heart. ''Of course it makes sense.'' Lori opened the rear door to the center for her. ''Now don't you have a game to practice for?''

''Yeah,'' Angela beamed, looking very much like a fifteen-year-old who'd had the weight of the world lifted off her shoulders. ''I do.'' And then she surprised Lori by throwing her arms around her and hugging her. ''Thanks,'' she mumbled against her shoulder.

The next minute, Angela bolted and rushed into the building.

And that, Lori thought, was the way a fifteen-year-old was supposed to behave. Impulsive and happy.

''What was that all about?''

Startled, the door handle slipped out of her hand. She swung around to see Carson standing almost behind her. Where had he come from?

She took in a breath, then released it. Her stomach felt oddly jumbled, as if it was under attack. When *would* this baby stop tap dancing? It had been doing it for the past twenty-four hours or so. ''Who let you out of your cage?''

He'd been worried. When he hadn't seen her for the past two hours, he'd assumed that she hadn't been feeling well and had decided to go home. It wasn't like her to leave without saying something. Calling her at home had gotten him nowhere. Calling the hospital had done the same.

He hadn't known what to think. Leaving Rhonda in charge, he'd gone out for a walk to try to channel this sudden directionless energy that was threatening to undo him. He'd just turned a corner when he'd seen Lori's car pull up. He'd lost no time in hurrying over.

''I wanted to clear my head,'' he told her.

She looked up at the sky. It was one of those hazy days that people associated with Southern California. ''Too much smog out here for that today.''

He knew what she was trying to do. ''I've gotten used to it and don't change the subject. Where the hell have you been and what's up with Angela?''

She knew she should have told him before she left, but she also knew that he would have tried to talk her out of it, or flat-out told her she couldn't do this because there were rules to consider. All she could consider was Angela's welfare.

"I took her to see my gynecologist."

Carson's chiseled jaw dropped almost an inch. "Lori—"

She held up her hands before he could launch into a lecture. "I know, I know, I was meddling and I'm not supposed to, but damn it, Carson, the girl thought she was pregnant."

Dark brows gathered like storm clouds. "The girl also has a mother."

"So? Ma Barker was also a mother. She got her sons killed. And then there was Catherine de' Medici. She had scores of children. She also loved poisoning anyone she thought was her enemy—"

At times, her penchant for being a walking trivia trove got annoying. "I don't need a random history lesson, Lori. We're talking about parental rights here."

"No," she contradicted passionately. "We're talking about a young girl's life." She stuck her chin out pugnaciously. "You didn't talk to Angela's mother, Carson. I did. Or tried to. She sounded like she could care less about her daughter." She fisted her hands where her waist would have been under different circumstances, ready to fight him on this. "And if you're going to talk about rights, what about Angela's rights? What about her right to peace of mind?"

She could make a statue want to cover its ears. "Don't play lawyer with me, Lori. You won't win." His anger was calm, controlled. And maybe a little intimidating for all its quiet. "I wouldn't be here if I didn't care about the rights of these kids and what they're entitled to. I also know we wouldn't be able to survive a lawsuit. It would shut St. Augustine's down."

In her opinion, there were far too many lawyers in the world, ready to go to battle and disrupt lives over petty issues. She was secretly glad that Carson had left those ranks.

"What lawsuit?" she demanded heatedly. "I just took her into my doctor so that she could find out if she was pregnant or not. She's not about to tell her mother I did that. She wants to put the whole thing behind her. Angela and her mother aren't exactly the *Gilmore Girls.*"

"All right, so what did you find out? Is she pregnant?"

Her anger melted into a smile. He liked watching the transformation and told himself he shouldn't. "No, stress is throwing her timing off, that's all. She also got a little education in the fickleness of young studs." He raised his eyebrow, waiting for Lori to elaborate. "She told her boyfriend she thought she was pregnant and he split. Said it wasn't his. His undying love died." She shook her head. The girl was looking for love in all the wrong places. "Damn near broke her heart."

That sounded far too sensitive for the girl he was acquainted with. "She said that?"

"She didn't have to. Her eyes did."

"You read eyes now?"

She looked up into his. Still as unfathomable as always, she thought. Most of the time, the man was a walking mystery to her. But that didn't mean she wasn't willing to try to change that. ''I read anything that'll give me a clue.''

''Lori, you're going to turn my hair gray.''

She cocked her head, trying to picture him with streaks of gray woven through his black hair. ''Gray looks good on some men. Makes them distinguished.''

He laughed shortly, shaking his head. ''You've got an answer for everything, don't you?''

''Pretty much.''

''You should have been the lawyer.'' The other side would have been waving a white flag in no time, Carson thought.

She grinned. ''If I had been, I would have given you a run for your money.''

His eyes slid over her abdomen. ''Right now, I don't want to see you running anywhere. Matter of fact, I'd rather not see you, period.''

''You know you don't mean that.'' She patted his face. ''I light up your day.''

The ironic thing was, he thought as opened the door for her and they walked back into the building, she was right. Not that he was ever going to tell her. If she knew, there'd be no living with her.

There was hardly any living with her now.

Despite the fact that the baby insisted on being restless, Lori spent the rest of the day at the center. She'd seen all the kids off, had talked to Angela again before the girl went home and had told Rhonda that she would lock up. There were no Lamaze classes tonight and she didn't relish the idea of going home just yet.

She wondered if Carson was in the mood to catch a quick bite. Making her way to his office, she found him the way she had last week. Frowning over something on the computer.

Probably the budget again. He hadn't said a word about her idea since she'd framed it for him. It was time to prod him. ''So, have you given my suggestion any thought?''

Carson blinked as he looked away from the screen. No matter how long he stared, the number just wouldn't change. ''What suggestion?''

Was he playing games, or had he really forgotten? ''About the fund-raiser.''

''No.'' He'd been hoping the impossible, that she would drop the matter.

The word had a final ring to it. She might have known. With Carson, everything was an uphill fight. ''Why?''

''Because it was a dumb suggestion when you made it, and it's still a dumb suggestion now.'' He saw exasperation flit over her face and knew he was in for it. Trying to cut her off wasn't going to work, but he tried anyway. ''Fund-raisers are for national causes, national charities. Medical research.''

''Not everyone wants to toss their money into a large pile.'' He was an intelligent man, why didn't he know that? ''There are a lot of people who feel better backing the little guy.''

His mouth twisted into a cynical expression. ''Well, they certainly don't come any littler than St. Augustine's.''

Was he being sarcastic, or just downplaying the

center's influence on the neighborhood teens? She took offense for the center. And for him.

"Oh, I don't know. It's had positive effects on people's lives over the years. Look at how you turned out."

She struck a nerve. "Right. I don't think *People* magazine's going to be breaking down my door anytime soon, asking for an interview."

She wasn't about to let him throw stones, even at himself. *Especially* not at himself. "You were a kid who came from these mean streets and you became a successful lawyer."

That was only half the story. His ex had jeered the rest at him when she'd announced that she was going to get a divorce. "Who gave up working at a lucrative law firm to come back here and periodically bash his head against a wall."

That wasn't all there was to the story. "Because he was compassionate," Lori pointed out.

How could he argue with her when she was trying to defend him? He smiled despite himself. "Do you always have to have the last word?"

Her eyes danced as she looked up at him. "Only when I'm right."

"And just who decides that?"

"Me," Lori replied simply, knowing she was baiting him. "And God."

He sighed, shaking his head. Maybe he should call it a night after all. He was bone tired. It had been a long day. Carson pressed buttons on the keyboard, closing the computer down. "So now you talk to God."

"Every night."

"And does He talk back, or do you intimidate him, too?"

She honed in on what she took to be a slip. "Do I intimidate you?"

Carson gave her a look that was meant to put her in her place. "No, but you try."

"Do not," she countered glibly. "I just like to champion a cause, that's all." She frowned, wishing he'd listen to reason. She just *knew* the fund-raiser would erase that furrow between his eyebrows. At least temporarily. "And I hate seeing you being so stubborn when you're wrong."

He wondered what it felt like, to always feel you were right, to always be on the side of the angels. "Maybe I'm not."

"But maybe you are," she insisted. "Don't you think you owe it to yourself—and the center—to find out?"

Didn't she understand how presumptuous all this sounded? And how humiliating it could be? "What if we gave a fund-raiser and nobody came?"

Her parents had instilled the ability within her to always see the bright side of any situation. "Then the kids at the center would have a lot of good food to eat for a week." But that wasn't going to happen. She firmly believed that. "What if we didn't give a fund-raiser and people were willing to come?"

The woman just wouldn't stop, would she? "Lori, you're talking nonsense."

She took offense at the cavalier way he dismissed the idea. "I never thought you'd be afraid."

She knew just how to press his buttons, even when he thought he'd put a lock on them. ''I'm not afraid, I just don't want to look like a fool.''

Didn't he get it yet? ''Caring about something doesn't make you a fool.''

What did it take to pull the shades from her eyes? And why did a woman who had so much go wrong for her seem determined to continue looking at life through rose-colored glasses?

''But thinking that I can get other people to care about what I care about just on my say-so does. Don't you understand that? Now drop this, Lori, before you make me lose my temper.''

She frowned at him. *Stubborn idiot.* ''Is that supposed to make me shake in my shoes?''

He could feel his temper beginning to fray. ''It's supposed to make you stop babbling, although I'm beginning to think only duct tape will accomplish that.''

Yelling at him had never been the way to win. She tried again. ''Let me talk to my friends,'' she pleaded. ''You know I'm right.''

Enough was enough. Standing up, he towered over her. ''What I know is that if you don't stop nagging, I'm going to have to fire you.''

Her eyes narrowed. ''You wouldn't dare. You need me.''

He'd gone too far to make a U-turn now. ''Try me.''

''You'd really fire me?''

''If you don't stop, yes.'' Why wouldn't she just back off? Something had to make her.

Anger flared in her eyes. ''All right, then, maybe I'll just quit.''

Damn it, this had gone too far. Why didn't she ever cry ''uncle''? ''You can't apply for unemployment if you quit.''

''Oh, so now you're worried about me?''

He flipped the computer back on. He was staying. Adrenaline had just given him his second wind. ''Damn it, Lori, I'm always worried about you. Now go home and let me try to squeeze blood out of a stone.''

''The only stone I see is the rock between your ears. Now if you—''

She stopped so abruptly, he looked up. She was wincing and her face was pale. ''What's the matter?''

Lori had trouble drawing the air back into her lungs. It had all but whooshed out of her when the tap dance the baby was doing had turned into a Charleston. At double-speed.

Followed by an incredible surge of unadulterated pain.

Lori looked down at the floor and then at him with stunned amazement vibrating through her. This was too early. She wasn't supposed to be early.

There was no arguing with the facts. ''I think my water just broke.''

It was happening.

Chapter Six

She had to be kidding, Carson thought. Her water hadn't broken. She wasn't due yet. These kinds of things happened dramatically only in sitcoms and movies.

"Look, if this is some kind of ploy to try to get me to see things your way—"

But the look on her face told him that he had better start taking this seriously.

Lori splayed her hand over his desk, her fingers spreading out as far as they could reach. Pain was vibrating through every part of her body. This hurt like the devil.

"Trust me, I'm not that good." She measured out every word, as if there wasn't enough air to make it to the end of her sentence if she wasn't careful. "If you want visual proof—"

Carson was on his feet instantly. He rounded the desk and hurried over to her side. Damn it, why now?

Why not when she was with some female friends who had a clue what to do?

He peered at her face, hoping against hope that it was a false alarm. ''You're sure?''

She stared straight ahead, afraid to even move her eyes. Afraid that if she did, the pain would suddenly accelerate. ''Uh-huh.''

His brain refused to absorb the information. Or maybe he was hoping that if he denied it enough, it would cease to be true. ''You're in labor.''

''Oh, yeah.''

She said it with such conviction, all hope to the contrary died. Did he touch her? Offer support? Keep clear in case she needed space? He felt like an alien in a foreign land. ''What do you want me to do?''

The pain was taking a step backward. It was becoming manageable. She slanted her eyes toward him. ''Knocking me out sounds pretty good about now.''

If she could quip, then maybe the situation wasn't as dire as he thought. But there was one thing he knew for sure. ''I've got to get you to the hospital.''

Lori tested the waters slowly and nodded her head just a fraction of an inch. The pain was withdrawing, taking its sharp, pointy instruments with it. Thank God.

''Second best,'' she allowed, although oblivion still held its allure. This was just the beginning and part of her didn't feel as if she was going to be up to it. No choice, she thought.

Very slowly, she released her grip on the desk and covered her belly protectively with her hand.

Carson never took his eyes off her. Should he put

her in his chair and push her out to the car? Carry her? He'd never felt so unsure about what to do in his life. "Can you walk?"

A half a smile curved her mouth. Amid her fear that the pain would return, twice as strong, twice as big, at any moment was a sweetness that was flittering over her soul. She couldn't recall ever hearing Carson sound this gentle, this concerned.

"My legs still work, Carson. It's my middle that's under attack."

If she wasn't asking him to carry her, he wasn't going to volunteer. Dignity was an important factor to every human being. He left her with hers. "Okay, then let's go."

"Right."

She wanted to walk out on her own power. She'd had a thing about hanging tough, especially since Kurt had died. But the weakness that was assaulting her knees drove nails of fear through her. She looked at Carson, not saying a word.

She didn't have to. He slipped his arm around her shoulders, silently giving her the support she needed. Lori blessed him for it.

Once outside, he guided her over to his car. She looked back at hers, parked three spaces over against the building. "What about my car?"

This was no time to launch into a debate over which car to use. He'd driven the sedan today and his was the roomier vehicle. He had a feeling that she was going to need all the space she could get right now.

"I'll have someone drive me back for it and I'll

drop it off at your house.'' One arm around her, he took out his key and unlocked the passenger side. ''Your car's the least of your problems right now.'' Very slowly he lowered her onto the seat and then helped her swing her legs inside. He didn't bother masking his concern when he looked at her. ''You sure you don't want me to call 9-1-1?''

If anyone had ever asked her, she would have said that Carson was incapable of being this gentle. Who would have thought?

She did what she could to assuage his concern. ''No 9-1-1. I'm just in labor, Carson, not in the early stages of delivery.''

He had his doubts. Lori had this superwoman attitude about her that got in her way more than once. Especially now. He didn't want to take any unnecessary chances. ''You sure?''

He kept asking her that. She could feel the edges of her temper peeling away and knew she was being unreasonable. With effort, she curbed her tongue. ''As sure as I can be.'' She looked at him as he got in behind the wheel, turning only her head, afraid a new onslaught of pain might start at any sudden movement. ''Hey, I'm new at this kind of thing, Carson. I'm playing it by ear.''

He turned on the ignition. ''It's not your ear I'm concerned about.''

Lori's eyes fluttered shut, as if that could somehow seal the pain away from her. ''Just drive,'' she breathed.

Something was happening. She wasn't sure if it was a contraction, but it felt like it might be one. If not, some invisible force was going at her with a giant, jagged can opener in one hand, a sledgehammer in the other. How could women have more than one baby after going through this?

He started to put the car into drive, then saw that she still hadn't buckled up. ''Get your seat belt on,'' he ordered.

Lori grabbed the strap, trying to pull it around herself but it wouldn't give. ''How about if I just brace my feet against the floor and you drive as fast as you can?''

Now she was scaring him. Maybe he should just call the paramedics. ''That bad?''

She shifted her eyes toward him and tried to smile, knowing he needed to see the effort more than she needed to make it. ''It's not good.'' Her throat felt dry as she swallowed. ''Just get me to Blair, please, Carson.''

It was all she needed to say. He reached over and pulled the seat belt up and over her bulk, then sank the tongue into the groove, snapping it in place.

''I'll get you there as fast as I can,'' he promised.

Couldn't be fast enough for her, she thought. ''Sounds good to me.''

Gunning the engine, Carson peeled out of the small parking lot behind the center. He made his way onto the street, snaking in front of a deep purple Camaro. The latter's driver leaned down on his horn in protest over the sudden maneuver. Carson never looked back.

Amber lights blinked, on their way to becoming red as Carson sped through one light after the other, his goal the southbound freeway. Somehow, he managed to make it through each light before it turned red.

"If you're trying to scare me into delivering the baby in the car, you just might be successful."

He didn't even spare her a look, his eyes intent on the road.

"That's exactly what I'm trying to prevent." The last thing in the world he wanted was for her to have the baby with only him in attendance. The very idea scared the hell out of him. All he could think of was that women still died in childbirth.

He made it to the on-ramp of the 405. Like a racer at the Indianapolis 500, Carson wove his car in and out of the various lanes of traffic until he finally crossed over firmly painted double yellow lines and merged into the carpool lane a full fifty feet before it was legally allowed.

Lori was afraid to hold her breath, afraid that if she did, if would somehow terminate her labor and throw her headfirst into the delivery. But her pulse was definitely racing as she watched Carson's progress.

"You could get a ticket for that." The words came out breathlessly.

"A cop would be nice around now." He glanced in his rearview mirror. No such luck. "He'd get us to the hospital faster."

She managed to find the control on the armrest and pressed until the window rolled down. She was perspiring so much she was afraid she was going to dissolve in a puddle soon. "So this racing madly and breaking laws is actually a plan."

"I've always got one."

It sounded good, but it was a lie. Carson liked to think that most if not all of his life was proceeding according to schedule if not some kind of outright plan. But lately, he had to admit he'd been flying by the seat of his pants. It had begun with his divorce, which had hit him with the force of a small-time bomb. His brother's death the following year had devastated him. And now this thing that hummed between Lori and him confounded him so totally he had trouble remembering what day it was. If there was still some kind of a plan to his life, other than running the center, it had somehow gotten lost in the shuffle. The only plan life seemed to have for him was chaos.

He glanced at Lori as he pressed down on the gas pedal. The speedometer needle was flirting with numbers that went far above the ones posted on the speed limit signs. He saw that Lori had one hand braced on the dashboard. Her knuckles were white. Was that from the pain?

What else would it be, idiot? he mocked himself. "How are you doing?"

She was trying to breathe as regularly as possible. All she really wanted to do was scream in frustration. "I've been better."

He took the connection to the 55 southbound, telling himself that it wouldn't be that much longer. "Damn it, Lori, why didn't you go home the way I've been telling you to?"

Here it came again, that pain that took her entire body prisoner, squeezing every part of her. She struggled to stay grounded. "If I had, I'd be going through this alone right now."

That wasn't his point. He zipped around a car that was going too slow for him, mentally cursing at the driver. ''You'd also be closer to the hospital and maybe if you weren't so hell-bent on doing everything as if you weren't pregnant, you wouldn't have gone into labor in the first place.''

That was unrealistic and they both knew it. ''I've been circling my due date for days now. I would have had to have gone into labor eventually.'' She looked at his stony profile. Was he angry at her? No, that wasn't it. She realized he was worried about her, but she wished he could show it with soft words instead of snapping at her. ''Just not around you.'' She clenched her hands in her lap as another wave began to roll over her. She pushed the question out before she couldn't form it. ''Would you have preferred it that way?''

''Yes,'' he bit off.

Well, Carson was nothing if not honest, she thought. He wasn't given to charming lies, the way Kurt had been. She'd seen that as one of Kurt's shortcomings. Still, right now she would have liked to be lied to. She couldn't even say why. Or why she suddenly felt like crying.

''I see. Well, when we pull up at the hospital, you can just push me out the door,'' she retorted. ''I'll roll right in. You don't even have to come to a full stop.''

He hadn't meant to hurt her feelings. The sting of guilt had his anger flaring higher. ''Damn it, Lori, I just mean I'm not any good at this.''

That made two of them. Lori struggled to get a grip on her fear. "Neither am I."

"But you taught Lamaze classes at the hospital," he pointed out. "You had all that background training. You know what's coming." As far as he was concerned, the whole process was as mysterious as plucking a rabbit out of a magician's hat.

As if any of her training helped, she thought in disgust. "Knowing what's coming and being caught right in the middle of it are two entirely different things." She tried to think of something a man could relate to. "It's the difference between watching a war movie and being smack in the middle of a real battle."

"Point taken." The off-ramp was right ahead. He'd made a twenty minute trip in ten. "We're almost there. Won't be long now."

Oh God, here came another one of those things. Even harder than before. It wasn't supposed to be happening this way. She wasn't ready yet. Maybe in another year. "Easy for you to say," she panted.

He didn't like the sound of that. Why was she making those noises? He looked at her. "Lori?"

She shook her head, not answering. Instead, her eyes were fixed on some nebulous point beyond the windshield and she was taking short pants the way she'd shown other women how to do countless times in the class.

Except that this time, it was for real.

She began to feel light-headed.

"Lori, what's going on?" he wanted to know.

"Why are you breathing like that?" Was she going to pass out on him?

She felt as if all the air had been let out of her. It was over, the strange urge to expel all of her organs at once had passed. For now.

Lori blew out a long, cleansing breath then looked at him. Why did he insist on annoying her with all these questions? "Weren't you at your daughter's birth?"

He shook his head. It was one of the main regrets of his life. "I was in the middle of a high profile trial." His mouth twisted grimly. "Jaclyn didn't want me there. She wanted the prestige of having me win."

Even in her present condition, she knew enough to try to navigate past the rapids and toward clearer waters. "Did you?"

"Yeah."

Her heart went out to him. "Then I guess she got what she wanted."

A sigh of resignation escaped his lips. "She always did."

Maybe it was dumb, but she'd never really played it safe when feelings were concerned. And she had a very tender spot in her heart for Carson. Jaclyn was cold for having treated him this way, like an object, a means to an end. He deserved better than that. He deserved someone who loved him for the man he was, not the man someone wanted him to be.

"But you didn't."

That was the mother of all understatements. "I missed Sandy's birth." He'd looked forward to that, counting the days. Jaclyn had tricked him. "I didn't even know she was in labor until after the fact. Jaclyn had gone in and had labor induced to get the whole thing over with.'' Those had been his ex-wife's words. She'd regarded the miracle of their daughter's birth as something odious to get out of the way.

Lori clutched the overhead strap, bracing herself for the next tidal wave of pain. ''How did you ever get so caught up with such a calculating woman?''

He shrugged. Because he'd been lonely. Because Jaclyn had been a stunning woman and knew how to ply her trade. She'd seen him as her ticket to the right circles. All she had to do was get him there. But he'd been blind to all of that. All he'd seen was someone whom said she'd loved him, someone who he thought he loved.

''Seemed like a good idea at the time. Besides, Jaclyn wasn't calculating then. At least,'' he allowed, ''not that I noticed.'' He supposed that had been his fault. ''I was too busy proving myself at the firm.'' It all seemed like it had happened a million years ago.

They were off the freeway. There were only five more long blocks to the hospital.

''Almost there,'' he told her again, hoping that would put her at ease. Or as at ease as she possibly could be at a time like this.

''I'm holding you to that,'' she murmured, beginning to slip back into the web of pain with its steel threads. She shut her eyes tight.

And then she felt a sudden, abrupt jerk.

Lori opened her eyes and saw the line of cars before them. Just like that, traffic had come to almost a dead stop. It looked as if they were in the middle of a parking lot.

This couldn't be happening. She tried to sit up straight and succeeded only marginally. Her body felt as if it was rebelling against her. "What's going on?"

Carson swallowed a curse as he made a calculated guess. "Must be an accident up ahead. Maybe it'll clear up soon." Even as he said it, he didn't believe it. He looked at her. "Can you hang in there?"

She pressed her lips together and nodded, but Carson had serious doubts.

His view was obstructed by the tan SUV in front of him. Frustrated, Carson opened the door on the driver's side.

Lori looked at him. Was he leaving? "What are you doing?"

"Seeing how far this jam extends."

He got out and took hold of the roof, and then climbed up on the doorsill. The extra inches of visibility only showed him more traffic. A whole sea of traffic. It looked as if nothing was moving well past the hospital turn-off. In the distance, he thought he detected red and yellow lights, but that didn't do them any good here.

He got down again and looked into his vehicle.

"Well?" she asked.

He knew she wasn't going to like what he had to tell her. "Doesn't look like it's going to clear up anytime soon."

"Swell." Heat traveled up and down the sides of her body and the pointy instruments of pain were back, jabbing her in all the inappropriate places. She couldn't remain like this indefinitely. "So how do you feel about my delivering in your car?"

There was nowhere to pull off, nowhere to go in order to give her even the smallest measure of privacy. The road was straight and completely exposed all the way past Hospital Road.

There was only one thing to do. Straightening, Carson closed the door on his side.

Panic came crashing down, fueled by hormones that had gone completely awry. What was Carson doing? Where was he going?

She tried to crane her neck as he disappeared from view. The next thing she knew, he was opening the door on her side of the car. She looked at him in confusion. "What's going on?"

"We're going to have to walk there," he told her. He began to take her arm to help her out of her seat.

She pulled it back. "Maybe you, but not me." She was through trying to act tough. "I can't be John Wayne any longer."

Carson laughed dryly. "John Wayne wouldn't have been in this position," he assured her.

He tried to reassess the situation. They couldn't just stay here, waiting for the traffic to clear and he wasn't about to have her deliver her baby in the back of his car. It wasn't sanitary. Besides, all sorts of things could go wrong, not to mention that he didn't want her to have to deal with the embarrassment of having people possibly looking in and seeing her go through the ordeal.

He made up his mind. There was only one thing to do. "You don't have to walk."

''Flying is not an option.'' She was trying very, very hard to keep her growing panic at bay. Her hormones felt as if someone had loaded them into a slingshot and fired. Right now they were ricocheting all over the place.

''No flying,'' he assured her. Taking her by the arm, he eased her out. The next thing she knew, she was in Carson's arms.

Was he crazy? ''Carson, you can't walk to the hospital carrying me like this.''

He had already begun to walk. She was lighter than he'd expected, even with the extra weight. ''Why not?''

''Because I'm too heavy.'' If she'd had the strength, she would have jumped down, but that was really not possible.

Carson smiled at her. ''Been meaning to say something to you about that. You'd better cut out those extra starches.''

She looked back at his vehicle. Had he even locked it? ''What about your car?''

He was aware of the dirty looks that his abandoning the car had garnered. But once Lori was out of the vehicle, the horn blasts from the cars directly behind him had ceased. Everyone familiar with the area knew how close they were to Blair Memorial and the woman in his arms was very obviously pregnant. Adding two and two together wasn't difficult.

''It's not going anywhere.''

She threaded her arms around his neck, knowing she needed to put up more of a protest. But it was hard when she was having trouble catching her breath. ''I can't let you do this.''

If he'd called 9-1-1, she'd be in better hands than his right now. He should have gone with his first instincts. All he could do now was get her there as fast as possible. ''Don't see as how you have much say in the matter. Now stop talking, the hot air is making you heavier.''

She looked at the road ahead of them. Tree-lined, it still made her think of San Francisco. ''Carson, it's uphill all the way.''

''Then you'll owe me. I'll remind you of this every time you start getting argumentative.'' He forced a smile to his lips as he looked down at her. ''Guess we'll be talking about this a lot.'' He felt Lori stiffen against him. ''Bad?''

''Not good,'' she murmured. God help her, it wasn't fair to him but she felt safe in his arms. Unable to do anything else, she buried her face against his shoulder. ''Thank you, Carson.''

Her warm breath penetrated through his shirt, spreading small waves of something he wasn't about to explore through his chest. ''Don't see how I have much say in the matter, either.''

That was so like him. ''Just accept gratitude once in a while.''

He shifted her weight slightly in his arms as he crossed the street and began up the next block. ''I'll see what I can do.''

Chapter Seven

Carson's stride lengthened as he came down the slight incline that led from the sidewalk to the rear entrance of Blair Memorial's Emergency Room. He knew he was jostling Lori with each step he took, but it couldn't be helped.

Her breathing was becoming labored. He could tell by the way she stiffened that she was struggling against another contraction. "Hang in there," he told her. "We're almost there."

She merely nodded in response, pressing her lips together.

"I've got a pregnant woman in labor here," he announced loudly the instant the ER electronic doors sprang open for him.

Within moments an orderly came rushing up, pushing a gurney before him. A nurse followed in the man's wake. Another nurse was on her heels. Questions were being fired at him from all directions.

"Are you the father?"

"Is she hurt?"

"How far along are her contractions?"

"Is her doctor on staff here? Has he been called yet?"

Carson tried to make sense of all the words coming at him. "No. No. I don't know. I think so. No." If there were any other questions in need of answers, he couldn't untangle them from the rest. He looked to Lori for clarification.

There was pain written across her face, but she was alert. For someone in the throes of labor, she still looked pretty damn good, he thought. But then, she'd always looked pretty damn good to him.

Lori wet her lips. In contrast to the rest of her, they were horribly dry. She wasn't even sure she could push the words out between them.

"My doctor's Dr. Sheila Pollack," she told the intern who came up to join the circle of people gathering around her. "There was no time to call her."

A low-level din rose in her ears, closing in around her senses.

Carson was moving back.

He was withdrawing.

Panicked, Lori raised herself up on her elbows just enough to grab hold of his forearm. Her fingers gripped it as tightly as she could manage.

"No." Dark eyes looked at her questioningly. "Stay," she entreated.

Very gently, he tried to disengage himself. For a little thing, Lori had one hell of a grip.

"Lori, they'll take care of you."

Not like he would, she thought frantically. She wanted him with her. Suddenly, she didn't feel like a superwoman—more like vulnerable and afraid. She needed his familiar face in her corner, because it would give her something to focus on.

''No, I want you.'' She looked at the fresh faced intern for support. ''He's my coach,'' she told the bespectacled man.

Stunned, Carson stared at her. This was certainly news to him. She'd never even approached him with the slightest hint that she wanted him with her when she went into labor. There were certainly other places he wanted to be, up to and including the hull of the *Titanic*. ''I'm your *what?*''

''Coach.'' She licked her lips, her tongue almost sticking to them. ''Please?''

''Page Dr. Pollack,'' the intern instructed the taller of the two nurses. ''Tell her one of her patients is about to deliver.'' He raised a brow as he looked at Lori. ''I'm sorry, I didn't get your name.''

It was Carson who snapped the answer out. ''Lori O'Neill.'' She'd slid her fingers down to his wrist and had clamped a death grip around it. ''Lori, you can't be serious. Where's your real coach?''

A contraction started. There wasn't much time for her to answer. She twisted and arched on the gurney. Why did it have to hurt like this? She knew that there were women who had gone through almost a painless delivery, why couldn't she be like one of them?

''I...don't...have...one.''

She never ceased to amaze him. The woman taught

Lamaze classes, for heaven's sake. How could she not have a coach of her own?

The old saying about the shoemaker's children going barefoot struck a hard chord.

The ER head nurse shouldered Carson to the side. "If you're going to coach her," the heavyset woman advised, "you'd better come this way." She looked as if she would brook no nonsense, but her deep brown eyes were kind. "Maternity ward's on the fifth floor and we need to get her up there right away." She nodded toward the orderly. "You know the drill, Jorge."

A row of brilliant white teeth flashed as the short, powerful man took over the gurney and began pushing it out of the ER toward the service elevators.

All he had to do was stop walking. Pull his hand out of her grasp and stop walking, Carson thought. That was all. God knew he certainly didn't want to be part of something so intimate as the birth of Lori's baby.

He wasn't the baby's father and he and Lori were only…

They were close. He and Lori were close. And she needed him.

The argument was over before it was ever begun.

Easing his wrist out of her grasp, Carson took her hand in his and hurried along beside the gurney as the orderly guided it to the back elevators.

He wasn't cut out for this kind of thing. He didn't know how much more he could take.

They had placed Lori in one of the small birthing

rooms. It was cheerfully decorated in an effort to evoke a soothing atmosphere for the miracle that was wrestling its way into the world. But there was nothing cheerful about what Lori was going through.

He was standing beside Lori who was writhing in pain on the bed. The battle had been going on for over six hours with no end in sight.

Carson had never felt so damn useless in his whole life.

Exasperated, he looked at the maternal-looking woman who had just finished checking on Lori. ''Can't you do something about this?'' he demanded. ''Look at her, she's in pain.''

''Yes, sir, I know.'' The nurse's voice was calm, as peaceful as he felt agitated. ''It's all part of the process.''

That was no answer. ''Well, part of the process is sadistic,'' he snapped.

Carson's voice peeled away the haze forming around her brain. Taking his hand, Lori offered the nurse an apologetic smile. ''You'll have to…forgive him.… He…means well, but…his…social graces… are…the first…to go…under…fire.''

The white-haired woman merely laughed, her ample bosom heaving. ''Don't worry about me, honey. I've seen and heard them all. After fifteen years in maternity, I've got a hide like a rhino.'' She smiled at Carson as she exited the room. ''Your wife'll be fine.''

''She's not my wife,'' he protested, but the nurse had already left the room, on her way to the next station on the floor.

He said that with so much feeling, Lori thought. She felt guilty about forcing him to stay. ''I'm sorry…for…putting you through…this.'' She tried to hurry her words out, afraid that any moment, another contraction would cut them short. The effort was draining. ''You can…go…if you…want to.''

Oh, he wanted to all right. Very much. But now that he was here, he couldn't just leave her. To walk out on her now when she was like this seemed almost inhuman, not to mention damn cowardly. Like it or not, she needed him and he was here for the duration.

He shrugged, looking down at her. ''I can stick it out if you can. You've got the tougher assignment.''

She tried to smile. ''Tell me…about it.'' And then her eyes widened like exploding cornflowers and she squeezed his fingers hard.

''Another one?'' It wasn't really a question. The way she was crushing his fingers told him all he needed to know. Carson wondered if he would ever fully regain the use of his right hand once this was over.

Unable to answer, Lori nodded. Pressing her lips together, she struggled to hold back the scream she felt gurgling in her throat.

Damn it, why couldn't he do something to help her? he thought angrily. Why couldn't *someone* do something? ''The nurse said it wouldn't be long now,'' he repeated. The promise didn't comfort either one of them.

''All…depends…on your…perspective.'' Right now, it was feeling pretty much like an eternity to her.

He looked at the pink pitcher on the side table. Water was condensing along its sides like falling teardrops. ''Want some more ice chips?'' He was already reaching for the pitcher, needing to do something besides look at her helplessly.

But Lori moved her head from side to side. Ice chips wouldn't help. Her mouth was dry the second the chips melted.

''Only...if they have...knock-out drops...in...them.''

It was going to be over with soon. Soon, she promised herself. Lori tried to focus on a point in time in the future when this was behind her, but the pain kept anchoring her to the moment. There were only small respites now, far shorter than the waves of pain that came in their wake.

How much more could she take? she thought in desperation.

Taking out his handkerchief, Carson gently mopped her brow before the perspiration could fall into her eyes. Suddenly, every bone in her body looked like it was stiffening.

Lori bit back another scream. ''Get...the...doctor!'' she ordered, her voice gravelly.

He clutched her hand, giving her something to hold onto to. She cut off his circulation. ''Why? What's wrong?''

Wrong? What did he think was wrong? She was exploding, that was what was wrong. ''The baby's... coming.''

He hesitated. She'd said this before. ''It's been coming for the last six hours.'' Six years was more like it to him.

Why was he arguing with her? ‘‘Now… It’s… coming…NOW,’’ she insisted.

He’d already called the nurse into the room three other times. Each time Lori had been certain that the delivery was imminent, but she wasn’t dilated far enough.

One look at Lori’s face and any thoughts of trying to reason with her fled. Carson went to the door again.

He looked up and down the hallway. The nurse was just coming out of the room next to Lori’s.

‘‘I think she’s ready this time.’’

The nurse was patience itself. There wasn’t even a glimmer of skepticism on her face. ‘‘Then let’s go see, shall we?’’

Preceding him into the room, the nurse went straight to the foot of Lori’s bed and positioned herself on the stool placed there. Carson looked away as she pulled back the sheet and examined Lori.

With a smile, the woman rose from the stool and dropped the sheet back into place. ‘‘Looks like this time, you’re going to have yourselves a baby.’’

Carson stared at her in disbelief. He’d begun to feel that the baby was never going to come. ‘‘You mean she’s really having it now?’’

The nurse nodded. ‘‘That’s what I mean.’’ She looked at Lori. ‘‘You’re completely effaced. Ten centimeters. I’ll go get Dr. Pollack.’’

Lori dug her heels into the bed for traction. ‘‘Hurry,’’ she pleaded.

The woman was already gone.

Alone with Lori, Carson sank his hands into his

pockets. He glanced toward the closed door. "I should go."

She looked at him, not comprehending the words. "What?"

How could a single word make him feel so guilty? It wasn't his place to be here. "This is too personal, Lori. You don't want me here."

Her head was spinning. "Yes." She pushed the word out between clenched teeth. One of the monitors moved as she raised her hips from the bed. There was no hiding place from this. "I…do."

Forming an arch, her whole body looked like a sine curve on a graph.

She put her hand out, her fingers fanning the air frantically, unable to reach him. He knew that all he had to do was just take a step away, then another and another until he reached the other side of the door.

He moved back to the bed. Back to Lori and what had somehow become his responsibility.

Taking her hand, he stroked her hair. "It's going to be all right."

She hung onto the assurance as if it was a lifeline pulling her out of the swirling whirlpool. Consumed by another contraction, harder than all the rest. "Promise?"

"Promise."

The look in her eyes told Carson she was grateful for the comfort. And for his remaining in the room with her.

A tall, slender blonde wearing green scrubs entered the room. "I hear we're having a baby in the next few minutes.'' Dr. Sheila Pollack gave off a calming, confident aura the moment she walked into the room. She looked at Carson. ''Hello, I'm Dr. Sheila Pollack.'' Her smile was quick, confident. ''But you've probably figured that part out by now.''

''Carson O'Neill. I'm her brother-in-law,'' he felt compelled to add.

''Nice of you to be here, Carson.'' Sheila took Lori's other hand in hers and gave it a comforting squeeze. ''Ready to bring this baby in?''

''More…than…ready.''

''Then let the games begin.'' Sheila flashed her a smile and positioned herself at the foot of the bed. She moved the sheet aside. One quick look was all that was needed. ''Oh yes, I'd say that you were more than ready. It's a lovely evening for a baby to be born.''

''I…can…push?'' It was all she'd wanted to do for the past half hour.

Sheila nodded. ''Absolutely. On my count.'' She raised her eyes to Carson, her smile encouraging. ''I want you behind her, Carson, supporting her shoulders. Raise her off the bed,'' she instructed. When he complied, she nodded. ''That's it. All right, Lori, this is it. On three. One—two—three. Push!''

Lori squeezed her eyes shut, squeezed with the rest of her body as well. She held her breath as she pushed as hard as she was physically able.

She was beginning to feel light-headed when she heard Sheila order, ''All right, stop.''

She fell back, exhausted, against Carson's hands. They felt strong, capable and all she wanted to do was somehow shrink down into nothingness and hide within them. But then she stiffened as another contraction seized her in its jaws.

Sheila looked at the monitor, seeing the contraction before it arrived. ''Okay, Lori, again. One—two—three, push!''

Lori had no choice in the matter. It was as if the baby, eager to finally come into the world, pushed for her. Holding her breath, she bore down so hard, bursts of light began to dance through her head and behind her shut eyelids.

Propping her up, Carson brought his face in close to hers from behind. ''Can't you do a C-section?'' he prodded the doctor. This didn't seem right, having someone suffer like this.

''She doesn't need a C-section,'' Sheila assured him. She managed to do it without sounding patronizing. ''She's doing just fine, really.'' Sheila smiled at Lori. ''Aren't you, Lori?''

Lori felt as if she could hardly draw in enough air to sustain herself. It was leaving her lungs faster than it was coming in. She barely nodded in response to her doctor's question.

''Depends...on...your...definition...of...fine.''

The look she gave Lori was nothing if not empathetic. Sheila had two children of her own and knew about the pain of childbirth from both sides of the delivery room. She took a deep breath, as if to brace herself for Lori's ordeal. ''Okay, ready?''

Lori wanted to say no, she wasn't ready, but suddenly there was this overwhelming urge to push again and she was swept away with it. She made a noise that passed for agreement.

Behind her, she could feel Carson propping her up again. Offering up quick fragments of all the prayers she could think of, Lori closed her eyes and began to push again.

She was a hell of a lot stronger than he was, Carson couldn't help thinking. He would have been wiped out by the pain. "You can do this, Lori. C'mon, just a little more."

Lori realized that Carson had lowered his head and was uttering the words of encouragement into her ear. They echoed in her head as she bore down a second time, pushing so hard she thought she was going to pass out from the effort.

And then she heard it, heard the tiny wail.

Was that her? Was she making those noises?

No, she realized, the sounds were coming from somewhere else. From her baby.

Her baby.

Lori's eyes fluttered open again and it was like coming out of a deep, gut-wrenching trance.

"Baby?" It took all the strength she had just to utter the single word.

"Baby," Sheila confirmed, pleased. "You have a lovely baby girl with ten fingers and ten toes." She looked up at Lori, beaming.

The nurse beside her took the infant and wrapped her up in a sparkling white blanket. The tiny wail ceased as her huge eyes seemed to sweep around the room, as if she was as amazed to be here as Lori was amazed to finally have her here.

"Would you like to hold her?" Sheila's question was addressed to Carson.

He began to say no, that the joy of being the first to hold this new life belonged to Lori. But one look at the tiny being now nestled against the attending nurse's maternal breast and he knew he was a goner. He fell hard and instantly in love.

Carson looked to Lori for permission. She seemed to understand what he was silently asking her and she nodded her head.

"Yes," he murmured.

The nurse transferred the infant to his arms. They closed protectively around the baby.

The infant was so light, she felt like nothing. And like everything.

Carson had no idea that it could happen so fast, that love could strike like lightning and fill every part of him with its mysterious glow. But it could and it did. It coated him completely, leaving nothing untouched, nothing unaltered.

This tiny life form was deeply embedded in his heart.

"She's beautiful," he told Lori. "But then," he looked at her, "I guess that was a given."

Was that a compliment? Or was her head just fuzzy because of this ordeal? Lori wasn't sure. It wasn't like Carson to say something nice like that, but then, she wouldn't have thought he'd carry her for blocks uphill to the hospital, either.

And then she remembered. "Oh God, Carson, your car."

He'd completely forgotten about that. It had probably been towed away by now. It was going to take some doing to find where it had been taken. He was going to have to call someone to come and get him once he left the hospital. Details, just details. What mattered was that Lori and the baby were all right.

"Good thing we didn't take your car."

Very gently, he lay the infant in the crook of Lori's arm. Stepping back, he looked at mother and daughter and thought that he'd never seen anything more beautiful, never seen Lori looking more radiant. Not even at her wedding to his brother.

Something stirred deep within him, struggling to rise to the surface. Self-preservation instincts had him trying to keep it down, to push it back to where it could exist without causing any complications.

Back to where it had existed all this time without seeing the light of day.

"She has your eyes," he told Lori.

Lori raised hers from her baby's solemn face to his. "And your expression."

"She's young. You'll teach her."

Lori smiled, feeling very content and very, very tired. She looked at him meaningfully. "Yes," she said softly, "I will."

Chapter Eight

They descended upon her en masse, just as they had when they had first gotten together. The ladies of The Mom Squad walked into her single care unit, bearing gifts, good wishes and chatter, all of which Lori welcomed with both arms.

The women were all slender now, living testimony that there was life after pregnancy and delivery. Though she'd espoused the theory time and again for the benefit of the mothers-to-be who populated her Lamaze classes, Lori was genuinely relieved to see it in practice so close at hand. That meant that there was hope for her, too.

Each of the three women hugged her in turn, smelling heavenly and ushering in sunshine.

"Boy," Joanna Prescott, a teacher herself, teased as she stepped back, "leave it to the teacher to be the only one to follow rules and have her baby the prescribed way." She raised a brow. "In a hospital."

Their resident reporter, Sherry Campbell, was more than willing to join in the good-natured razzing. ''Not like me, in a cabin almost a hundred miles from a certified hospital.''

''Or me,'' Special Agent Chris ''C.J.'' Jones reminded them, ''on the floor of the FBI task office dedicated to tracking down the Sleeping Beauty serial killer.''

As far as she was concerned, Joanna felt she had the others beat by a mile. ''Oh, and the lawn in front of my burning house was better?''

''Stop.'' Lori held her hands up to hold back the competitive comparisons. ''You're all making me feel deadly dull.''

Sherry looked at her in mock surprise. They were all privy to the particulars of the infant's arrival. She, like the other two women, had also met Carson O'Neill the night he'd had to pick Lori up from class because her car was in the shop.

''Oh, I don't know, having a man, who clearly looks like a Greek god, carry you in his arms for five blocks to get to that hospital isn't exactly shabby, you know.''

Lori didn't want the women to get the wrong idea. Without looking, they had all managed to find the kind of life partners that most women only dreamed about. But that hadn't happened to her. Carson would probably have been horrified to learn he was cast in that kind of role. ''He's my brother-in-law.''

C.J. pinned her with a knowing look. ''He's a fox,'' she pointed out.

Lori shook her head. Incurable romantics, all of

them. Including the FBI Special Agent, who should have known better. "You're making something out of nothing."

But C.J. wasn't about to back off. Not when she knew she was right. She'd seen the way Carson had looked at Lori when the latter had been busy answering a question for a straggler. It wasn't the kind of look a brother-in-law directed at his brother's widow. Not unless there was an strong undercurrent of feelings involved.

"I think you're making nothing out of something," C.J. contradicted. As Lori opened her mouth to protest, C.J. added, "Don't forget, it's my job to look beneath the surface. From what I've witnessed, I'd say that the man has definite feelings for you."

Lori sighed. The woman was incorrigible. "Of course he has feelings for me. I'm his late brother's wife and we always got along." She shrugged vaguely. "As far as I know, I'm the only one he's ever talked to about his ex-wife."

Triumphant, C.J. exchanged looks with the other women. "Aha."

She wasn't about to let her thoughts drift that way, no matter how tempting that route might be. "No 'aha,'" Lori told her, "just 'uh-huh.'"

Sherry piled the newly opened gifts that they'd brought together and placed them on the side shelf for Lori. "Sweetie, you pushed out a baby. I really hope you didn't push out your common sense along with her, too."

Lori dug in. "I've always had more than enough to spare."

Sherry's eyes dance. "See that you do," she advised meaningfully. "Nothing worse than slamming the door shut when opportunity comes knocking."

"Opportunity?" Joanna teased. "Is that what you call it now?"

Sherry laughed. "I call it anything it wants to be called. All I know is that if I hadn't gone after that story about Sinjin, I wouldn't have wound up giving birth in his cabin with him acting as a midwife. And, I wouldn't be looking down the right side of a wedding date now."

"That's you, not me," Lori pointed out, then added, "Thank you all for your good thoughts, but you're letting your imaginations run away with you. Carson is just a very good man, that's all."

"Well you know what they say," C.J. told her. "A good man is hard to find and the three of us have just about cornered the market. Carson may be the last of his breed left. I say go for it."

Lori wasn't about to let any latent hopes for any sort of meaningful relationship be nurtured by these women. If Carson occupied a special place in her heart, it was just because he was kind and good and had been there for her when she needed him most. To think anything else was just asking for trouble. She'd had enough of that already.

Lori shifted in her head. "So tell me what's been going on in your lives since we last got together."

It was all the lead-in the others needed.

"I've brought a visitor to see you."

Lori had just begun to drift off. After the Mom

Squad had left, she'd spent the latter part of her morning getting thoroughly acquainted with her brand-new daughter. The nurse had taken the baby away not ten minutes ago, leaving her to take a short nap before lunch arrived.

Carson's voice emerged out of the dream that had begun to form and registered in the back of her mind.

He wasn't in her dream, he was here. In her room. Lori struggled against the curtain of sleep that was surrounding her and forced herself to pry open her eyes.

When she did, she saw Carson walking into the room. He wasn't alone. He'd brought his daughter Sandy with him. At six foot two, Carson towered over the five-year-old who was holding tightly onto his hand.

Lori pressed the top arrow on her guard rail. The back of her bed began to rise slowly until she was sitting up so she could look at her niece. "Hi."

With her thick, straight black hair and electric blue eyes, Sandy O'Neill was a small female version of her father. The little girl smiled shyly at her. Huge, kissable dimples appeared in each cheek.

"Hi," she echoed.

This really was a surprise, Lori thought. She hadn't seen Carson's daughter since Christmas. Jaclyn had given him exactly one day to spend with the little girl. Or, more precisely, six hours. He'd made the most of it. The three of them had shared the time together.

Warm, sweet and quick to laugh, Sandy was everything her mother wasn't. "Have you seen the baby yet?" Lori asked her.

Sandy moved her head from side to side, the tips of her straight bob moving back and forth against her cheeks. Her eyes never broke contact with hers. ''No. Daddy wanted to come here first.''

''We thought you might want to come with us,'' Carson explained.

The man continued to be an endless font of surprises. ''That was very thoughtful of you.''

Carson snorted. ''Don't make a big deal out of it,'' he told her gruffly. ''I wasn't sure if I could pick the kid out of the crowd, that's all.''

That was a crock and they both knew it. Why was being recognized as a good man so hard for him to accept? ''The nurses can always help steer you in the right direction, you know.''

''Yeah, well...'' Shrugging, he let his voice trail off. He released Sandy's hand, nodding at her instead. ''You need help getting up?''

Lori reached for the robe that was stretched out on the end of her bed. Her smile was warm, grateful. ''A strong arm to lean on might be nice. By the way, who's taking over my place at the center?''

He doubted that anyone could take Lori's place. She gave a great deal of herself to the kids. A lot more than he was paying her for. ''For now, Rhonda's pulling double shift.''

Lori thought of the younger woman. ''She must be loving that.''

''Actually, it's not too bad,'' he told her. ''She just had another big fight with that worthless jerk she's hooked up. They broke up and she has a lot of extra time on her hands. So this is working out.''

''Every cloud has a silver lining,'' Lori murmured, pushing her arms through the sleeves of the robe.

''So you keep trying to tell me,'' he muttered. The tone of his voice told her that he was no closer to believing that than he'd ever been.

Lori paused to look at him. ''Only because it's true.'' Throwing off the light blanket, she slowly swung her legs down, trying not to allow the pain in her lower half impede her. She scooted to the edge of the bed. ''Sandy, can you get my slippers for me?''

The little girl looked eager to be of use. With a solemn face, she crouched down on the floor and elaborately peered under the bed. With a small cry of triumph, she gathered up the slippers and held them against her chest as she stood up again.

''These?''

Lori smiled warmly at her. ''Absolutely. But I'm, going to need them on the floor, honey.''

''I'll take it from here, Sandy.'' Taking the slippers from his daughter's hands, Carson placed them on the floor in front of Lori. ''Here,'' he offered, holding out his hand, ''just hold onto me.''

''Can't Aunt Lori stand up?'' Sandy asked, concern pinching her small face.

In response, Lori smiled at the little girl's concern. ''I'm just a little wobbly, honey, that's all.''

Lori curled her fingers around the hand Carson held out to her. Holding on tightly, she stood up, sliding her feet into the slippers. It wasn't her first time on her feet. Since the delivery, the nurse had been by twice to chase her out of bed and to help her take a short, painful walk down the hall and back to her room. But her legs still felt rubbery and weak.

She was holding on to Carson more than she would have liked. ''You might regret this offer,'' she warned him.

''Let me worry about that.'' Carson tucked her arm through his, pressing it against his side to anchor her. ''We'll take it slow,'' he promised.

She looked at him for a long moment. ''Yes, I know.'' Her tone was as pregnant as she had been a short while ago.

Carson pretended not to notice. It was easier that way than dealing with the thoughts that kept crowding his head, or the feelings that kept crowding his soul. He looked at her. ''Ready?''

She took a deep breath, catching her lower lip between her teeth before saying, ''As I'll ever be.''

Sandy watched her with wide eyes that were so much like her father's. ''What's the matter, Aunt Lori? Are you sick?''

Lori was hanging onto his arm, slightly hunched. ''Aunt Lori's got a big hurt,'' Carson explained tactfully.

''Does it hurt to have a baby?''

''Sandy,'' Carson warned. He'd told his daughter about the baby being in ''Aunt Lori's tummy'' because he believed in being as straightforward as possible with her. But he didn't want her asking any probing questions.

''Just a little, honey,'' Lori lied. She saw Carson looking at her with dubious surprise. ''Well, I don't want to scare her,'' she whispered.

He merely nodded, the corners of his mouth curving slightly.

They had passed the nursery on the way from the elevators. Even at her tender age, Sandy had already demonstrated to Carson that she possessed complete recall. He envisioned a future without limits for his little girl. Dancing ahead of them on her toes, Sandy led the way to the nursery.

She made Lori think of a little fairy princess. Right now, Lori was envious of Sandy's light-footedness. ''It was nice of you to bring her,'' she told Carson.

He took no credit. ''I told her about the baby. She wanted to come.''

There was more to it than that. He'd told her that his ex-wife was not congenial when it came to visitation rights. ''How did you manage to spring her?''

He cut down his stride considerably for Lori's sake. He could feel her digging her fingers into his arm. ''Wasn't hard. Jaclyn and her husband left for Hawaii day before yesterday. Sandy was left with the housekeeper.''

Who undoubtedly had orders not to let the child see her father, Lori thought. ''So you charmed the pants off her.''

His laugh was dry, short. ''You've got me confused with Kurt. He was the one who could charm articles of clothing off women.'' A talent that had gotten his brother in trouble more than once. ''Besides, Adele is almost sixty,'' he said referring to the housekeeper. ''Her pants are very firmly in place.''

''I think you underestimate yourself, Carson. You might not have a golden tongue, but that doesn't make you any less charming or attractive.'' Pausing, she cocked her head as she regarded his profile. ''Joanna Prescott thinks you're a hunk.''

Carson frowned at the assessment. ''Joanna Prescott should have the prescription to her glasses checked,'' he suggested.

''She doesn't wear glasses.''

''Maybe she should start.''

''Oh, I don't know, you do look pretty good in the right light.''

When they were growing up, Kurt had always been the good-looking one. His role had been to be the dependable one. To hear anyone refer to him any other way always raised his suspicions. Carson eyed her now. ''You want me to leave you stranded here?''

She raised her free hand in a mock oath. ''I'll behave.''

He raised a skeptical brow aimed in her direction. ''That'll be the day.''

Sandy was standing on her tiptoes with her face pressed against the large bay window. There were three long rows of bassinets displayed. ''Can we pick out any one we want?'' Sandy wanted to know. She shifted from toe to toe excitedly.

''She's not an ice-cream cone, Sandy,'' Carson told her patiently. ''Each of these babies already belongs to someone.''

Sandy turned partway from the window, looking up at her father. ''Which one belongs to us?''

''The baby belongs to Aunt Lori, not us.''

''We can share her,'' Lori told Sandy with a wink. The girl looked up at her, pleased.

Carson picked his daughter up so that she could have a better view. ''It's that one, over there.'' He pointed out a pink cheeked baby in the third row, the second bassinet from the right end.

From this distance, the name tags were hard to make out. Lori cocked her head as she looked up at him. ''I thought they all looked alike to you.''

Lori was grinning at him when he looked at her. Putting his daughter down, he shrugged. ''She looks more familiar than the others do.'' He set Sandy down. ''Did I guess right?''

Lori looked at him knowingly. ''You didn't guess at all.''

He supposed there was no point in lying about it. ''Yeah, well maybe I was here before. When they put her in her bassinet last night.''

She wouldn't have thought he would do that. But then, Carson was doing a lot of things she wouldn't have thought him capable of as little as eight months ago. ''You followed the nurse?''

He shrugged. ''Just wanted to be sure they didn't lose the kid.'' Was it his imagination, or did Lori's arms tighten slightly through his?

''Why is it that I never noticed how sweet you were before?''

He didn't have to look at her to know she was smiling. broadly. ''Maybe because you were never delirious with pain before.''

She took her case to Sandy. ''Your daddy's a nice man,'' she told the little girl.

In response, Sandy turned from the bay window with its large selection of babies that had kept her so fascinated and looked up solemnly at her father. She nodded her head vigorously. "I know."

In turn, Lori looked at the man at her side, her point won. "Out of the mouths of babes."

He raised a single eyebrow. "You talking about Sandy or yourself?"

"Scoff if you must, Carson, that doesn't change anything. You're a lot nicer than you want people to know about."

He merely shook his head. Former lawyer or not, he knew better than to get into a debate with Lori. "Like I said, delirious."

The day nurse assigned to the rooms in Lori's section peered into the room. "Are you all set?"

More than sct, Lori thought. She was going home. Barely two days after the delivery and she was going home to begin her life as a mother.

The first step of an eighteen-year journey, she thought.

She glanced down at the suitcase on her bed. Carson had brought it to her the morning after she'd delivered. Except for her nightgown, her robe and the slippers she'd bought expressly for her hospital stay, she hadn't taken out anything. All three items were back in the case.

"All set."

"Let's not forget the most important item." Pushing the door open with her shoulder, the nurse came all the way into the room. Lori's baby was in her arms. "Can't be a mom without one of these."

Nerves danced and retreated. Smiling, Lori took the baby into her arms. ''No, I guess you can't.''

The nurse stood beside her for a moment. She patted Lori's arm. ''You'll do fine.''

She had her doubts about that, Lori thought, fervently wishing her mother was still alive. For a whole host of reasons. ''Can I hold you to that?''

''For as long as you'd like.'' The nurse adjusted the baby's receiving blanket around her. ''Remember, any questions, Blair has a new mom hot line. Night or day, just call,'' she instructed. ''There'll always be someone to answer your questions.''

Lori knew that. It was something she told the women at the Lamaze classes. It was something for them to cling to. Now it was her turn, Lori thought. The baby books she'd read were all well and good, but nothing beat talking to someone who had already experienced what she was going through.

''How long am I going to be considered a new mom?''

The nurse smiled at her. ''Just until after they go off to college.'' Taking out a card, she tucked the telephone number into Lori's purse on the table. ''Remember, night or day,'' she repeated. ''Now then, who's taking you home?''

''I am.''

As if he'd been waiting in the wings for his cue, Carson strode into the room, looking bigger than life to Lori. She smiled a greeting at him. ''Hi.''

He was running late and there was nothing he disliked more than being late. ''There's some kind of construction going on along Blair Boulevard,'' he said by way of explanation.

The nurse nodded, obviously familiar with the problem. ''They've started widening the road.''

Carson frowned. He was a firm believer in not fixing things that weren't broken. ''The road was fine the way it was.''

Lori grinned. ''Don't mind him, he doesn't like progress.''

''I've got nothing against progress. It's gridlock I don't like.'' He paused to look at the baby, then asked Lori, ''You ready?''

She looked around. ''Let me see, suitcase, baby, yes, I'm ready.''

Carson glanced toward the nurse. ''Do I need to sign her out?''

Lori answered for her. ''You're not springing an inmate from an asylum, Carson. You're just taking home a very antsy new mom.''

The word caught his attention. ''Antsy?'' She'd already given birth, what was there to be antsy about? ''Why?''

''Just afraid I'll do something wrong, that's all,'' Lori confessed.

He tried to laugh her out of it. ''That's a first. It never stopped you before.'' Carson grew serious. ''This isn't going to be any different than anything else you've ever done.''

He was supposed to be the pessimist here, not her. ''Since when did you get so blasé?''

He'd done a little attitude adjusting these past few weeks. Circumstances had forced him to do some reassessing. "Since I found out that if life knocks you down, you just have to stand up again."

Taking her elbow, he helped Lori into the wheelchair and then waited until the nurse placed the baby back into Lori's arms. Carson moved behind the wheelchair, taking control. He nodded at the other woman. "Okay, let's roll."

The nurse picked up the vase of flowers that was still in the room. Lori had given away the other flowers, sending them on to the children's ward and to the chapel on the first floor. But the pink and white carnations the nurse was holding had come from Carson. She wanted to take them home with her.

Lori craned her neck to look at him as he pushed her out of the room. "Thanks for coming to pick me up."

"I had to. I was afraid you'd thumb a ride if I didn't." Coming to the elevator banks, he pressed for a car. It arrived almost instantly.

His answer was typically flippant. "Why can't you just let me say thank you?"

He pressed for the first floor. "Had anyone ever been able to stop you from saying anything?"

"You've tried more than once," she pointed out. The passing floors flashed their numbers at them as they went down to the first floor without stopping once.

"Don't remember succeeding, though."

The elevator doors opened. Carson pushed the wheelchair down the long, winding hallway, hardly paying attention to the arrows that guided him to the entrance. He knew the way by heart now.

His car was parked just ahead in the temporary zone. There was a valet standing beside it. "By the way," Carson began as he guided her through the electronic doors. "I'm spending the night."

Chapter Nine

She'd stared at Carson in stunned silence as the nurse momentarily took the baby from her. She continued staring as he helped her out of the wheelchair and into the car. It wasn't until the baby was back in her arms and they had pulled away from temporary loading zone that Lori regained possession of her tongue.

"What do you mean you're spending the night?" She had to have misheard him. "Spending what night where?"

He'd thought he'd been clear enough. Carson glanced at her just before he merged to the left and entered the flow of traffic. "Are you on any medication?"

"Don't change the subject," she warned. "What did you just mean back there?"

Carson frowned as a sports car cut him off. "Same thing I mean here." In deference to the fact that he wasn't alone in the car, he swallowed the curse that rose to his lips. "I'm staying at your house tonight."

The offer had come out of nowhere and it wasn't like Carson. She grinned, wondering if he was aware of how it sounded. "This is a little sudden, don't you think?"

Carson slanted her another look, certain she couldn't mean what he thought she meant. Certain she couldn't be feeling what he'd felt. She was a widow, she'd just given birth and he was the guy who was always just there, that's all.

Wasn't her fault he'd been feeling things lately. That helping her deliver her baby had somehow placed a very different focus on their relationship for him. That her upbeat, warm personality had finally managed to cut through the corrugated fencing he'd kept around his soul. That was his problem, not hers.

But he was more than willing and able to help her with what was her problem. Adjustment.

He winged it. "Sudden? You've been pregnant for eight months. There's nothing sudden about it. I just figured you might need help the first night."

He got that right, she thought. Still, he was the last person she would have thought would realize the fact. The man kept astounding her.

"And you're volunteering?"

He queued onto the freeway ramp. There was some sort of traffic jam on the other side, but except for a few rubbernecks who slowed down to look, their side moved along at a good pace. "Don't see anyone else in the car, do you?"

Just when she thought he was being as nice as he

was possibly able to be, Carson upped the ante. "Just the baby, but she's a little too young to be changing her own diaper," Lori said.

His expression was impassive, unreadable. "Sounds like her mother might be a little too young to change her diapers."

He was covering, she thought. Making a flippant remark about how young she sometimes acted in order to hide something. She wasn't sure what he could possibly want to hide. It couldn't be what she hoped it was. Any excess feelings Carson O'Neill had were all sent special delivery to his daughter. There wasn't anything else left over.

No matter how she was beginning to feel about him.

Because her own feelings were oddly vulnerable now, she retreated to the same flippant ground where he'd taken shelter. "Hey, I've taught men who were all thumbs how to diaper a baby."

She had book knowledge, he had something better. "A doll," he pointed out, "you taught them how to change a doll. The real thing's different." For one thing, it moved a great deal more than a doll did, he thought, remembering his first time. That he'd changed his daughter's diapers wasn't something he'd ever advertised. The information went against the image he liked to project, the one he felt comfortable with. That of an unapproachable authority figure.

But for Lori, he was willing to temporarily abandon that image.

She studied his profile, trying to picture him with baby powder in his hand and a dirty diaper waiting for disposal in front of him. ''And you'd know about the real thing?''

His expression never changed. ''I've got Sandy, don't I?''

''You diapered Sandy?''

He could hear it in her voice, she was going to start teasing him any second. ''What, am I talking a foreign language?''

''Apparently.'' She knew he wouldn't have revealed this to just anyone and was truly surprised that he trusted her with this information. It touched her. ''I just can't picture you diapering a baby, that's all.'' Her voice became more serious, more thoughtful. ''I guess I really don't know you as well as I thought.''

He'd never liked the idea of being thought of as an open book. Open books had no privacy and privacy was of paramount importance to him. ''There's a lot about me you don't know.''

''Apparently,'' she murmured again.

But she was willing to learn, Lori added silently. More than willing.

The door was open, but Carson knocked anyway. He didn't feel right about just walking in. After all, it was her bedroom and he didn't belong in it.

When Lori turned her head toward him, he told her, ''I think the baby's hungry.''

Giving in to Carson's insistence, she'd lain down for a few moments. Until she had, she hadn't realized just how exhausted she really felt. This first day was taking more out of her than she'd imagined.

A few moments had easily stretched out into twenty minutes.

Lori sat up, dragging a hand through her hair. She felt guilty about being so inactive. This was her baby and for the past hour, Carson had been the one taking care of her.

Still standing in the doorway, Carson avoided looking in her direction as he explained, ''I can't warm up her meal for her.''

She was breast-feeding Emma. Lori smiled to herself as she rose. A lot he knew. He'd been warming up the vessel that contained the baby's meal since he'd brought her home. Longer.

Did he even have a clue about the way he'd been affecting her? Would it scare him if he knew? ''I'll be right there.''

''No need.'' He walked into the room with Emma. ''I brought Mohammed to the mountain.''

She laughed, opening the top button of her blouse. ''So now I look like a mountain?''

Carson slipped the infant into the crook of her arm, being very careful not to brush his fingers against anything they shouldn't be coming in contact with. ''Figure of speech. You don't look like a mountain. You look terrific.''

A compliment. Was he even aware he was paying it? She raised her eyes to his. ''Really?''

Carson flushed. ''I don't say anything I don't mean.'' As if aware of how close he was to her, he took a step away from the bed. ''Just sometimes I say too much.''

Her eyes met his. That would be the day. Clams were more talkative than he was. ''I don't think so, Carson. God knows no one is ever going to accuse you of being a chatterbox.''

He took another step back, then stopped. ''I leave that to you.''

With the baby pressed against her breast, Lori opened another button on her blouse, and then another. ''Thanks a lot.''

With effort, he tore his eyes away, although this time it wasn't easy. Noble intentions only extended so far. ''Um, I've got some...stuff to see to.''

She saw the pink hue creeping up his cheeks. ''Are you embarrassed?'' Lori stopped unbuttoning her blouse. She'd never thought that anything could embarrass Carson. ''You were there at her birth.''

''If you recall,'' he addressed the wall above her head, ''I was positioned at your other end.''

The man was positively adorable. ''And you didn't look?''

''Nope. Figured you needed your privacy, even at a time like that.''

She didn't know of any other man quite like him. ''You really are amazing, you know that?''

''Like I said,'' he jerked his thumb toward the hall and beyond, ''stuff.''

With that, Carson pivoted on his heel and withdrew, moving a little quicker than Lori thought the situation warranted.

The sound of her soft laughter accompanied him out into the hall.

* * *

He was an early riser. He always had been. When he awoke at morning, he was surprised that the baby hadn't interrupted his sleep. Newborns woke up every few hours and made their presence known. He'd fully intended to spell Lori. Instead, he'd slept like a dead man.

Some help he was, Carson thought, disgusted with himself as he made his way into the kitchen. He had every intention of making breakfast for them both.

Entering, he discovered that Lori had gotten there ahead of him. Her back to him, she was just opening the refrigerator.

''What are you doing out of bed?'' He wanted to know.

Hurrying, she'd almost dropped the plate of butter she was taking out. She set it on the counter, taking a deep breath to steady her pulse. ''I believe it's called making breakfast.''

He glanced toward the stove. There was more than enough in the frying pan for two people. This wasn't working out the way it was supposed to.

''I didn't stay over for you to make breakfast for me.''

He made it hard to say thank you, Lori thought. ''No, you stayed over to see me through my first night and I appreciate that more than you'll ever know.'' She divided the contents of the frying pan between the two plates she had waiting on the counter. Scrambled eggs filled each. ''Now, I can't carry you to a hospital, I can't help you give birth and I can't be your moral support in a time of muted crisis.'' Placing the frying pan into the sink, she ran hot water into it, then shut it off. "The very least you can do is let me make you breakfast."

He was accustomed to lukewarm breakfasts eaten at his desk at the center. Even when he'd been a lawyer, he'd eaten in his office. "I was thinking of picking up something at a drive through."

Fat, served up medium warm, she thought. The toaster gave up its slices. Moving quickly, she buttered two for him. "Is that how you eat?"

He shrugged. Food was something to sustain him, not something to look forward to. "Most of the time."

"Then I've been remiss." Arranging the toast around his eggs, she placed his plate on the table. "You are hereby invited over for any meal of your choice any time you want." Grabbing a fork and a napkin, she set down both beside his plate. "Now sit."

He was trying to help her cope, not give her more work. "I'm not about to come barging in on you—"

She fixed him with a look. "Sit!"

He didn't feel like getting into an argument first thing in the morning. He planted himself on a chair. "Yes ma'am."

"Better." Taking her own plate, she sat down opposite him in the small nook. There was bacon on her plate. She noticed he looked at it. "I didn't make any bacon for you because I remembered you didn't like it."

They'd never had breakfast together. "How do you know I don't like bacon?"

"Kurt told me." Picking up the curled bacon slice in her fingers, she broke a piece off and popped it into her mouth. "I remember things." A smile curved her lips as she looked at him. "Like that argument we never finished."

He was already sampling his portion. He had to admit, this beat cardboard eggs in a foam box seven ways from sundown. "What argument?"

"More like a discussion, really," she amended, watching his face. "Just before you did your hero thing."

She was talking about that damn fund-raiser, wasn't she? "It wasn't a hero thing and if you want to pay me back for anything, you'll drop the subject."

That far she wasn't willing to go. "You know I'm right."

Why had he even thought she'd give up on this? "What I know is that once you get hold of a subject, you can be a damn pain in the neck about it." She said nothing, merely continued to look at him as she ate. Why did that make him feel like squirming inside? He knew she was wrong about this. "You know, this isn't going to do you any good. I still think it's a bad idea. It's not going to work," he insisted.

"Yes, it will," she countered. Finishing her bacon, she leaned in over the table, her eyes excited. "I already talked to Sherry and Joanna about it when they came to the hospital and they think it's a great idea."

He forced himself to look down at his plate. Looking into her eyes made him lose his train of thought. "Your friends' opinions notwithstanding—"

She knew what he was going to say. That they were

her friends and had to side with her. But that wasn't the point she was trying to make. ''And they're both engaged to billionaires.''

The information temporarily brought his train to a halt before it could even exit the station. ''Billionaires?''

She nodded her head, aware that she'd managed to temporarily derail him. ''St. John Adair and Rick Masters. Adair's the head of—''

''I know who he is, who they are.'' He hadn't been living in a cave, after all. Even if his ex-wife hadn't lived and breathed the society page, the names would have been familiar to him. But even so, he didn't see this half thought out idea of hers taking off. ''And these billionaires would be willing to come to a weenie roast at the center.''

She ignored his mocking tone. ''Your problem, Carson, is that you don't think big. And that you have no faith,'' she added for good measure. ''I also know a caterer. She'd be willing to do this for cost.''

Now there was a nebulous word, Carson thought. ''Whose cost?''

''It'll be underwritten,'' she assured him. Either one of the two men's foundations would be more than willing to take on the expense in exchange for the goodwill. ''And, I've already developed a theme and everything.''

''A theme?'' he echoed. What the hell did that have to do with anything?

As if reading his mind, she said, ''Can't have a fund-raiser without a theme. Sherry's a former newscaster who's a reporter now,'' she went on, ''and her father is retired from the *L.A. Times,* so publicity is not going to be a problem—''

He leaned back in his chair, looking at her. She'd had a baby less than three days ago. Most women in her position would still be trying to pull themselves together, not pulling together a fund-raiser for high rollers. ''You've got this all worked out, don't you?''

She took a bite out of her toast. ''All except for you saying yes.''

''Does that even matter?'' As far as he could see, she was ready to steamroll right over him.

How could he say that? The center was his baby, his domain. She was just trying to help. ''Of course it matters.'' And then she grinned. ''It also matters that this'll be written up in the society pages.''

''Society pages?'' he echoed. Was Lori trying to tell him that she had something in common with his ex-wife? That she craved the limelight, too? ''Why should that matter?''

''So Jaclyn can eat her heart out, of course.'' She knew that he wasn't the vengeful type, but that was all right. She was vengeful for him. ''I want her to realize that she lost a catch *and* a chance to come floating in on your arm at a really big charity event.''

He laughed, shaking his head. ''You're letting your imagination run away with you.''

''No, I'm not.'' She finished her toast. ''I just have to have imagination for the both of us, so it seems as if I have too much. What do you say?''

He kept a straight expression. ''If I said no—''

She wasn't sure if he was being serious or not.

With Carson it was hard to tell. "I'd hammer away at you until you said yes."

"That's what I thought." Maybe it wasn't such a bad idea after all. Not that part about Jaclyn. He didn't care anymore what the woman thought, only that she was a good mother to Sandy. But the center could definitely use the money. "Let me think about it."

"Really?"

There was something about the way she looked when she widened her eyes like that that got to him. Made his stomach feel like jelly.

Maybe it was time to go. He rose to his feet. "I told you, I never say anything I don't mean."

Lori was on her feet as well. "You won't regret this."

And then, moved by the moment and by everything he'd done that had led up to this point in time, she pulled on his shirt, drawing him down to her level. When he bent his head, a query in his eyes, she raised herself up on her toes and brought her mouth up to his.

He stopped her at the last minute, placing his fingertips against her lips.

Stunned, she looked up at him. Was he rejecting her?

There was a dab of strawberry jam at the corner of her mouth. He slowly rubbed it away with his thumb. His eyes never left hers.

"I know you're a go-getter, but there are some things a man likes to initiate himself. At least the second time around."

He knew he should have just walked away. It would have been the sensible thing to do. But he'd been battling too many emotions lately to be sensible. He cupped her chin in his hand and brought his mouth down to hers.

Carson kissed her with all the feeling that had been churning within him. Kissed her the way he'd been wanting to ever since she'd first kissed him. Ever since, a part of him realized, he'd first seen her on his brother's arm, her eyes sparkling, her manner bursting with the kind of sunshine he had never believed people were capable of exuding.

One look at Lori and he'd been proven wrong.

She tasted of strawberries. He'd always had a weakness for strawberries. And even if he hadn't, he had a feeling that he would have developed one now.

He deepened the kiss, knowing it was a mistake, knowing it would only make him want more. Want her. It was crazy and it was something that he would keep to himself until his dying day, but he knew in his heart that he wanted her.

Wanted Lori not for an hour, not for a night, but forever.

Because even in her stubbornness, she embodied everything he had ever wanted in his life, everything he had ever wanted in a woman. The last bone of contention he'd had with his brother was the way Kurt took Lori for granted.

Had Lori been part of his life, Carson knew he would have never treated her that way, never taken her for granted for even one moment.

But that choice wasn't his. Wouldn't be his.

But if only for the moment, he allowed himself to pretend that it was.

He was making her head spin and her blood rush. She'd never been with another man other than Kurt, but suddenly, she felt as if everything inside of her was being pulled to this man. It wasn't possible, not yet, because strictly physically she wasn't ready.

But that didn't mean that the rest of her wasn't. That the rest of her didn't ache to be his in every sense of the word.

She dug her fingers into his shoulders, trying to steady herself. Wouldn't that be a surprise for him, she thought, to know what she was feeling?

Or maybe, just maybe, it wouldn't be that much of a surprise.

At least, she could hope.

A stab of guilt had him withdrawing. What the hell was he doing, taking advantage of her when she was so vulnerable? What had gotten into him?

"I'd better get going," he murmured. "The center's not going to run itself."

"Carson—"

"Call me if you need anything."

She smiled, watching a six-foot-two man beat a hasty retreat out the door. If she did call him, she thought as she heard the front door closing, it would be because she only needed one thing.

Him.

Chapter Ten

By the time Carson arrived at St. Augustine's, he'd made up his mind. He was only going to call. Just a simple call to check in on Lori and the baby. If even that.

He sat down at his desk, bracing himself for the task he'd put off the past couple of days. Searching for funds to reallocate so that the center's bills could be paid this month. It was a hell of a juggling act.

After all, he argued, his mind slipping back to Lori, he'd already done more than his fair share when it came to helping her out. More than most men would have. He'd filled her refrigerator, brought her home from the hospital and stayed over her first night home with the baby.

Not that she'd really needed him. She'd seemed to manage fine on her own. Just as she'd said.

Just as, he thought, she'd always done.

Maybe it was just his own need to be needed. He

sighed, dragging a hand through his hair. Damn it, he was beginning to sound like one of those afternoon talk shows. Muttering an oath under his breath, he turned his attention back to his unbalanced budget.

No, he wasn't going over tonight, he thought for the hundredth time that day as he regarded the stone-cold, borderline petrified hamburger on his desk. If he couldn't get his mind more than a few inches away from Lori, well that was his problem to deal with, not hers. Things wouldn't improve if he went over.

Besides, Carson shut his eyes, momentarily surrendering the budget battle he was engaged in, he knew if he did show up at Lori's house, she would only start yammering at him again about the fund-raiser. There was no way he wanted to hear any more about that, especially not in his present state of mind.

No, he was going to give her some space. Go home after work and get some well-deserved rest of his own. He'd call her once he got there.

Maybe.

Or maybe he'd just call her now and get it over with. Carson eyed the sickly salmon-colored telephone beside his deceased hamburger, feeling as if he were involved in an exhausting physical tug-of-war rather than just a mental one.

''Hey, boss man.'' Without bothering to knock, Rhonda swung the office door open and stuck her dark head in. ''I think you've got yourself a problem.''

That was an understatement, he thought, then realized that she had to be referring to something at the center.

A problem. Good. Something to sink his teeth into. Something to get his mind away from things it shouldn't be dwelling on. Splaying his hands on his desk, he rose to his feet. "Such as?"

She looked unwilling to go into detail. Or perhaps unable. Rhonda wasn't the most articulate person in the world. Not like Lori, he thought. Lori liked to use ten words when three would suffice.

Rhonda nodded toward the hall. "I think you'd better come and see this."

In desperate need of diversion, he still didn't know if he liked the sound of that. But then, Rhonda wasn't the type to tackle things on her own. She was a firm believer in passing on things that she deemed weren't part of her job description.

Not like Lori. Lori tackled everything as if it was her private crusade.

Damn it, O'Neill, give it a rest. The woman's not a saint. What the hell's gotten into you?

He needed a woman, he decided abruptly. Someone to ease the physical tension that had to be at the root of all this. He refused to entertain the idea that there might have been another cause, another solution. Anything that had to do with feelings was going to be left out in the cold.

"What is it?" he asked again. Rhonda led him across the first floor toward the stairwell on the other side of the gym. They cut a wide path around the basketball court.

"One of the guys came and told me that the water

in the boys' shower was cold. I was going to have Juan check that out when Alda told me the same thing was happening in the girls' shower. So I had a hunch and went down into the basement.'' Stopping at the door that led to the basement, she paused significantly.

Carson knew it was because she wanted recognition for her initiative.

Moving in front of her, he opened the door. A long, narrow stairway led down to the basement. It reminded him of something that would have been found back East or up North. For the most part, there were no basements in Southern California. Not in any of the newer buildings. But St. Augustine's Teen Center had originally been an unwed mothers' shelter that had been renovated in the sixties. The building itself was over fifty years old. And not wearing its age well.

''And what did you find there?'' He held on to the rickety banister as he went down the stairs. They creaked under his weight.

''That.'' Rhonda pointed to the inch of water that graced the dirty basement floor. She made no effort to go down the final two steps, the last of which was partially submerged. Instead, she indicated the culprit in the corner. ''Looks like you need a new water heater.''

He bit back a few choice words. Damn, this wasn't going to be cheap. Never mind the cost of the water heater, plumbers were worth their weight in gold.

For a moment, he seriously regretted the altruistic emotions that had caused him to turn his back on the law firm and take up the mantle of shepherd for this dysfunctional flock.

"What was your first clue?" he asked sarcastically.

"The water on the ground."

She was serious. He'd forgotten that humor was something that was usually wasted on Rhonda. Not that there was any in this situation.

Frustrated, Carson dragged his hand through his hair, looking at the mess. Some of the center's gym equipment was stored down here and it didn't take an expert to see that it was ruined.

Well, at least Lori was going to be happy. The thought did nothing to improve his mood. Against his will, Lori was going to get her way. He was going to have to put his faith in a fund-raiser. There was no other way he was going to find any money to repair the damage done by the flood and buy a new water heater.

Not to mention pay this month's electricity bill. Rates had gone through the roof this last year and there was just so much that could be cut back.

When it rained, it poured, he thought. He stared darkly at the dirty water. No pun intended.

She missed him.

There'd been barely two unattended minutes for her to rub together since Carson had left this morning. Visitors had begun dropping by her house within ten minutes of his departure.

But she still missed him.

Not only had each one of the women in the Mom Squad chosen to come by separately to offer encouragement and advise, not to mention to coo over the baby, but she'd also received visits from a good many of the women who had taken her classes and gone on to have their own babies. Everyone had brought gifts, food and insisted on spelling her, despite her protests that she didn't need any "spelling."

News of her delivery had spread quickly and some of the kids from the center had made the pilgrimage to her house as well. Angela had been the first and most enthusiastic. The look in her eyes told Lori that she'd fallen in love with Emma.

"Gonna have one of these myself one of these days," she vowed, then looked quickly at Lori and flushed. "The right way. After I finish school and after I get me a husband."

She was coming along, Lori thought. "Sounds good to me."

Angela stayed until her ride came to pick her up again. The teenager's impromptu visit meant a great deal to Lori.

But even with this endless parade of hot and cold running women who insisted on taking over and allowing her to "rest" and not do anything beyond breast-feed her daughter, Lori found herself missing him. Missing Carson. Even missing the way he frowned.

She knew it was futile to feel that way. Carson had gone more than the extra mile for her and there was no reason to think that he might come over tonight for some reason. Now that she had safely delivered the baby and had been brought to her own home, he could turn his attention to other important matters.

Without her there to help out, the center was going to take up all of his time. She knew Carson. He didn't believe in half measures.

Or in attachments, she thought as she shut the door on the last of her visitors, holding the baby in the crook of her arm. Carson had made it known to her in no uncertain terms that he was out of the relationship business as far as male and female interactions went.

Though he pretended otherwise, she knew that Jaclyn had hurt him much too much. He'd allowed himself to go out on a limb, to expose himself and become vulnerable and Jaclyn had sawed that limb right out from under him. There was no way he would risk that happening again, Lori thought. She caught a glimpse of herself in the hall mirror. Even with someone who was a great deal more trustworthy than that witch of an ex-wife.

They approached life differently, she and Carson. Kurt hadn't been anything like Jaclyn, but his irresponsibility had eventually worn down the effect of his charm. But she'd discovered that her less than perfect experience with marriage hadn't hardened her heart against further entanglements. It had just made her hopeful that the next one would be *the* one.

If it involved someone like Carson.

''Wouldn't your Uncle Carson just love to hear that?'' she murmured to Emma.

The infant was dozing against her breast. Lori paused for a moment, savoring the silence and just looking at the precious bundle in her arms.

Even after a fair share of dirty diapers and feedings,

it was still hard to believe that Emma was finally here. That the months of nausea, of waiting and worrying were over and that her daughter was finally here, finally part of her life.

"You're every bit as beautiful as I knew you'd be," she whispered to the sleeping face. "But you don't want to hear me carrying on, you want to get your beauty sleep." She began to walk up the stairs. "I warn you, though, you get too much more of that and the princes are going to start lining up at the door fifteen deep. You're not going to know a moment's peace." She grinned. "I suppose there are worse things in life."

Smiling to herself, she walked into the nursery and put the baby down for another nap.

She'd just adjusted the baby monitor when she heard the doorbell.

Was there anyone left in the immediate world who hadn't been by today? She wouldn't have thought so, but apparently there was.

The doorbell rang again before she had a chance to reach the door.

"Who is it?" she called out.

"I brought Chinese this time."

She felt her heart leap up in her chest. The grin spread across her lips instantly. "Carson?"

"Well, it's not the Good Humor Man." The grumpy voice took away all doubt. "Open the door, Lori. These cartons are hot and they're going to break through the bags at any second."

He heard her flipping the top lock. The next moment she threw the door open. The smile in her eyes went right to his gut and made him glad he hadn't talked himself into going home.

"What are you doing here?"

"Trying to bring you dinner." He elbowed his way past her. "Can we play twenty questions later?" Without waiting for an answer, he headed straight toward the kitchen.

She smiled to herself as she closed the door again. Carson was here and everything felt right. "Hello to you, too."

"Hello was implied," he told her curtly, sparing her a short glance over his shoulder. The woman looked better than she had a right to, given the circumstances. In jeans and a tank top, she looked as if she belonged on the cover of a magazine, not someone who had given birth a few days ago.

He forced himself to pay attention to what he was doing and not what he was feeling.

The cartons just barely made it to the counter before the paper bags they were in ripped completely. He took the containers out and bunched up the bags, tossing them into the garbage.

Lori came in right behind him. "You sound like you certainly got up on the wrong side of the chow mein serving."

She took out two soda cans from the refrigerator. Joanna, bless her, had come by earlier with groceries, saying she knew just what it was like, not having a family to fall back on.

Lori popped the tab on the first can and placed it beside a glass for him before repeating the action for herself. She regarded him for a moment. ''Anything wrong beyond ripped bags?''

''Yeah,'' he grumbled, looking down at her. ''You're right.''

The man certainly liked being enigmatic. The napkin holder was empty. She took out a handful from the pantry and slipped them between the two ends before moving the holder back to the center of the table.

She leveled a look at him. His expression gave her no clue. ''I'm right because there's something else wrong, or you're mad because I'm right? Give me a hint here, Carson. Twenty-four hours away from you and I'm getting a little rusty in my Carson-speak.''

He sighed, sliding his large frame onto a chair. ''You know, I don't know what you're talking about half the time.''

Lori gave him a bright smile. ''Which means that half the time you do. Always put a positive spin on things, Carson.''

She turned away to get two plates out of the cupboard and two forks. She would have taken out her chopsticks, but she knew that Carson was almost hopeless when it came to using them. He'd been nice enough to bring her dinner, she wasn't about to irritate him by flaunting her dexterity. He looked like he had enough on his mind.

''Now,'' she made herself comfortable at the table, ''why are you so extra grumpy?'' She thought of the likeliest explanation. ''Did something go wrong at the center?''

''Yes.''

It was like pulling teeth, but then, that was nothing new. "Are you going to make me guess?" Opening the carton with fried rice, she took out a portion for herself, then passed it on to him. "And if so, how many chances do I get?"

He regarded the carton before him, his expression dour. "The hot water heater broke."

She thought of the old hundred gallon tank. The one time she'd gone into the basement for equipment, the heater had startled her by groaning and making strange noises. "You knew it was only a matter of time, Carson. That thing was ancient."

He passed her the chow mein container. "Yeah, I know."

She knew where this was leading. To a place he was unwilling to go. "Got the money to fix it?" she asked innocently.

"The bottom dropped out," he told her. "It's beyond fixing."

She nodded her head, taking in the information. "Which means you need a new one." She thought of the stack of bills on his desk that he'd been juggling the last month. "Carson—"

He dropped his fork on the plate. "Now you see, that's why I'm angry."

Her expression just grew more innocent. "Because I said Carson?"

She knew damn well that wasn't what he meant. "Because of the way you said Carson."

Lori cocked her head, her eyes holding back a smile. "What way was that?"

"You're going to start nagging again." He looked

at her pointedly. She wasn't saying anything. "About that fund-raiser."

Lori turned her attention to the meal. "Nope, not me. I'm done nagging."

He looked at her incredulously. Lori might as well have said that she'd just died and gone to heaven. He figured it would take that much for her to desist. "You're done nagging," he repeated.

"Absolutely." She was innocence personified as she looked at him. "Well, it hasn't done any good, so there's no point in getting on your nerves. You're an adult, you'll figure a way out of this without my putting in my two cents."

"So that's it?" He didn't believe her, not for one second.

She savored the forkful of sesame chicken she'd slipped between her lips. He'd remembered her favorite, she thought. The man just kept on amazing her. "That's it."

"You're going to stop talking about the fund-raiser." He was waiting for a contradiction.

Her blue eyes were causing his stomach to tighten even though they were doing nothing more than talking about raising money for the center.

She raised her hand in a solemn oath. "Not another word."

Carson frowned. That wasn't the way he'd wanted to play it. He'd wanted her to push her cause and then, after some wrangling, he'd give in. He didn't want to just surrender without her laying siege to him.

But she left him no choice. His back was against the wall and it was either this or begin bankruptcy proceedings. He wasn't about to let that happen before he exhausted all other avenues.

He didn't like this avenue.

Carson blew out an angry breath. ''All right, you win.''

''Win?'' she echoed, a smile playing along her lips. She fluttered her eyelashes. ''What do I win, Carson?''

He realized she'd been putting him on. That didn't change the course of the conversation. ''We'll have the fund-raiser. It goes against everything I believe in to go out there with my hat in my hand, but there's no other way.''

She was delighted at the turn of events. She could finally be of some kind of real help to him.

''No hat in hand, Carson, I promise. When we get through with them, they'll be begging to give you money.'' Her appetite on hold, she pulled the pad over from the edge of the table. Her eyes were shining as plans began forming in her mind. ''We still need a theme.'' It took her only a second. Her eyes were gleaming as she announced, ''I know, we'll have a fifties party.''

This was already beginning to sound bad to him. ''What?''

''The center was built in 1951,'' she reminded him. ''You know, the era of the poodle skirt, slicked back hair and innocence—'' She winked. ''Or so they tell me.''

''Why do we need a theme?'' Even when his life had been on an upward swing and he'd been part of the firm, he'd always opted for simplicity.

"Two reasons. People like a worthy cause and people like having an excuse to dress up and have a good time." She knew what he was going to say and cut him off. "I know, not you, but most people. Anyway, we'll give them both."

"What 'we'?" His part in this, he thought, was just to give Lori her lead. "This is going to be strictly your operation."

"You make it sound like the invasion at Normandy." She made a few notes to herself. "This is going to be fun, Carson." She saw the dubious look on his face. "Trust me."

"I won't have to dress up, will I?" He didn't like the way her grin widened. He pushed back his plate. "Oh no, count me out. You run this whole thing. I'll be the invisible partner."

"Silent," Lori corrected. "Not invisible." She pushed his plate back toward Carson. "You have to be there."

This was going to be her show. She was doing it for the center. There was no need for him to even show up. "Why?"

"Because St. Augustine's is your center. I promise, you won't have to do anything but dress yourself." She winked at him again, sending off strange ripples through him. "I'll do everything else."

The thought of her dressing him suddenly flashed across his mind, causing havoc in his system before he shut it away. "You just had a baby. You're tired."

She put her own spin on it. "I just shed some baby weight, I'm energized."

He sighed, shaking his head. "I was afraid you'd say that."

But he couldn't quite get his voice to sound as disgruntled as he wanted it to. He knew he hadn't succeeded when he saw the pleased smile on her face. The vague thought that it was worth the price whispered across his brain before he had a chance to block it.

"Okay," she was saying, passing him an egg roll. "Let's get our guest list together."

"And she's off," he murmured.

The look she gave him curled through his belly and went straight to places that should have been left out of this.

He bit down hard on his egg roll.

Chapter Eleven

Carson stood staring at the outfit that Lori had left hanging on the inside of her hall closet door. She'd directed him to it as she went back into the guest room to put on her own costume for tomorrow's fund-raiser. She wanted him to see her in it.

There was a red jacket, faded jeans and a white T-shirt hanging in front of him, daring him to try them on. He glanced over toward the guest room. "You're kidding, right?"

Her voice came floating out of the room. "What's the matter, don't you like it?" She didn't give him a chance to answer. "Try it on, you'll look like James Dean. Or what he might have looked like if he hadn't died in that car accident."

"If he hadn't died in that car accident, he'd be an old man now."

He heard her sigh. "Then," she corrected. "The way he'd looked back then."

Carson picked up the red windbreaker's sleeve and shook his head. She couldn't be serious.

As if reading his thoughts, Lori called out, "You're not playing along, Carson. The fund-raiser has a fifties motif, remember?" She paused a second and he knew she was thinking, always a dangerous thing as far as Lori was concerned. "Would you rather dress up like Cary Grant in *Mr. Lucky* or *Houseboat?* That might be more your style, although the outfit is less recognizable. Dressed like that, you'll just be a man in a tux. Everyone's pretty much familiar with James Dean's jeans and red windbreaker from *Rebel Without A Cause.*"

That was just the trouble. He didn't want to look like an idiot, emulating a man who'd been dead for over forty-five years. "What are you wearing?" he wanted to know. "A poodle skirt and a sweater set?"

"Not quite."

Lori stepped out of the guest room. Carson's tongue was suddenly in danger of sliding down his throat.

She was wearing a white sundress that seemed to be a flurry of soft white pleats that caressed her curves with every move she made. The halter top showed off her shoulders to their advantage and his disadvantage. They displayed more white, creamy skin than he felt safe being around. Her legs were bare and she was wearing white, sling back high heels. Lori's light blond hair was teased and fashioned in a classic, familiar style that had been a sex goddess's trademark in the fifties. She even had a beauty mark near the corner of one side of her mouth.

Lori held out the skirt and twirled around one complete revolution for his benefit, her eyes barely leaving his face. ''So, what do you think?''

He'd never been one for movies, but he knew what he liked. ''Damn.''

She smoothed down the skirt. The outfit made her feel just this side of wicked. So did the look in his eyes. Whether he knew it or not, he made her feel like a woman again. ''Good damn or bad damn?''

''Just damn,'' he breathed, grateful that he still could. ''You look like—''

Knowing his limited range when it came to movie stars, she came to his rescue. ''Marilyn Monroe in *Seven Year Itch,* I hope.''

''Better.'' The halter accentuated her breasts and dipped down low. Realizing he was staring, Carson looked down at her waist. It was as slender as it had been the day she'd married Kurt. ''Nobody'd ever guess you just had a baby.''

Dimples flashed as she grinned. ''Unless I forget to use her drool cloth just before I go.'' She crossed to the closet where his costume was still hanging. ''So, what'll it be? Cary Grant or James Dean?''

Carson frowned. He hadn't even had a suit on since he'd left the law firm. He passionately disliked getting dressed up and donning a costume was even worse.

He closed the closet door, hoping to end the discussion. ''Couldn't I just be me? Nobody's going to look at me anyway, not if we walk in together.''

Did he even realize what he'd just said? Probably not. ''Why, Carson, that just might be the nicest thing you ever said to me.''

Feeling uncomfortable, he shoved his hands into his pockets. ‘‘I must have said something better than that to you.’’

‘‘Not that I recall.’’ Moving him aside, she opened the closet door again. This time, she took out the costume and draped it across the back of the sofa. ‘‘But don’t try to turn my head with compliments, I’m determined to get you into the full swing of this.’’ She regarded the costume, then looked back at Carson, trying to picture him in it. ‘‘Now, if you want that tuxedo, I can probably scare one up for you, but you have to tell me now. We don’t have much time.’’

She didn’t have to tell him that. The fund-raiser’s date had haunted him ever since he’d given her the green light three weeks ago. He’d never seen a woman work so hard so quickly. You would have thought that just adjusting to being a new mother would have been enough for her to handle.

‘‘And everyone’s coming.’’ He still couldn’t believe it. A hundred and fifty people had been invited to this wild scheme of hers. She’d even invited the other lawyers who had been part of his firm. He’d found that out when one of the senior partners had called in person to confirm. He’d almost called the whole thing off then, but one look at Lori’s radiant face as she went over plans with him had made him swallow his words before they’d ever had a chance to emerge.

She nodded. ‘‘According to their RSVPs, everyone’s coming.’’ Picking up the red windbreaker, she held it up against Carson. She liked the way it made him looked. Sexy, wild. ‘‘Actually, with Sinjin and

Rick Masters coming, we could opt for an intimate party of eight and still get enough money to keep you going for the next few years.''

Each of the two men had already separately let her know that they were more than willing to make generous contributions to the center, as well as lend their names to the function, thereby guaranteeing its success. It certainly did help to have connections, she mused.

''But the object of this little shindig,'' she said before he pounced on her comment like a drowning man grabbing a lifeline, ''is to get the center solvent for many years to come. Not to mention getting a few computers and a new roof for the place.''

The roof had been her addition last week. New computer was a brainstorm that came two days ago. He pushed aside the windbreaker. ''Why is it that every time I talk to you, the center's wish list has grown?''

She placed the jacket back on the sofa beside the jeans and T-shirt. ''Because I keep thinking of things that would be useful at the center.'' She'd already told him this part, but she saw no harm in repeating it. In typical male fashion, he probably hadn't been listening the first time around, anyway. ''If we had a class teaching them basic computer skills, those kids could get decent jobs and maybe save up some money so they could get into college when they graduated. To have that kind of a class, we need computers. And as for the roof, have you taken a look at it lately?''

''Yes, I have,'' he said curtly. Patching had all but reached the end of its usefulness. They needed a new one. The last Santa Ana winds had seen to that. ''Anything else on your wish list I should know about?''

She was standing toe-to-toe with him, very aware, suddenly, of his maleness. And of the fact that she was very, very attracted to him. ''I wish you were more flexible, but that's something I can't buy.''

He touched her hair and was surprised to discover that it wasn't stiff with hair spray. It felt silky against his hand. He found himself tangling his fingers in it. Tangling his soul in hers.

''Maybe you could trade for it.''

She tilted her face up to his. ''What would you like to trade?'' she asked in a low whisper.

He had no idea where that had come from or why he'd even said it. Maybe it was the perfume she was wearing. Or the way she looked like pure sin. Or the way she looked up at him, her eyes tempting him to abandon caution. To take another risk.

It was playing havoc on his thought process. On his desire.

''Let me think on it,'' he murmured just before he brought his mouth down to hers.

Every time he kissed her, it was easier to let go of his resolve not to. Each time he kissed her, he was more tempted than before to continue kissing her. To turn his back on everything he'd promised himself he would never do again.

He felt himself aching again. Needing again.

Warm waves of desire passed over Lori, drowning her. Thrilling her. She stood on the very tips of her toes and wrapped her arms around his neck, drawing her body against his. Savoring their closeness.

His heart was pounding as their lips drew apart. "Damn, but you make it hard, Lori."

She felt just the slightest bit fuzzy, just the slightest bit deliciously dazed. Her eyes searched his face. "What do I make hard, Carson? What?"

His hands were on her shoulders. It was himself that he was holding back, not her. "You make it hard for me to remember that you're my brother's wife."

That was still between them and it shouldn't be. "Widow, Carson, I'm your brother's widow, not his wife. Not any longer. And why do you need to remember that?"

Didn't she understand? "Because this shouldn't be happening. I shouldn't feel this way."

Feelings, he had feelings for her. Something inside of her sang. She could feel her pulse accelerating. "How, Carson, how do you feel? Tell me."

Her question undulated along his skin, along his mind. Like a siren's song, leading him to places that were far too dangerous for him to navigate around.

He had to leave. Now. Before he couldn't.

He didn't.

"Like this," he murmured against her mouth a moment before he kissed her again. Kissed her with a passion that broke through the steel bands he had wrapped around it.

He could feel his blood surging through his veins, could feel it roaring in his ears. Could feel his head spinning as he closed his eyes and let himself go, just for a moment.

No more than that, just for a moment.

Because a moment was all he could safely risk. Any longer and he knew that he would lose all control. Lose himself in her.

And that would be a very dangerous thing to do.

He wanted her. Wanted to make love with her. Wanted to feel her soft skin yielding itself up to him.

Too far, this was going to far.

With superhuman control, he reined himself in. Carson released her shoulders and drew his head away. "I'd better go."

Something inside of her felt like weeping, but she made an effort not to show it. "So, is it James Dean or Cary Grant?"

He shrugged. "You've already got the costume. It might as well be James Dean."

She grinned. Taking the jacket, jeans and T-shirt, she hung them up again in the closet. "Always knew you were a rebel at heart."

That wasn't all his heart was, Carson thought grudgingly as he let himself out.

She was in her element, Carson thought the next evening as he watched Lori work the festively decorated ballroom of the Grand Hotel.

Lori might have a degree in digital design, might be an aide at the center and teach Lamaze classes at Blair Memorial, but she was a born hostess. A born charmer.

Like Kurt, he remembered. Except that in her case, Lori used her gift to help others, not just to be self-serving. Once she'd broken him down and he'd agreed to having the fund-raiser, she'd taken off like a lit Roman candle, illuminating everything within her scope.

True to her word, she'd handled everything, the invitations, the catering, the sponsors. All she'd required of him was his presence and his tolerance. The latter involved wearing tight jeans and a jacket whose color would have never been even his fiftieth choice. But she had thrown herself into this so hard, he felt he couldn't really turn her down, even though he would have preferred spending the evening in the solitude of his home, waiting to have her come by and tell him how it went.

No, that wasn't quite true. He did enjoy being here, he had to admit, but only because it allowed him to watch her work the room.

Allowed him to watch her move like every man's secret fantasy, her slender hips moving just enough to undo every single man within eye range.

Well, maybe not every man. Masters, Adair and that special agent he'd been introduced to, Byron Warrick, all looked to be taken with the women who had accompanied them to this fund-raiser, but he'd noticed more than one man stare after Lori with a note of longing whenever she walked by. Her Marilyn Monroe outfit had only a little to do with it.

It made him feel possessive.

It made him feel, Carson realized with a start, jealous.

As if she was his to be jealous of, he admonished himself. Anything she might feel for him was obviously just tangled up with gratitude. He knew that.

She'd been in a bad place when Kurt had been killed and he'd come through for her. It would have been against his nature not to.

The danger here was getting caught up in the woman's smile. In the woman herself.

"Smile," she said, coming up behind him. "You're supposed to be having a good time."

The warm flush that went over him took a bit of doing to hide. "I am." He picked up a glass of white wine from a passing waiter and took a sip to prove his point. "Can't you tell?"

He wasn't fooling her. She'd watched him hang back all evening and had all but dragged him over when the press photographer had taken his pictures. "I've seen people looking happier in a dentist's waiting room, queuing up for a root canal."

"Just my way, Lori, you know that." He took another sip of the wine. He didn't usually care for wine, but this was surprisingly appealing. Or maybe it was just Lori going to his head. "You did a good job."

She looked around the large room. People looked to be enjoying themselves. And happy people were generous people. "It did turn out pretty well, didn't it?"

There was no vanity in her assessment, he noted, only pleasure. It occurred to him how terribly different she and his ex-wife were. Jaclyn would have been looking to get herself into every photograph, mentioned in every line of press.

For the first time, he noticed that Lori had a small drawstring purse hanging from her wrist. She held it up in front of him. "And I've gotten a lot of checks and pledges for the center.'' She was very, very pleased with herself ''We can afford twelve new water heaters and five roofs, stacked one on top of each other.''

In general, he disliked exaggeration. Hers only succeeded in amusing him. ''We'll just need one of each.''

She threaded her arms around his free one. ''Well, then we're going to have a great deal of money left over for a lot of other necessary things. The center's going to be giving computer classes,'' she suddenly remembered to tell him. ''Sinjin's seeing to that personally.'' She waved as the man and Sherry looked in her direction. ''One of the companies he owns manufactures computers.''

The woman was nothing short of incredible. She'd only thought of the idea a few days ago and already it was a reality. ''The kids are going to think you're some kind of fairy godmother.''

Turning toward him, she shook her head. ''No magic, Carson, just kind hearts. Like I've always told you, people are basically good if you just give them a chance to be.''

He'd been raised on the same mean streets that also housed St. Augustine's. His father had abandoned his family and everything he'd ever gotten he'd had to struggle for. And when he'd grown up, he'd dealt with all manner of criminals who needed representation. In addition, when he'd tried to bring meaning to his life, his wife had left him to look for someone with more promise and more money.

He shook his head. ''Sorry, I'm afraid I never saw

things that way. My world isn't exactly what you'd call rosy.''

Why did he always insist on painting everything in such dark hues? ''You help kids who might have been hopeless if you hadn't come into their lives, what's rosier than that?''

''You.''

He was doing it again, making her feel all warm inside. If she didn't know that it would embarrass him, she would have kissed him right there, in front of everyone. Instead, she just laughed.

''Well, that goes without saying.'' Taking his glass from his hand, she took a tiny sip. ''Just one,'' she told him when she saw the surprised look that came into his eyes. She gave him back his glass. ''For energy. There's still half a room to schmooze with.'' She looked at him, extending her hand. It would be so much better if he was at her side. ''Come with me.''

But he just shook his head. ''I'd only get in your way.''

She knew better than to push. With a sigh, she nodded. ''Have it your way.''

''That'll be a first.''

She left him with a smile. But she was back in a few minutes. The band was beginning to play another set. ''I need to take a break,'' she told him. ''Dance with me, Carson.''

''I don't dance, you know that.''

She was quick to contradict him. ''You don't dance fast dances.'' She presented her hands to him. ''This is a slow dance. You dance slow dances. I've seen you.''

''When?'' he challenged. He couldn't remember the last time he'd been anywhere with music.

''At my wedding. With me. Remember?''

He remembered. Remembered thinking that he had never seen anyone looking so radiant. ''But not since then.''

''It's like riding a bike.'' She threaded her fingers through his. ''It'll come back to you, I promise.''

''And if I step on your foot?''

She turned her face up to his, already swaying against him. ''I won't sue. Can't get a better deal than that, Counselor.''

''I suppose not,'' he allowed grudgingly.

She felt good in his arms. Too good. He let his mind drift again, fueled by a desire that had no place in their relationship, not even fleetingly. What did it take to get that through his head?

Apparently a lot more than it was taking now, he thought, inhaling the scent in her hair as she laid her cheek against his shoulder.

''Were Marilyn Monroe and James Dean ever an item?''

He felt her smile against the T-shirt, a warmth spreading through his chest on point of contact. ''Not that I know of. Why?''

''No reason. Just wondering.''

That showed a glimmer of imagination. He was coming along. Tiny, baby steps, she thought, but he was coming along. It was all she asked.

* * *

"I feel giddy," Lori told him, closing the door as Diane Jones departed. C.J. had insisted on lending her her mother as a baby-sitter for the evening. She had to admit she'd felt better leaving her daughter in such competent hands. Mrs. Jones had raised five children of her own. "Must be my second wind."

"Or your twelfth." She looked at Carson quizzically as she slipped out of her shoes. The woman was positively tiny, he thought. Like an ounce of dynamite. "I never saw anyone with as much energy as you have." It was two in the morning and by his count, Lori had worked almost round the clock today, supervising and getting everything ready for the event. "A dozen other women would have been exhausted by now."

"You mean a man wouldn't have been exhausted in my place?" There was amusement in her eyes.

"No, I always thought of women as the heartier breed." He unzipped his jacket. "And the deadlier one."

She saw the look in his eyes. "You're talking about Jaclyn, aren't you?"

He shrugged out of the windbreaker, tossing it on her sofa. He didn't want to go there tonight. "Just making a comment, that's all."

She didn't dislike many people, but she disliked Jaclyn for the way she'd hurt Carson. Disliked her with a passion. "Not all women are like Jaclyn, Carson."

It didn't matter one way or the other. "I'm not planning on running a survey."

She looked up at him. "I wouldn't think you'd have to."

"No," he agreed, cupping her cheek, "I don't."

He was sinking again, he thought, sinking into her eyes. Getting lost again. He had to be stronger than that. They had something good right now, something he enjoyed. He didn't want to ruin it by trying for anything more. Half of something was better than all of nothing.

"Lori, I don't think we should let anything happen."

Too late. "I'm sorry, Carson, I'm not as regimented as you are. I can't pencil in feelings. Or pencil them out. They just happen." And they had happened to her. Because of him.

He had to stop it now, before he did something even more stupid than he'd already allowed himself to do. Before he started kissing her and never stopped. "Well, maybe they shouldn't."

He looked troubled, she thought. And there was a panicky feeling taking a toehold inside of her. She needed help in banking it down. "Talk to me, Carson. What's wrong?" *What's wrong with us getting closer?* she wanted to cry.

She looked sad. Vulnerable. He wanted to stay and comfort her, but he knew that would be both of their undoing. He was perilously close to crossing a bridge that allowed no way back.

He had to leave before he couldn't.

Carson backed away. "Look, it's late and the baby's going to be waking up soon. You should get some rest."

"Fat chance," she muttered, staring at the closed door through the tears in her eyes.

Chapter Twelve

Lori paced the floor restlessly, unable to sleep. The clock on the nightstand was serenading 1:00 a.m. Emma was asleep in the next room and so should she be, but she couldn't. Hadn't been able to sleep for several nights now.

It was all Carson's fault.

He hadn't been over in a week. Not since the night of the fund-raiser. At work, it was as if they had suddenly become strangers. That was the way he was treating her. Politely, distantly. As if they hadn't just been on the brink of something far more meaningful, far more intimate.

And it was driving her crazy.

She had no idea how to approach him, how to scale this new glass wall that had appeared without warning between them. She could see him, but she couldn't touch him. Couldn't even make him smile.

Why?

Exasperated, she went downstairs to the kitchen. Maybe warm milk would soothe her, although she didn't hold out much hope.

She took out the carton and poured a glass, then placed it into the microwave. She set the dial for forty-five seconds, then pushed the start button so hard, the oven moved back on the counter.

Had they gone too far for him? That night of the fund-raiser, when he'd brought her home, had there been too many charged emotions between them? Had he suddenly withdrawn because the risk of what was ahead seemed too great for him to take?

The microwave dinged and she yanked the door open. Some of the milk spilled over the top. She mopped it up with a sponge and a sigh.

Damn it, if she was willing to venture out, why wasn't he? Risks were taken every day. It was a risk to leave the house every morning, to cross the street. Some people never made it back. Most did. Why couldn't he think that way?

The odds were in their favor. But only if they tried. *He* had to try.

She took a sip of the milk and burnt her tongue. With disgust, she poured out the rest in the sink.

He wasn't trying. And she was tired of doing the work for both of them. It wasn't the work she minded, it was getting summarily rejected that hurt. And continued to hurt.

Lori pressed her lips together. Drastic times required drastic measures. She'd done everything she could to be encouraging, now it was time to try something else. There was only one thing left as far as she could see.

She hadn't wanted to do this, but he left her no choice. She had to risk everything.

And perhaps be left with nothing.

But she didn't know what else to do.

Carson sat outside on his patio, looking up at the same full moon that was keeping Lori company. Though he had no way of knowing, the same sleeplessness dogging him that afflicted her.

He'd been keeping himself so busy, you'd think he'd be able to sleep at night when there should have been nothing left but exhaustion to tuck itself around him.

But he couldn't. And that was because there was something else besides exhaustion haunting him. There was Lori. His desire for Lori. Each day, it loomed a little larger, a little more prominent, and he hadn't a clue what to do about it.

It scared him, pure and simple.

He wasn't a man who scared easily. Carson liked to think of himself as someone who faced all of life's challenges head-on without flinching. And he had. So far.

But this, this was something different. This involved not risking his body, but his heart and that organ had sadly proven to be too fragile a thing to survive without layers of protection to keep it safe.

Even so, it had succumbed.

To her.

There was no kidding himself. All manner of arguments to the contrary, he was in love with Lori. Very much in love with Lori. And he knew where that path led. He'd only ventured out on it once and had been badly beaten back for his trouble. He wasn't any good at it. At relationships.

The scars had finally healed. This time. But what of the next time? What if he told Lori what was in his heart and she looked at him with pity? What if she didn't feel what he felt? Things would never be the same between them.

Or what if they gave it a try and the romance led nowhere? He didn't think he could endure the disappointment of that. Or of losing her in his life because he knew he would. Friends who turned into lovers never remained friends once the romance was over, no matter what promises they made to each other.

He didn't want to lose her.

It was better this way, nothing ventured, nothing gained.

Nothing lost.

Sitting behind his desk, Carson stared up at Rhonda. The words she'd just said in response to his question felt as if they had bounced off his ears without entering, without being absorbed.

For one small second, he felt confined, as if his office had suddenly turned into a coffin, sealing him into a tiny space.

After more than a week of playing hide and seek, of being everywhere Lori was not, he needed to talk to her. The computers for that class she was so keen on starting for the kids at the center had arrived. Since this was her baby, he couldn't just let the moment pass without interacting with her. Feeling that it was better to be in her company with someone else there, he'd asked Rhonda to have Lori come in.

Only to be told that it wasn't possible.

He had no idea why, but he had a bad feeling when the aide said the words to him. "Why? Didn't she come in today?"

Rhonda shoved her hands into her back pockets as she shook her head. "No."

For someone who loved to gossip, Rhonda was being oddly uncommunicative. "Well, did she call in sick?"

"No." Digging further into one pocket, she pulled out a wrinkled envelope. "She gave me this last night to give to you."

"Last night?" he echoed. Carson looked at the envelope she held in her hand. The bad feeling intensified. "Then why didn't you give it to me?"

"She made me promise I wouldn't give it to you until you asked about her." Rhonda put the envelope down on his desk. "She said she didn't think it would be for a few days."

That was crazy. "What, she thought I wouldn't notice she wasn't here?"

Rhonda raised her model-thin shoulders and then let them drop again carelessly. But her eyes were boring small, accusing holes into him. "That's what she said."

Carson muttered something unintelligible under his

breath as he tore open the envelope. The paper inside had only two sentences written on it: You win. I quit.

He stared at the words as if they were gibberish. Slowly, they finally registered in his brain. Was this some kind of a new game Lori had decided to play? "She says she quits."

"Yeah, I know." Rhonda rocked on the balls of her feet. Her tone told him that she'd been confided in while he had not. "Does this mean you want me to work more hours? Because I could use the raise in pay—"

He didn't want to talk about more hours, or pay raises. His brain felt as if it was suddenly under siege and a cloudy mist had encircled it. He waved her away. "I'll get back to you."

He wasn't even sure just when Rhonda withdrew. Maybe then, maybe a few minutes later. He just sat looking at the almost pristine piece of paper. The words in the center of the page were cold, austere. Lori hadn't even put down a reason.

Anger bubbled up within him, but he banked it down. He shouldn't be angry, he should be relieved. This was, he told himself, for the best. Because he didn't know how much longer he could continue to do the right thing. If their paths kept inevitably crossing, as they would at work, he knew it was only a matter of time before he did something stupid again.

Before he gave in to the ache that had become his constant companion and risked everything.

Possibly to be left with nothing.

He'd done that before, risked everything, but it had

been for a noble reason. He'd risked everything to help the kids at the center. And he'd wound up losing a wife in the bargain.

One risk was enough in anyone's lifetime.

He was just going to have to remember that.

Very slowly, Carson opened his middle drawer took out a manila folder. He slipped Lori's abbreviated letter of resignation into it.

Then filed it away.

That was that.

He slammed the drawer a little harder than he meant to.

He thought it would be better, but it wasn't. It just got worse.

Not having Lori around, knowing she wouldn't *be* around, only made the longing within his chest more acute. Nothing staved it off.

Nothing interested him. Not even working on the '54 Buick Skylark he'd been lovingly restoring in his garage every free moment he could spare. Working on it had seen him through his divorce. He'd thrown himself furiously into its restoration when Kurt had died. It had kept him sane then.

But not now. Nothing was working now. Not his visits with his daughter, who asked about Lori and the baby incessantly, not his job, not the Skylark. Nothing.

Throwing down the rag he'd used to polish a section of the passenger door, Carson went to get his car keys. He knew what he had to do.

* * *

Someone was leaning on her doorbell. Not ringing it, leaning on it. Turning the baby monitor up as she left the kitchen, she hurried to the front door.

The last person in the world she expected was standing on the other side.

Carson was wearing faded, paint-splattered jeans that had holes at each of the knees and a T-shirt that was torn in two places. He looked like a brooding rock star in search of a groupie and the right, elusive lyric.

''I never knew a human being could be so miserable and still live.''

She willed her pulse to return to normal as she closed the front door. Part of her had given up hope that he would ever turn up. It had been over three days since she'd handed in her resignation.

''Exactly what are you talking about?''

He turned on his heel, almost bumping into her. ''Why aren't you at work?''

She lifted her chin defiantly. ''Don't you remember? I quit.''

Yes, he remembered she quit. Quit the center, quit him. Nothing else had been on his mind for the past seventy-two hours. He'd lifted up the phone to call her so many times, he'd almost developed carpal tunnel syndrome in that hand.

His eyes narrowed as he looked at her. ''What are you doing for money?''

So that was it, he was still playing big brother? She didn't want a brother anymore, she wanted the man who had kissed her, who'd made her feel that there was something more for them. ''Don't worry about me.''

''What are you doing for money?'' he repeated. He knew her finances were shaky. Kurt hadn't left her with anything but bills.

Her voice became icy, distant. ''Sherry showed Sinjin some of my work and he asked me to handle the Web pages for his companies. The money's excellent and I can work out of the house most of the time, be around the baby. Everything's perfect,'' she fairly snapped.

Everything was perfect for her. Not so perfect for him. He was dying inside the way he never thought he could. He played the only card he felt he had. ''The kids at the center miss you. And Sandy misses you.''

And you? What about you? Can't you even tell me that much? ''And I miss them and her,'' she said tersely. ''I can volunteer some time on Sundays at the center.'' As to Sandy, she had no solution there, even though she loved the little girl as if she were her own. His time with his daughter was limited, she wouldn't very well tell him to drop Sandy off at her house and come back for her later.

Was she that determined to keep away from him, to severe all ties? He had no idea until now how much knowing that could hurt. His voice was very still as he said, ''I'm not around on Sunday.''

''Exactly.'' Her chin went up even more pugnaciously, daring him to say something. ''Isn't that the way you want it?''

''No.''

She had no idea what he meant, what he was thinking. Her intuition had completely deserted her.

"Then how *do* you want it, Carson? Because I'm tired of guessing. Tired of being slapped down." Her voice rose, crackling with all the emotion she was attempting to suppress. "Yes, that's right, Pollyanna has her limits, too. And getting pushed away a hundred and twelve times is mine."

Carson looked at her stonily. "It hadn't been that often."

"Damn it—" she threw up her hands, moving away from him before she did something she'd regret "—I'm exaggerating the number, not the situation. The way I always do. You'd think you'd know me by now."

He caught her by the shoulders and spun her around, forcing her to face him.

"I do," he said fiercely. "I know everything about you. I know the way your eyes light up when you have an idea, or when you've made someone come around. I know the way you laugh. High when something's funny, low when it's at yourself." His eyes searched her face, trying to see if he was getting through, if she understood what he was telling her. "I know the sound of your walk when you're coming down the hall at the center. Like harnessed energy just waiting to go off. I know the curve of your mouth when you smile. It's like sunshine, brightening everything it touches."

There was nothing but stillness for a long moment. She blew out a breath. "Well, you certainly do know the way to take the wind out of someone's sails."

He wanted to take her in his arms, to hug her to him, but he was afraid. Afraid that it was too late. So he stood there, still holding her shoulders, still searching for signs.

"I don't want to take the wind out of your sails, Lori. And I don't want to be adrift again. I thought I could back away, for both our sakes. But I can't." Suddenly aware that he was still holding her in place, he dropped his hands helplessly to his sides. "Nothing's right without you. Nothing fits anymore. Not my purpose, not my skin, nothing."

She was almost afraid to breathe. "So what are you saying?"

He felt like a drowning man, still searching for something to keep him afloat. "I was hoping you'd say it for me."

She wasn't going to make it easy for him. She had before, but if there was ever going to be anything for them, it had to be his turn, his sentiments.

"Uh-uh, I'm through putting words into your mouth. These have to be your own. I need to hear the words in your heart, Carson."

He wasn't any good at this, she knew that. His eloquence, such as it was, began and ended in the courtrooms he no longer frequented. "You already know them."

Lori shook her head. "Doesn't matter what you think I know or don't know. I have to hear it. To be sure I'm not imagining it."

Carson's dark eyes delved into hers, silently asking for help, for understanding. "You already know what's in my heart."

Maybe she was wrong. Again. Maybe he didn't really care. Maybe what he missed was the familiarity of having her around. If he didn't give her this, then he couldn't give her anything.

"How can I know what's in your heart?" she demanded. "Supposedly until a little while ago, *you* didn't even know what was in your heart. I need to hear the words, Carson."

He took a breath, leaping off the cliff. Risking everything. "I love you."

Tilting her head in his direction, she cupped her ear. Carson's voice had hardly been above a whisper. "Say again?"

A tiny amount of tension eased away. There was a hint of a smile playing on her lips. He glanced up toward the stairs. "I'll wake the baby."

She took a step closer to him. Maybe it was going to be all right after all. "It's worth waking up for."

He slipped his arms around her. "I love you." He waited. She said nothing. "Don't you have anything to say to me?"

Lori lifted her face up to his, a smile in her eyes. "It's about time."

He laughed shortly. She was paying him back. Not that he blamed her. "Don't you have anything else to say to me?"

She couldn't keep the grin back any longer as she fluttered her lashes at him. "You already know what I have to say to you."

He had that coming, Carson thought. "I need to hear the words."

"Yes," she said softly, "you do. We all do." It

was going to be all right. She didn't kid herself, the road ahead was going to be bumpy, but it was going to be all right. "I love you, Carson O'Neill, love you despite the fact that you are very possibly the stubbornest man on the face of the earth." She slipped her arms through his, locking them around his waist. "Love you for your generous heart, your way of never sidestepping a responsibility, and the fact that you are the world's best kisser."

That made him laugh. "How would you know? You haven't kissed the world."

He saw a devilishness enter her eyes just before she asked, "Want me to?"

"Don't even think about it."

He loved her, she thought. He really loved her. She hadn't been wrong and it felt wonderful.

She wanted more. "Why, Carson, why shouldn't I think about it?"

His arms locked tighter around her, bringing her closer to him until their bodies were touching. "Because you're mine."

"And?"

"And I'm yours."

After all this time, it was hard to believe he was finally saying what she'd wanted to hear him say. "Sounds pretty official."

"It will be," he answered matter-of-factly, "once we're married."

He had just succeeded in broadsiding her. She stared at him, wide-eyed. When the man leaped, he really leaped. "When did this happen?"

"It hasn't. Yet." She wanted words, all right, he'd

give her words. ‘‘Lori, will you do me the very huge honor of being my wife?’’

Excitement, happiness and a host of emotions she couldn’t begin to name all welled up inside of her. ‘‘I don’t know how much of an honor it’ll be, but yes, I will. You had me at Lori, you know.’’

‘‘No, I didn’t know. I didn’t know anything.’’ God, but he loved her. Why had he been so afraid of letting it out? This was Lori, and he’d always known that she was special. ‘‘Maybe that’s why it took so long.’’

She shook her head, negating everything that had come before this moment. ‘‘Doesn’t matter how long it took. That’s behind us. All that matters is now.’’

‘‘And forever. You still haven’t said you’d marry me,’’ he reminded her.

Lori stood up on her toes, her arms just barely reaching around his neck. ‘‘I thought that was understood.’’

He wasn’t about to make that mistake again. ‘‘From now on, nothing’s understood, nothing’s taken for granted. Everything’s spelled out.’’

Amusement shone in her eyes. ‘‘Could get wordy.’’

‘‘That’s all right,’’ he assured her, ‘‘I like the sound of your voice.’’

‘‘Good thing.’’ Her eyes were smiling at him. ‘‘Yes.’’

‘‘Yes, what?’’

‘‘‘Yes dear?’’’ And then she laughed. ‘‘Yes, I’ll marry you.’’

He realized that despite everything, he’d been holding his breath until this moment. Until she agreed.

"I'll leave the arrangements up to you. You're good at that sort of thing."

She wasn't about to fall into that trap again. "Uh-uh. From now on, we're doing it all together."

That sounded a great deal better to him than he thought it would have. But then, the fact that the bargain was sealed with a kiss might have had something to do with it.

* * * * *

SOCIAL GRACES

by

Dixie Browning

DIXIE BROWNING

is an award-winning painter and writer, mother and grandmother who has written nearly eighty contemporary romances, Dixie and her sister, Mary Williams, also write historical romances as Bronwyn Williams. Contact Dixie at www.dixiebrowning.com or at PO Box 1389, Buxton, NC 27920, USA.

One

Standing in the middle of the bedroom, dangling a pair of Chanel slingbacks by the stiletto heels, with a sleeveless black Donna Karan slung over her shoulder, Val Bonnard stared at the partially open closet and listened for the scratching noise to come again. Shivering in the chill air, she glanced quickly at the window. With the wind howling a gale, it might be only a branch scraping the eaves. What else could it be? She was alone in the house, wasn't she?

She was alone, period.

Swallowing the lump that threatened to lodge permanently in her throat, she glared at the closet door. It was ajar because there wasn't a level surface in the entire house. All the doors swung open, and all the windows leaked cold air. The temperature outside hovered in the low forties, which wasn't particularly cold for Carolina in the middle of January, but it felt colder because of the wind. And the dampness.

And the aloneness.

She was still glaring when the mouse emerged, tipped her a glance, twitched its ears, then calmly proceeded to follow the baseboard to a postage-stamp-sized hole near the corner of the room.

It was the last straw in a haystack of last straws. Grief, anger and helplessness clotted around her and she dropped onto the edge of the sagging iron-framed bed and let the tears come.

A few minutes later she sniffed and felt in the pocket of her leather jeans for a tissue. As if pockets designed to display starbursts of rhinestones could possibly harbor anything so practical.

Sniffing again, she thought, it's not going to work. What on earth had she expected? That by driving for two days to reach a quaint, half remembered house on a half remembered barrier island she would not only escape from crank calls, but magically exchange grief for perspective? That a lightbulb would suddenly appear above her head and she would instantly know who was responsible for Bonnard Financial Consultants' downfall, her father's disgrace, his arrest and his untimely death?

Time and distance lent perspective. She'd read that somewhere, probably on a greeting card. She'd had more than two and a half months. Time hadn't helped.

As for distance, she had run as far away as she

could run, to the only place she had left. Now she was here with as many of her possessions as she could cram into her new, cheap, gas-guzzling secondhand car, in a village so small it lacked so much as a single stoplight. She had even escaped from those irritating calls, as there wasn't a working phone in the house. Her cell phone with its caller ID didn't seem to work here.

There wasn't a dry cleaner on the island either, and half her wardrobe required dry-cleaning, most of it special handling. "Why not whine about it, wimp?" she muttered.

At least focusing on trivia helped stave off other thoughts—thoughts that swept her too close to the edge.

It had taken all her energy since her father had died to settle his affairs and dispose of the contents of the gabled, slate-roofed Tudor house that had been home for most of her life. Although stunned to learn that it was so heavily mortgaged, she'd actually been relieved when the bank had taken over the sale.

The rest had gone quickly—the disposal of the contents. Belinda and Charlie had helped enormously before they'd moved to take on new positions. She and Belinda had shared more than a few tears, and even stoic old Charlie had been red-eyed a few times.

In the end, all she'd brought south with her was her hand luggage, three garment bags and three banana boxes, one filled with personal mementos, one with linens, and another with the files she'd retrieved from her father's study.

In retrospect, everything about the past eleven weeks had been unreal in the truest sense of the word. There'd been a bottle of special vintage Moët Chandon in the industrial-sized, stainless-steel refrigerator, waiting for her birthday celebration. Her father had bought it the day before he'd been arrested. "Belinda has orders to prepare all your favorite dishes," he'd told her the night before, looking almost cheerful for a change. The old lines and shadows had been there, but at least there'd been some color in his face.

She'd asked several times before if anything was worrying him. Each time he'd brushed off her question. "Stock market's down," he'd said the last time, then he'd brightened. "Cholesterol's down, too, though. Can't have everything, can we?"

She'd chided him for spending too much time downtown and been relieved when he'd promised to take her advice and start spending more time at home, even though she knew very well he would spend most of it closed up in his study with *Forbes* and the *Wall Street Journal.*

For her birthday she had deliberately arranged to have dinner at home with only her dad instead of the usual bash at the club. She had planned to mellow him with the champagne and find out exactly what had been eating at him. But early on the morning of her thirtieth birthday a pair of strangers who turned out to be police officers had shown up at the door and invited her father to accompany them downtown.

She'd seen the whole thing from the top of the

stairs. Barefoot and wearing only a robe and nightgown, she had hurried downstairs, demanding to know what was happening.

The spokesman for the pair had been stiffly polite. "Just a few questions, miss, that's all." But obviously that hadn't been all. Her father had been ashen. Alarmed, she'd called first his physician, then his lawyer.

The next few hours had swept past like a kaleidoscope. She didn't recall having gotten dressed—she certainly hadn't taken time to shower, much less to arrange her hair before racing outside. Belinda had called after her and told her to take her father's medicine to the police station, so she'd dashed back and snatched the pill bottle from the housekeeper's hand.

They'd had only brief minutes to speak privately when the officer in the room with him had gone to get him a cup of water. Speaking quietly, as if he were afraid of being overheard, Frank Bonnard had instructed her to remove all unlabeled paper files from the file cabinet in his study and store them in her bedroom.

Confused and frightened, she had wanted to ask more, but just then the officer had returned. Her father had nodded, swallowed his pills and said, "Go home. I'll be there as soon as I get through here."

That was the last time she'd seen him alive. Before he could even be bonded out, he'd suffered a fatal coronary.

Now, peeling a paper towel from the roll on the old oak dresser, Val blew her nose, mopped her eyes and sighed. She'd been doing entirely too much of that lately. Great, gasping sighs, as if she were starved for oxygen.

What she was starved for were answers. Now that it was too late, she wondered if it had been a mistake to leave Greenwich. She could have rented a room, possibly even an apartment. If there were any answers to be found, they would hardly be found halfway down the East Coast in a tiny village her father had visited only once in his entire life.

On the other hand, the auditors, the men from the Financial Crimes Unit, plus those from all the various government agencies involved, were convinced they already had their man—their scapegoat—even though they'd made another token arrest. And even if she were to unravel the mess and prove beyond a shadow of a doubt that her father was innocent, it was too late to bring him back. The best she could hope to do was to restore his reputation.

Light from the setting sun, filtered by ancient, moss-draped live oaks, turned the dusty windows opaque. So many things on the island had changed since she'd last seen this old house, she would never have found it without the real estate agent's explicit instruction.

Just over a week ago she had called the agency that managed the property she'd inherited from her great-grandmother, Achsah Dozier. A few hours ago, following the agent's instructions, she had located Seaview Realty. While the office was scarcely larger than a walk-in closet, the woman seated behind a desk cluttered with brochures, boxes of Girl Scout cookies and what appeared to be tax forms, seemed friendly, if somewhat harried.

"Marian Kuvarky." The woman nodded toward the nameplate on her desk. "Glad you made it before I had to close up," she said, handing over a set of keys. "I'd better warn you, though—I still haven't found anyone to give the place a good going-over since the people who were renting it moved out. You might want to check into a motel for a few days."

Val had come too far to be put off another moment. Besides, she couldn't afford a motel. Even in the dead of winter, beach prices would seriously erode her dwindling funds. "I can take care of a little dirt, just tell me how to find my house." She was hardly helpless. She had looked after a three-room apartment with only a weekly maid before she'd moved back home to Connecticut.

Ms. Kuvarky, a youngish blonde with tired eyes and an engaging smile said, "Okay, but don't say I didn't warn you. Take a left once you leave here and turn off onto the Back Road."

"What's the name of it?"

"Of what?"

"The road."

"Back Road. It's named that. I had the power turned on after you called. I forgot if I told you or not, but the last renters left owing for two months. I would have had it ready to rent out again once I found somebody to do a few minor repairs, but like I said over the phone, my cleaner's out on maternity leave. She says she'll be back, but you know how that goes. I'm sort of coasting for now, trying to get through the slack season. I cleaned two places myself last weekend.''

Val had been too tired to involve herself in the agent's problems. Her stomach hadn't stood the trip well, as she'd nibbled constantly on junk food, more from nerves than from hunger. ''I brought linens. You said the house was furnished,'' she reminded Ms. Kuvarky.

The agent had nodded. ''Pretty much all you'll need, I guess, but it's sort of a mishmash. I wrote to your father about the repairs—those are extra—but I never heard back. Anyway, there's so much construction going on these days, even between seasons, it's hard to find dependable help.''

Ms. Kuvarky had promised to call around. Val remembered thinking that if the place had a roof and a bed, everything else could wait.

Now she wasn't quite so sure.

The last thing the rental agent had said as Val had stood in the doorway, trying to get her bearings in a village that had nothing even faintly resembling city blocks or even village squares, was ''By the way, if you happen to be looking for work and know one end of a broom from the other, you're hired.''

She'd been joking, of course. It might even come to that, Val told herself now, but at the moment she had other priorities. Starting with getting rid of her resident mouse.

* * *

The power was on, that was the good part. The bad part was that there was no phone. Or maybe that was the good part, too. A few crank calls had even managed to get through call-blocking before she'd left Greenwich, but they could hardly follow her to a place where she didn't have a working phone.

There was no central heat, only an oil heater in the living room and an assortment of small space heaters scattered in the other rooms. She'd managed to turn the oil heater on. The thing hadn't exploded, so she assumed she'd pushed the right button.

The water heater was another matter. She let the hot water faucet run for five minutes, but luke was as warm as it got. That's when she'd discovered that her cell phone didn't work. She'd tried to call Ms. Kuvarky, and the darned thing blanked out on her. No signal.

All right, so she would think of herself as a pioneer woman. At least she had a bed to sleep in instead of a covered wagon somewhere in the middle of the wilderness. She was thirty years old, with a degree from an excellent college—and although she was somewhat out of her element at the moment, she'd never been accused of being a slow learner. However, repairing major household appliances just might stretch her capability close to the breaking point. Sooner or later—probably sooner—she would have to look for a paying job in order to hire someone to do the things she couldn't figure out how to do herself.

One thing she definitely could do was clean her

house. That accomplished, she could start going through her father's files, looking for whatever he'd wanted her to find that would enable his lawyer to reopen his case posthumously and clear his name.

There *had* to be something there. Otherwise, why had he made that strange, hurried request? He could've had no way of knowing that he'd be dead within hours of being arrested.

Bitter? Yes, she was bitter. But grief and bitterness weren't going to solve any problems, either those facing her here or those she'd left behind.

She stood, crossed the small room and kicked at the baseboard. ''All right, Mickey, your time is up. Sorry, but I'm not in a sharing mood, so pack up your acorns or whatever and move out.''

By no standards was the house she'd inherited from Achsah Dozier comparable to the one she'd left behind. The original structure might have been modernized at some point since she'd last seen it, but the white paint was peeling rather badly and a few of the faded green shutters dangled from single hinges.

At least the gingerbread trim on the front eaves was intact. She remembered thinking in terms of a fairy tale when she'd been told as a child that the fancy trim was called gingerbread. The fact that her great-grandmother had actually baked gingerbread that day, the spicy scent greeting them at the front door, had only enhanced the illusion.

Marian Kuvarky had mentioned that a few years before she'd died, Achsah Dozier had had part of the old back porch turned into another bedroom and bare-bones bath with its own separate entrance, in case she needed live-in help. Since her death, it had occasionally been rented separately. Val briefly considered the possibility and decided that she wasn't cut out to play landlady.

On the other hand, unearned income was not to be sneezed at.

Dropping the shoes and dress she'd been clutching, she headed downstairs in search of cleaning materials. Before she could even consider sleeping in the room, she had to do something about the mice-and-mildew smell, either air it out or scrub it out. It was too cold to air it out.

It occurred to her that if Ms. Kuvarky had any idea of just how little she knew about the domestic arts, she would never have offered her a job cleaning houses, even as a joke.

Later that evening Val stepped out of the rust-stained, claw-footed upstairs bathtub onto a monogrammed hand towel. She hadn't bothered to pack such things as tablecloths, dresser scarves or bath mats, knowing that short of renting a trailer, she had to draw the line somewhere.

She had augmented the lukewarm water with a kettle of boiling water brought up from the kitchen. One kettle wasn't enough, but by the time she'd heated another one, the first would be cold, so she'd settled for lukewarm and quick.

Now, covered in goose bumps, she swaddled her damp body in a huge bath towel. Aside from being grimy and smelly, the house was also drafty. There was a space heater between the tub and the lavatory that helped as long as she didn't move more than a foot away from the glowing element. At least with all the drafts, carbon monoxide wouldn't be a problem. As for the danger of an electrical fire, that was another matter.

Note: have the water heater repaired.
Note: have the wiring checked.

Which reminded her—what about insurance?

"Welcome to the real world, Ms. Bonnard," she whispered a few minutes later, flipping an 800-count Egyptian-cotton king-sized bottom sheet over the sagging double-bed mattress.

She'd pulled on a pair of navy satin pajamas, a Peruvian hand-knit sweater jacket and a pair of slipper socks. January or not, wasn't this supposed to be the sunny south?

Fortunately, she'd crammed two down-filled duvets in around her suitcases, one of which she'd immediately tossed over the ugly brown plaid sofa downstairs. The other one was miles too large for the double bed, but its familiar paisley cover was comforting. That done, she collected a pen and notepad and settled down for some serious list making, ignoring the reminder from her stomach that except for pretzels, popcorn and two candy bars, she hadn't eaten since breakfast. Starting early tomorrow she had a million things to do to make this place even marginally livable before she could concentrate on searching her father's files for evidence of his innocence.

Nibbling the white-tipped cap of her Mont Blanc, she reread the shopping list. Table cloth—one had standards, after all. Mattress cover—she definitely didn't like the looks of that mattress, even after she'd flipped it. Oh, and a bath mat. She'd have to ask where to buy linens here on the island.

On to the next list. Tea, bagels, other foods, preferably already prepared. Wrinkling her nose, she added mousetraps to the list. And cleaning supplies.

A clean house was something she'd always taken for granted. After graduating from college she'd lived in small apartments, first in Chicago, then in Manhattan—always in upscale neighborhoods. She had moved back to her father's house after he'd suffered his first small stroke, and soon after that she'd gotten involved with a few of the local charities. It was what she did best, after all—manage fund-raisers for worthy causes. She had frequently acted as her father's hostess, although most of his business entertaining had been done at the club.

Looking back, it had been a comfortable way to coast through life. Not particularly exciting—no major achievements—but certainly comfortable.

''Definitely room for improvement,'' she murmured, her voice echoing hollowly in the old house.

Tired, hungry, but oddly energized, she surveyed her surroundings. Gone were the familiar French wallpaper in her old bedroom, the mismatched but well-cared-for semi-antique furniture, the faded oriental rug and her eclectic art collection. Here she was confronted by gritty bare floors, dark with layers of varnish—naked, white-painted walls, dusty windows, and the lingering aroma of mouse spoor.

Okay. She could handle that. The sand, she'd quickly discovered, hid in the cracks between the floorboards so that each time she went over it with a broom, more appeared. She could live with a little sand. This was the beach, after all. Even if she couldn't see the ocean from here, she could hear it.

She added window spray and bathroom cleaner to the list, hoping there would be directions on the bottles in case she got into trouble. More paper towels. Sponges. Rubber gloves, although she probably wouldn't be able to wear them without her hands breaking out. Her skin was inclined to be sensitive.

Note: take down the for rent sign on the front lawn.

The lawn itself was a mess, but once she was through scrubbing the entire house, maybe she could paint the front door a bright color to deflect attention from that and the rest of the peeling paint until she could afford to landscape and repaint the entire house. There was nothing wrong with old, but she preferred old and charming to old and neglected.

One more note: find position that pays in advance.

Leaning back on the two down-filled pillows, she closed her eyes. "Dad, what am I going to do?" she whispered. "Charlie, Belinda—Miss Mitty, where are you when I need you?"

The only sound was the plaintive honking of a flock of wild geese flying overhead. It was barely nine o'clock. She *never* went to bed before eleven, often not until the small hours of the morning.

Her last memory before sleep claimed her was of her father being led outside to an unmarked car while she stood in the doorway, too stunned even to protest. One of the officers pressed her father's head down and urged him into the back seat.

It had been Sunday, the morning of her birthday. Belinda had made blueberry pancakes for breakfast. Frank Bonnard, an early riser, had evidently been in his study. He'd been dressed in flannels, an open-necked white shirt and a navy Shetland sweater when Charlie had answered the door. Val remembered thinking much later that if the ghouls could have stuffed him into a pair of orange coveralls before marching him out in front of the single reporter who had probably tuned in on the police radio and followed them to the Belle Haven address, they'd have done it.

That had been only the beginning. Within hours, the press had swarmed like locusts. Shortly after that the phone calls had started. Despite all the blocking devices, a few people managed to get through with variations ranging from "Where's my money?" to "Frank Bonnard owes me my pension, dammit. Where is it? What am I supposed to do now?"

The calls had ended when the police had put taps

on all three phone lines. Not until recently had she wondered why they'd ceased. How could the callers have known their calls could be traced?

The calls had stopped, but not the nightmares. Both asleep and awake, she had replayed the scene that morning back in late September a thousand times. A pale, stiff-faced Charlie stepping back from the wide front door to allow the two men inside. Her father emerging from his study and carefully closing the door behind him. Belinda, one plump hand covering her mouth as she stood in the dining-room doorway.

In less than twelve hours her father had been dead. Pestered by reporters, auditors and men in bad suits who seemed to think they had every right to invade her home, Val had tried desperately to cram her emotions deep inside her and lock the door. When confronted, she'd quickly learned to answer with one of several replies that included, "I don't know," "No comment," and "My father is innocent."

A part of her was still in hiding, but she had to know the truth, even in the unlikely event that the truth turned out to be not what she wanted to hear. Back in Greenwich she'd been too close for any real objectivity. Here, once she settled down to it, she would be able to think clearly. Then at least the callers who wanted to know where their money was would have an answer, even if it was one that wouldn't do them any good.

Valerie Bonnard slept heavily that night. Sometime before daybreak she awoke, thinking about the mouse she'd seen and all the others she'd heard and smelled. Were mice carnivorous? They were grain-eaters, weren't they?

Oh, God…now she'd never get back to sleep.

Eyes scrunched tightly shut, she rolled over onto her stomach. On her own firm, pillow-top mattress, prone had been her favorite sleeping position, never mind that her face would be a mass of wrinkles by the time she reached forty. On a mattress that sagged like a hammock, it was a toss-up as to which she'd succumb to first—strangulation or a broken back.

Grax, if this was your bed, no wonder your back was rounded, she thought guiltily. Her great-grandmother's given name had been Achsah, pronounced *Axa.* As a child, Val had shortened it to Grax. From her one brief visit, she remembered the old woman with the laughing blue eyes and short white hair. Wearing a duckbill cap, a cotton print dress and tennis shoes, she'd been working in the yard when they'd driven up. On their way to Hilton Head, her parents had taken a detour along the Outer Banks so that Lola, Val's mother, could introduce them to her grandmother.

To a child of seven, the trip had seemed endless. Her parents had bickered constantly in the front seat. Odd that she should remember that now. Looking back, it seemed as if it had been her mother who was reluctant to take the time, not her father.

They'd spent the night at a motel, but they'd eaten dinner in the small white house in the woods. She remembered thinking even before she'd smelled the gingerbread that it looked like Aunty Em's house in the Wizard of Oz.

Grax had served boiled fish—she'd called it drum—mixed with mashed potatoes, raw onions and bits of crisp fried salt pork. As strange as it sounded, it had turned out to be an interesting mixture of flavors and textures.

Her mother hadn't touched it. Her father had sampled a few forkfuls. Val, for reasons she could no longer recall, had cleaned off her plate and bragged excessively. She'd eaten two squares of the gingerbread with lemon sauce that had followed.

That had been both the first and the last time she'd seen her great-grandmother. Two years later her parents had separated. Her father had been given custody—had her mother even asked? At any rate, Lola Bonnard had chosen to live abroad for the next few years, so visitation had been out of the question. Val had gone through the usual stages of wondering if the split had been her fault and scheming to bring her parents together again.

She would like to think her mother had attended Grax's funeral but she really didn't know that, either. Her relationship with Lola Bonnard had never been close, even before the divorce. Since then it had dwindled to an exchange of Christmas cards and the occasional birthday card. It had been her father's lawyer who'd handled Grax's bequest, arranging for someone to manage the house as a rental. At the time, Val had been living in Chicago working for a private foundation that funded shelters and basic health services for runaway girls.

"I'm sorry, Grax," she whispered now, burdened with a belated sense of guilt. "I'm embarrassed and sorry and I hope you had lots and lots of friends so that you didn't really miss us."

No wonder the house felt so cold and empty. How many strangers had lived here since Grax had died? There was nothing of Achsah Dozier left, no echoes of the old woman's island brogue that had fascinated Val at the time. No hint of the flowers she'd brought inside from the Cape jasmine bushes that had once bloomed in her yard. Lola had complained about the cloying scent and without a word, Grax had got up and set the vase on the back porch.

Val made a silent promise that as soon as she got the house cleaned and repaired, she would see what could be done with the yard.

But first she had to go through those files, discover what it was her father had wanted her to find there, and clear his name. Frank Bonnard had been a good man, an honest man, if something of an impractical dreamer. He didn't deserve what had happened to him.

Two

John Leo MacBride studied the encrusted mass of plates and cutlery that had been brought up from one of the Nazi submarines sunk during the Second World War off the New England coast. He considered leaving a few as he'd found them instead of soaking them all in an acid solution, prying them apart and cleaning them up. The before-and-after contrast would make a far more interesting display at the small museum that had commissioned the dives.

He glanced at the clock on the wall of his stepbrother's garage where he'd set up a temporary workspace a couple of months ago when Will had called, asking for help. So far, about all he'd been able to do was to keep Macy, Will's wife, from making matters worse. That and stay on the heels of his lawyer, who might as well be back chasing ambulances for all the good he'd done his client.

Mac had been standing by chiefly to offer moral support, which was more than Macy was doing. Instead, she seemed almost to be enjoying her role as the wife of a man who was currently awaiting trial for embezzlement. She'd had her hair highlighted two days after Will had made bail, and since then had managed to get a fair amount of facetime with the media.

Bonnard's daughter, by contrast, had avoided the worst of the feeding frenzy. He could think of a couple of reasons why she might have managed to avoid the spotlight, but social clout didn't mean her old man wasn't guilty as sin.

Will's only crime, Mac was convinced of it, was being too trusting. Less than a year after being given a partnership, Will had gone down in the corporate shipwreck along with Frank Bonnard, founder and CEO of the privately held financial consulting firm. Bonnard had paid for his sins by dying of a massive heart attack almost before the investigation got underway.

Will had hired an inept lawyer—an old law-school classmate. A lawyer himself, as well as a CPA, he'd been planning to present his own defense when Mac had talked him out of it. He was sorry now that he had.

But the money was still missing, and after nearly three months, the trail was murkier than ever. Current thinking was that funds had been bled off gradually over a period of years rather than months, probably funneled from one offshore account to another until it was impossible to trace either the source or the destination.

No one was talking. Bonnard because he was dead, Will because he was clueless, his lawyer because if the jerk had ever passed a bar, it wasn't a bar that served drinks. The guy was a lush.

Mac had tried his own brand of logic on the case, running down the short list of suspects. The Chief Financial Officer, Sam Hutchinson, had apparently been cleared. Currently on an extended leave of absence to be with his terminally ill wife, he'd been the logical suspect. His computers, his files—everything that bore his fingerprints, had been impounded. He'd come through it all clean. Will liked the guy. Only hours before he'd died, Bonnard himself had vouched for him.

As for Bonnard, late founder and CEO of Bonnard Financial Consultants, not even death had offered protection. Once the flock of outside auditors dug in, both he and Will had been swept up in the dragnet.

It was shortly after that that Mac had moved his base of operations from an apartment in Mystic, near the aquarium, to Will's Greenwich home. He was currently living in the small apartment over the garage, finishing up a few tasks from his last commissioned dive.

BFC was a small regional firm, nothing like some of the big outfits that had hit the reef over the past few years. Not that the impact on the victims was any less devastating, as BFC had specialized in handling retirement funds for a number of small area businesses.

To give him credit, back when the economy had taken a dive a few years ago, Bonnard had borrowed heavily against his fancy house and pumped the funds back into the company, a fact that had quickly come to light. It didn't exactly fit the profile of a high-level embezzler to Mac's way of thinking, unless at the same time he'd been shoring up the business with one hand to allay suspicions, he'd been bleeding off profits with the other. Slick trick, if you could pull it off.

Bonnard's only heir was a daughter. The feds had run her through the washer just as a precaution, but so far as anyone knew she had never been involved in any way with her father's business. Will was convinced she wasn't a player.

Will's wife, Macy, wasn't so generous, but then, Macy was inclined to be jealous of any attractive woman, especially one who'd been born with the proverbial silver spoon. Even Mac had to wonder if the investigators had gone easy on the daughter because of her looks and her social position. He wasn't sure how big a part sympathy played in such a case, but the fact that her father had died on his daughter's thirtieth birthday might have had an effect. The press had made it a big deal. He remembered seeing that same pale, stricken face—flawless cheekbones, haunted gray eyes—replayed over and over on every recount during the week immediately after Bonnard's arrest—an arrest that had been followed almost immediately by his death.

Ironic to think that Bonnard might have got clean away if it hadn't been for a junior accountant who had mistakenly mailed out 1099s for a tax-free municipal fund to a number of clients and been forced to do amended forms. Evidently the matter had landed on the desk of a snarky IRS agent. One question had led to another; an outside auditor had been called in, and the whole house of cards had come crashing down. Bonnard had gone to his dubious reward, leaving his junior partner to take the fall.

That's when the scavenger hunt had shifted into high gear, drawing in the FBI, the Financial Crimes Unit, the state auditor's department and the IRS, not to mention a bunch of media types with Woodward and Bernstein complexes. But with all that manpower, they were no closer after nearly three months to locating the missing money, much less tracing it back to its source.

Which damn well wasn't Will Jordan.

Mac's single bag was packed, the Land Cruiser's tank topped off. He was ready to head south the minute Shirley, his hacker friend, gave the word. Not that hacking was even needed in this case, as public records were open to everyone who knew, geographically speaking, where to look. But when he needed information in a hurry, it helped to know someone who could make a computer sit up and sing the "Star Spangled Banner."

Valerie Bonnard's only asset of record at this moment was a modest trust fund that wouldn't kick in for another five years, and a small property she'd inherited in a place called Buxton, on North Carolina's Outer Banks. Mac was generally familiar with the area—what marine archeologist wasn't familiar with the notorious Graveyard of the Atlantic? There was even a new museum by that name on the island. From what he'd been able to find on the Internet, most of the island that hadn't been taken over by Park Service or National Wildlife had been developed over the past few decades.

Ms. Bonnard, using a dummy corporation, could have been investing steadily in some high-dollar real estate down there. Shirley hadn't been able to tie her to anything specific, but it would have been a smart move on the part of La Bonnard, especially considering the erratic stock market. Whether or not she'd socked away the missing funds in investment-grade real estate, it was as good a place to start as any.

One of the perks of being a freelance marine archeologist was large chunks of unregulated time. Unlike Will's, Mac's lifestyle was both portable and low maintenance, although Will's was probably about to change even more drastically in the near future. Mac had a feeling that once this nightmare was over, his stepbrother might have lost more than a junior partnership, an upscale house and a few club memberships. Macy was looking restless now that the publicity had died down. She just might walk, which would be no great loss in Mac's estimation.

* * *

The drive took two days, allowing for frequent breaks, in his fourteen-year-old, rebuilt Land Cruiser. Mac spent the first night in the Norfolk region. Late in the afternoon of the second day, having spent a few hours in one of the area's maritime museums, he pulled into a motel in Buxton and booked a room, intending to spend the first half hour flexing various muscles under a hot shower.

At age thirty-seven he was beginning to realize that stick shifts were hell on left knees. A friend had warned him, but he wasn't about to trade in his customized vehicle, with the locked compartments designed specifically to hold his diving gear and the ergonomic seats that helped minimize fatigue. It might take him a bit longer to bounce back after a long drive, but normally he looked on the bounce-back time as a chance to catch up on his reading. He'd even tossed in a few books at the last minute, in case he had any down time. Not that he planned to hang around any longer than it took to uncover a lead that would shift the focus off Will.

If Mac had a weakness—actually, he admitted to several—it was books. Aside from diving gear, books were his favorite indulgence. Mostly history. The stuff fascinated him, always had. But reading could wait until he'd pinned the Bonnard woman down and got the information he needed.

A fleeting image of him pinning La Bonnard down on a big, soft bed drifted across his field of vision. He blinked it away before it could take root.

The desk clerk was young and inclined to be chatty. It took Mac all of two minutes to get the location of the residence of the late Achsah Dozier, as this wasn't the kind of place where street addresses did much good.

"I didn't really know her, I've only been here a few years," the young woman said. She'd looked him over and touched her hair when he'd walked into the lobby, but evidently decided on closer examination that he wasn't that interesting.

Not altogether surprising. He still had all his hair and teeth, and he'd been asked more than once if he worked out at a gym. He didn't. The type of work he did tended to develop the legs and upper body while it pared down the waist and hips. On the other hand, his face had once been compared to a rockslide.

Besides, he had a couple of decades on the bubblegum-chewing kid, who was saying, "I think Miss Achsah used to live on the Back Road."

In certain pockets of population, he'd learned, *Miss* was an honorary title given to women over a certain age, regardless of marital status. When the first name was used, it generally indicated that there were a number of women with the same surname.

"You go out the door and turn left—" The young clerk continued to talk while Mac mentally recorded the data. "I heard her house was rented out after she died, but I don't think there's anybody living there now. Marian Kuvarky over at Seaview Realty could tell you."

Something—call it a hunter's instinct—told him that the Bonnard woman was holed up in her great-grandmother's house, probably keeping a low profile until things cooled down. If she had a brain under all that glossy black hair she had to know she was probably still considered "of interest" by certain authorities, even if they hadn't found anything to hold her on.

The smart thing would have been to go someplace where she had no ties and wait until the heat died down. After say, six months—a year would be even better—with what she had stashed away in an offshore account, she could settle anywhere in the world.

With what she *allegedly* had stashed away, he corrected himself reluctantly. So far, he was the only one doing the alleging, but then, he had a personal stake. Will hadn't embezzled a damned thing. In the first place, his stepbrother couldn't lie worth crap, and in the second place, if he could've got his hands on that kind of money, his wife would've already spent it. Macy could easily qualify for the world shopping playoffs.

Mac was good at extrapolations. As a marine archeologist, it was what he did best. Study the evidence—the written records, plus any prevailing conditions, political or weatherwise, that might affect where a ship had reportedly gone down. Not until he had thoroughly examined all available data and given his instincts time to mull it over was he ready to home in on his target.

In this case the field had officially narrowed to two suspects: Bonnard and Will. Eliminate Will and that left only Bonnard—or in this case, Bonnard's heir. The auditors were still digging halfheartedly, but the case had been shoved to the back burner as new and bigger cases had intervened in the meantime. Which left poor Will dangling in the wind, his next hearing not even on the docket yet.

Mac made up his mind to wait until morning to scope out the house. He even might wait another day before making contact, but no longer than that. He needed answers. Will wasn't holding up well. He'd lost weight, he had circles under his eyes the size of hubcaps, and his marriage was falling apart.

Timing was crucial. He didn't want to spook her, but neither could he afford to wait too long. The feds hadn't been able to find anything to hold her on, not even as a witness, but to Mac, the logic was inescapable. That damned money hadn't just gone up in smoke. Someone close to Bonnard held the key. The man had been divorced more than twenty years; he'd never remarried. So far as anyone knew, he'd never even had a mistress. A few brief liaisons, but none that had lasted more than a few months. The press had gone after the ex-wife, now reportedly in the process of shedding husband number three. There was no love lost between her and Bonnard, so if she'd known anything it would probably have come out. Another dead end.

By process of elimination, it had to be the daughter. Millions of bucks didn't just slip through a crack in the floor like yellow dust in a gold-rush saloon. Someone was waiting for the heat to die down to claim it. And he knew who the most logical someone was.

Valerie Stevens Bonnard, Mac mused. He knew what she looked like, even knew what make car she drove. He'd seen her around town a couple of times when he'd been in the area visiting Will last spring. Cool, flawless—sexy in a touch-me-not way. Talk about your oxymorons.

He'd even spoken to her once. Will had gone to some BFC function at the country club while Mac was spending a few days in Greenwich on his way back from DC last summer. He'd forgotten his prescription sunglasses and called to asked Mac to drop them off.

Mac had been changing the fluid in his transmission when he'd answered the phone and hadn't bothered to change clothes, intending to leave the sunglasses with an attendant. Driving the same weathered Land Cruiser, he had just squeezed into a parking place between a Lexus and an Escalade when Ms. Bonnard drove up in Mercedes convertible. Evidently she'd mistaken him for one of the groundskeepers, because she'd informed him politely that service parking was in the rear. She'd even smiled, her big gray-green eyes about as warm as your average glacier.

So yeah, he knew what she looked like. There was no chance she would recognize him now though.

She'd summed him up and dismissed him in less than two seconds flat.

* * *

Val was good at any number of things, among them organizing intimate dinner parties for fifty people and overseeing thousand-dollar-a-plate fund-raisers. She excelled at tennis, skiing and hanging art shows. She'd been drilled in what was expected of someone with her privileged background from the time she could walk.

Now, faced with an oven that was lined with three inches of burned-on gunk she burst into tears, only because cursing was not yet among her talents.

She wiped her eyes, smearing a streak of grime across her cheek and glared at the rattling kitchen window. There had to be a way to keep the wind from whipping in through the frames. How had the previous tenants managed to stay warm?

They hadn't, of course. Probably why they'd moved out, leaving the place in such a mess. Three of the rooms had air-conditioner units hanging out the windows. No one had bothered to remove or even to cover them, much less plug all the cracks around them. She had stuffed the cracks with the plastic bags from her first shopping foray, for all the good it did.

Neither the space heaters nor the ugly brown oil heater were a match for the damp chill that seemed to creep through the very walls. Hadn't anyone in the South ever heard of insulation?

She added a roll of clear plastic and a staple gun to the growing shopping list that included more of the sudsy cleanser, another six-pack of paper towels and a few more mousetraps. The plastic would have to serve until she could afford storm windows.

After hours spent scrubbing, most of the downstairs rooms plus her bedroom and the upstairs bath smelled of pine cleanser instead of mice and mildew. She'd ended up buying live traps instead of wire traps, even though they'd cost more, because while she refused to share her new home with rodents, she wasn't into killing. Spiders, roaches and mosquitoes, perhaps, but nothing larger.

Her new lifestyle, she was rapidly discovering, called for a drastically new mindset. Belinda and Charlie, her father's housekeeper and man-of-all-work, had spoiled her, she'd be the first to admit. Now, instead of taking her comfort for granted, she was forced to acquire a whole battery of new skills. In the process she was also acquiring an impressive array of bruises, splinters and broken fingernails, not to mention a rash on her left hand from the rubber gloves she'd tried to wear. French manicures and sleek hairstyles were definitely things of the past. After the second day, she hadn't bothered to apply makeup, only a quick splash of moisturizer and, when she remembered it, lip balm. Instead of her usual chignon, she wore her hair in a single braid that, by day's end, was usually frazzled and laced with cobwebs—or worse.

On the plus side, she was too busy to waste time crying. Hard work was turning out to be a fair remedy for grief. Somewhat surprisingly she was even making a few friends. Marian Kuvarky at the real estate office, the clerk at the hardware store who had advised her on mousetraps, and the friendly woman at the post office where she'd rented a mailbox. She'd asked questions of all of them, everything from where to find what on the island to what kind of weather to expect.

"Expect the unexpected, I guess," the postal worker had said, "This time of year we might get seventy-five degrees one day and thirty-five the next. Not much snow, but lawsy, the winds'll sandblast your windshield before you know it. By the way, did I tell you that you have to come here to collect your mail? None of the villages on the island has home delivery."

Which reminded her—she needed to get started mailing change-of-address notices now that she had an official address.

But first she had to finish scrubbing the tops of the kitchen cabinets. She'd given up on the oven for now—didn't know how to use the darned thing, anyway. But sooner or later she was going to defeat that thick black crust if she had to resort to dynamite.

Once she finished the kitchen she would tackle the back bedroom and bath in case she got desperate enough to look for a tenant. Meanwhile she needed to take down that half-hidden sign in the front yard. Or maybe just cover it for the time being. While she hated the idea of compromising her privacy, it might be a way of bringing in an income until she could look for work. Marian's offer of a job cleaning houses had been a joke...hadn't it?

Standing on the next-to-the-top step of the rickety stepladder she'd retrieved from a shed in the backyard, Val steadied herself by draping one arm over an open cabinet door while she wiped off the last section of cabinet top, wincing as her shoulder muscles protested. Hard to believe that only a few months ago she'd thought nothing of dancing all night, playing tennis all morning and spending the afternoon hanging a benefit art exhibit.

At least she no longer had trouble sleeping. A fast warm shower, a couple of acetominaphen caplets and she was out like a light. Over the past few months she'd lost count of all the nights she had lain awake, tunneling through endless caverns in search of answers that continued to elude her. Answers to questions such as, who could possibly have embezzled so much money without anyone's noticing in a small firm that was bristling with accountants? Oh, she'd heard all about the fancy shell games—most of them actually legal—that were played by some of the largest accounting firms. The fact remained, why hadn't anyone noticed until it was too late? What had happened to the money?

And why on earth hadn't she gone for an MBA instead of wasting her time on folk music, literature and art history?

Although, not even a Harvard MBA had kept her father from being taken in. But then, Frank Bonnard's strength had been pulling ideas out of the blue, working out an overall plan and counting on a select team to carry out the details. The team in this case had consisted of Sam Hutchinson, who'd been gone practically the whole year, and therefore couldn't have been involved, and the administrative assistant whom she'd never met before the woman had been asked to leave. Val had a feeling Miss Mitty might have engineered that, as evidently the newcomer had encroached on territory the older woman considered hers alone.

And of course, there was Will Jordan, the new junior partner who'd been indicted along with her father. He was probably guilty. The prosecutors must have thought so, as he was still out on bond.

To be fair she had to include Miss Mitty, longtime family friend and her father's efficient and insightful, if unofficial assistant. Not that she was in any way a suspect, but Mitty Stoddard had been there from the beginning. If she hadn't retired back in August she'd have known precisely where to start digging. While she might not have a college degree, much less a title, the woman was smarter than any of the younger members of the team gave her credit for being, Val was convinced of it.

Val made a mental note to try again to reach her. She'd dialed the number she'd been given countless times over the past several weeks, always with the same results. Not a single one of the messages she'd left had produced results. At first she'd been too distracted to wonder about it, but now she was beginning to be seriously concerned. If Miss Mitty was ill, it might explain why she had suddenly announced her retirement and moved to Georgia to be close to a newly widowed niece. She hadn't wanted anyone to worry about her.

Come to think of it, Miss Mitty had never really trusted Will Jordan. As a rule, people whom she didn't trust rarely remained at BFC very long. Jordan was an exception. If Mitty Stoddard didn't trust a person there was usually a sound reason, even if it wasn't apparent at the time. Val was sure she had voiced her reservations where it would do the most good, but for once in their long association, Frank Bonnard must have disagreed with her.

Val sighed. She desperately needed someone to bounce her ideas off, and Miss Mitty would be perfect. Under all that lavender hair lurked a surprisingly keen mind. Darn it, it wasn't like her not to return a call. The last thing she'd said before boarding the plane to Atlanta when Val had driven her to the airport was, "You call me now, you hear? You know how I feel about your young man." Val had been engaged at the time. "But then, you won't listen to an old woman. I guess I can't blame you." She'd laughed, wattles swaying above the navy suit and lacy white blouse with the tiny gold bar pin fastening the high collar. "Once you set the date, you let me know and I'll make plans to come back. Belinda and Charlie are getting along in years—the last thing they need is a big, fancy wedding."

Belinda was two years younger than Mitty Stoddard, and no one knew Charlie's exact age. As it turned out, Miss Mitty had been absolutely right about Tripp Ailes, but that wasn't the reason Val was so desperate to get in touch with her now. Was she even aware of all that had happened since she'd moved to Georgia? The collapse of BFC had been big news in the northeast for a few weeks—the *Wall Street Journal* had covered it, with updates for the first week or so. But it had probably been worth only a few lines in the business section of the *Atlanta Constitution,* or whatever newspaper Miss Mitty read now.

She would keep on trying, but in the meantime she had work to do before she could settle down with those blasted files. If there was a method in her father's filing system, she had yet to discover it. Brilliant, Frank Bonnard had undoubtedly been; organized, he was not.

Absently, she scratched her chin, leaving another smear of dirt. After waiting this long, the files could wait another day or two. She was making inroads on years of dirt and neglect—the pungent aroma of pine cleanser now replaced other less-pleasant smells, but it was still a far cry from the fragrance of gingerbread and Cape jasmine she remembered from so long ago.

"Up and at 'em, lady."

She didn't budge from the chair. She could think of several things she'd rather be doing than scrubbing down another wall. Shagging golf balls barefoot in a bed of snake-infested poison ivy, for instance.

Okay, so she was procrastinating. Scowling at the heap of filthy paper towels on the floor, she admitted that sooner or later the house would be as clean as she could get it and then—*then*—she would focus all her attention on going through her father's files with a fine-tooth comb.

Not even to herself would Val admit the smallest possibility of finding evidence of her father's guilt.

Three

A few hours later, with both the furniture and the downstairs windows sparkling—on the inside, at least—Val collapsed onto one of the freshly scrubbed kitchen chairs. She kicked off her Cole Haans and sipped on a glass of chilled vegetable juice, hoping that that and peanut butter constituted a balanced diet.

The ugly green refrigerator probably dated from the sixties. It was noisy and showing signs of rust, but at least it was now clean, inside and out. And if it wasn't exactly energy efficient, neither was she at the moment.

Marian had relayed the promise that her phone would be hooked up sometime today, which was a big relief. New number equaled no crank calls. She'd had to go outside and stand near the road to get even an erratic signal on her cell phone. After today, though, she could hook up her laptop, deal with her e-mail and check out the Greenwich newspapers to see if there'd been any new developments since she'd left town.

That done, she'd better start composing a résumé. Unfortunately, the only kind of work in which she had any experience was the kind that paid off more in satisfaction than in wages.

''Ha. How the mighty have fallen,'' she said, dolefully amused.

How much would a private investigator charge to dig into her father's records? The same records that had been turned inside out by swarms of experts?

Too much, probably. Anything was too much, given her present circumstances. Besides, even if she could have afforded to hire an investigator, she wasn't sure she could trust him with her father's personal files. Was there some code of ethics that said a private investigator had to turn over any incriminating evidence he might find?

''Dad, I'm out of my element here, you're going to have to give me a hint,'' she whispered now. Will Jordan might be still under investigation, but Val had a feeling he was going to find some way to pin the whole thing on Frank Bonnard. Why not? Her poor father was in no position to defend himself.

Val was feeling more inadequate with every day that passed. If she got lucky and found evidence that would vindicate her father, then she could be charged with concealing that same evidence. Couldn't win for losing. Classic case, she thought ruefully.

Finishing the last of her vegetable juice, she wiped her watering eyes with a grimy fist and went to see who had just pulled into the front yard. Marian had mentioned stopping by later today on her way to pick up her daughter at preschool. Still blinking, Val peered through the newly cleaned glass panel beside the front door. Or maybe it was the phone people.

It wasn't Marian. The vehicle that had just pulled up behind her own didn't look like any telephone van she'd ever seen. It wasn't even a van, it was a junker—a collection of mismatched parts. As for the driver…

Did she know him? There was something vaguely familiar about that thick, sun-streaked hair, the angular features—the wide shoulders that threatened the seams of his navy windbreaker. Her gaze moved down past the narrow hips to a pair of long legs that looked powerful even under loose-fitting jeans. He was definitely what her friends called a hottie. And the rush of sudden warmth she felt sure wasn't coming from that creaking old oil heater.

He stopped beside the sprawling palmetto that fanned out to cover the for rent sign she'd forgotten to take down. Bracing his legs, he shaded his eyes against the harsh sun and surveyed the front of her house. Not only was his face oddly familiar, but there was something about his stance—feet apart, one thumb hooked in the pocket of his jeans, that nudged the backside of her memory.

Could she have seen him somewhere? At the post office? The grocery store? She might've forgotten those rugged, irregular features, but that indefinable quality that was loosely referred to as sex appeal for want of a better word, would be hard for any woman to overlook. He had it doubled in spades, as the saying went.

Could she have met him before? She'd be the first to admit that her mind was stuffed with so many details, she had trouble remembering whether or not she'd even had breakfast this morning, much less what it had been.

Oh, well…peanut butter toast and hot tea, that was a given.

Still, even his vehicle looked vaguely familiar, and cars weren't her thing. She'd driven the one her father had given her for her twenty-sixth birthday until two weeks ago when she'd traded it in for something larger, older and a lot cheaper, plus a nice amount of cash.

On the other hand, how often did one see a rust-brown-and-primer-gray SUV that looked as if it had been pieced together from junkyard components? With yellow molded plastic seats, no less.

She stepped back from the panel of glass beside the door, unwilling to be caught staring if he came any closer. The last time she'd felt this fluttery sense of uncertainty she'd been fifteen years old. On a dare, she had asked a certain seventeen-year-old boy to a dance and nearly thrown up before he accepted.

He took his time looking the house over—the uneven shutters, the mended porch post, the ever-so-slightly sagging roofline—almost as if he were sizing up what it would take to fix it.

And then the light dawned. This must be the handyman Marian had promised to find. Of course! That would explain his interest in the house. He was mentally preparing an estimate.

The question now was whether or not she could afford him.

"I'm sure I can rent it for you once we get it fixed up," Marian had said. "There's a growing market for low-end housing." And Grax's old house was certainly that, as much as it pained Val to admit it. "The last couple rented it as a fixer-upper," the rental agent went on to say. "Trouble is, they didn't fix anything, so you're probably going to have to put some money into bringing it up to standard before I can advertise it again. Look, why don't I call around and see who I can find to do the minimum?"

Val had nodded, not knowing what else to say. Catch-22. She had to spend money she didn't have to make money she desperately needed.

His deck shoes made no sound on the porch. She swallowed hard. *I really can't afford you, but oh, how I need you.*

Want you?

"Don't even go there, woman," she muttered.

His jacket was open slightly, revealing a gray sweatshirt bearing the letters OD'S HO. Underneath the soft, loose-fitting clothing he looked solid as a slab of hardwood. Pecs, abs—from here she couldn't see the gluts, but she had no doubt they were every bit as splendid as the rest of the glorious package. Compared to this man, her ex-fiancé on his best day wasn't even a blip on the horizon.

Standing just inside the front door, she waited until he'd knocked twice before opening the door. "Yes?" She had the eyebrow lift down pat, having learned it at an early age from Charlie, who, she was convinced, had picked it up from watching "Masterpiece Theater."

"Miss Bonnard?"

For a moment she was startled that he knew who she was, but of course, Marian would have given him her name. Hopefully, she'd also told him that Val could afford only a minimum of basic repairs.

She nodded. It would have helped if he'd had a high-pitched nasal drawl. Instead, his voice was better than Belgian chocolate. "If you'll come around to the back, I can show you what needs doing first." Everything needed doing first. Mentally, she tried to prioritize what absolutely had to be done, whether or not she could afford it.

Instead of taking her implied suggestion that he go around outside, the tall stranger stepped through the door and glanced around curiously, making her aware all over again of the shabby, mismatched furniture and the boxes still waiting to be unpacked.

"Back this way, then. The shower, I think first of all. It barely trickles when I turn it on and then it takes forever to drain." She glanced over her shoulder as she led him down the hall. ‘‘You can do plumbing, can't you?’’

‘‘Nothing major, I'm not licensed, but maintenance, sure.’’

‘‘Ms. Kuvarky might have told you, I'm considering renting the back bedroom separately.’’ She hadn't been, not seriously, but with what she'd been spending lately on cleaning supplies, the slightest income would help. ‘‘So I'd rather start there if you don't mind.’’

After that, she decided, the hot-water heater and then the windows. Maybe the roof. Patching, not replacing. It hadn't rained since she'd been here, but she didn't relish the thought of waking up in a cold, wet bed, and she'd noticed a few suspicious stains on the ceiling.

‘‘I'll have to get my tools.’’

‘‘Oh, well…of course. I mean, it doesn't have to be done today, although…’’

He nodded, pursing his lips.

Mesmerized, she stared at his mouth, then shook herself back to reality. The back end of the house was freezing. The back door didn't fit any closer than the front. She needed this man for practical purposes. The last thing she wanted to do was scare him off before he even agreed to take the job.

After a cursory glance at the ugly, closet-sized bath, he turned his attention to the tiny adjoining bedroom. Val studied the room objectively, trying to see it through the eyes of a stranger. That mattress definitely needed tossing, but at the moment she couldn't afford to replace it. The furniture was old, but hardly old enough to be called antique. Not that there was anything really wrong with it that a lick of paint and a little judicious sanding wouldn't remedy. Anyone with half a brain could figure out country chic.

She shook her head. Repairs first. Interior decorating later, if at all. "I can bring one of the spare heaters down from upstairs and put it back here while you work. Oh, by the way—do you know anything about space heaters?"

"I know they're probably not cost-effective, depending on the local power rates."

She sighed. "I was afraid of that. There's an oil heater in the front room, but it doesn't heat much beyond that. How on earth do you suppose people used to get by?"

"Furnaces have been around a long time. Aside from that, fireplaces, quilts." He grinned unexpectedly. It was as if the sun suddenly burst from behind a cloud. "Long johns."

She blinked and said, "Yes, well…there were two fireplaces originally, but they've both been boarded up. I'm not sure the mice haven't been chewing on the cords of some of the heaters, so you might take a look while you're here." She paused, tapping her lower lip with her fingers, wondering how much of him she could afford.

Stop it! Don't even think what you're thinking.

"How much?" he asked. His eyes were the color

of single malt whiskey, only not as warm. Noticeably cool, in fact.

"To, uh—to do the work? I guess that depends on what needs doing most and how long will it take. I don't even know your hourly rate." The fleeting expression that crossed his face was impossible to interpret. She didn't even try.

"I mean, how much rent are you asking? What kind of terms?" he said.

If there'd been a chair close, Val would have dropped down on it. As there was only a three-legged stool, a sagging iron-framed bed and an oak dresser, she leaned against the doorframe and stared at him, her mouth open like a guppy waiting to be fed. "The, uh—the going rate, I suppose."

Whatever the going rate was. It probably varied wildly in different parts of the country.

"Kitchen privileges?"

God, yes. If the man could cook, she might consider paying *him.* She couldn't afford many more restaurant meals, and she was growing tired of peanut butter three times a day.

She assumed an air of competence she was far from feeling and hoped he bought it. "That's negotiable," she said coolly.

He nodded, gave the place one last look, then turned and headed down the hall toward the front door.

"You're leaving?" She hurried after him, wanting to plead with him to stay, but for all the wrong reasons.

"Tools. Be back in an hour."

Tools. Right. "What about...that is, how much—?"

At the door, he glanced over his shoulder. "A week's rent in exchange for fixing the plumbing and seeing to any other minor repairs."

She followed him outside. "Does that include doing something to my water heater and checking to see if the roof leaks?" she called after him.

Instead of answering, he lifted a hand, swung up into the driver's seat and swerved out onto the narrow blacktop called Back Road.

She stood there for several minutes, arms wrapped around her body for warmth, and wondered what had just happened. Had she really hired herself a handyman? Had she actually rented out her back room?

Had her fairy godmother touched her with a wand and produced...

Well, hardly Prince Charming, but maybe someone even better?

And yes, his gluts were every bit as good as the rest of him, she couldn't help but notice as he'd strode across her front yard.

Too keyed up to go back to work, Val considered the possibility that her renter-repairman might not be back. She hadn't even asked his name, and now she was too embarrassed to take her cell phone out to the edge of the road to call Marian and admit that she'd hired the man without even asking that much.

Where was her brain? You'd think she had never screened a single applicant or volunteer. That was part of her job—to keep troublemakers from worming their way inside and causing trouble. Activists. These days, for every worthwhile cause, there was almost always some group of malcontents with a different agenda.

This time she didn't have a cause, at least none that anyone else could know about. When and if he came back she would have him sign an agreement spelling out the terms of...whatever. Rent versus work with a possible sidebar on kitchen privileges. While she was at it she would also ask for references. If there were rules covering renters and rentees, they probably differed down here. Just about everything else did. Imagine having to drive to the post office to collect your mail.

Welcome to the real world, chicky.

That was what Tripp, her ex-fiancé, used to call her. Chicky. She'd hated it. He'd known it, which probably was why he'd done it. He'd loved to ruffle her feathers. The harder he tried, the more determined she'd been not to be ruffled. It was a game they'd played, one she had never particularly enjoyed.

Shivering, she backed up to the oil heater. She almost wished he could see her now, in all her grime. Pondering the possibility of adding another layer over her silk undershirt, her cashmere pullover and the boiled wool cardigan, she thought longingly of a deep, hot soak, with a handful of whiteflower bath salts. And as long as she was wishing, she might as well have a Sibelius symphony playing softly in the background, a warm toddy within easy reach and towels staying warm on a heated towel rack.

Dismissing the wishful dream, she collected a stack of change-of-address cards, located her pen, her address book and a roll of stamps, then settled at the coffee table. This was one task she could do herself and cross it off her list. Trouble was, the to-do list was growing faster than she could do.

The first name in her address book elicited a grimace. Ailes, Timothy III, other wise known as Tripp. Amherst, Yale law, junior partner in his father's law firm at age thirty-two. All-around jerk who had given her a two-carat engagement ring six months ago and asked for it back less than a week after the scandal broke.

''Sorry, chicky-poo.'' She scratched through the name and went on to the next entry.

No point in letting her dentist know where she was, she would hardly be seeing him again anytime soon. Fortunately she'd already had her teeth braced and bleached.

Her three closest friends—tennis partners, bridge partners and confidantes Felicity, Sandy and Melanie, had avoided her after the scandal broke. As stunned as she'd been by all that had happened, including her father's death, that had hurt her terribly. By the time they'd made the first overture it was too late. Numb with grief and still in shock, she had never returned their phone calls.

Now she addressed a card to each woman. They could respond or not, it no longer mattered. It was highly unlikely that they'd ever again be moving in the same circles.

"And you know what?" she murmured, staring at the out-of-date lighthouse calendar hanging crookedly on the far wall. "I don't even care any longer."

She made it all the way through the Ms before setting aside the stack and wandering into the kitchen in search of something edible. The choices were peanut butter or cheese and salsa on whole wheat.

She *had* to find work soon. Starving wasn't an option, and she didn't know how to beg. Not on her own behalf, at least.

He wasn't coming back. He'd said he was going to get his tools, but how far did he have to go?

Outside the hardware store, Mac tossed the newly purchased hand tools into the back of the Land Cruiser, considered picking up a sub before heading back and decided against it. He could grab something to eat after he'd checked out of the motel and moved into the fox's den.

Talk about luck. He'd figured on engineering an accidental meeting in a day or so, working his way into La Bonnard's confidence and picking up any crumbs of information she might let slip before applying the thumbscrews.

Something told him he might be in for a few surprises. The lady wasn't quite what he'd expected. Either that or she was a damned fine actress. Recalling the first time he'd heard her voice, he'd nearly laughed aloud this time when she'd tried to send him around to the back door. By all means, let's not forget our respective places.

With any luck, hers was about to change. The last time he'd spoken to him, his stepbrother had blamed the lack of progress on a combination of local politics, ego, ineptitude and territorial interests, which made for a pretty unsavory stew. Mac wasn't quite sure yet where Ms. Bonnard fit in, but she was definitely a player. Had to be. The lack of makeup and the smear of dirt on her face had thrown him for a minute, but once he was out of range, cool logic had kicked in.

The last time he'd seen her—the day he'd delivered Will's sunglasses—she'd been wearing white linen pants, a navy shirt and a green linen blazer. Her hair had been twisted into one of those classy-looking bundles on the back of her head, with tortoise-shell chopsticks sticking out the sides.

Today's version—grimy face and hair that hadn't recently seen a brush—took some getting used to. Always open to a fresh challenge, Mac told himself there was much to be learned here, starting with why the heiress-apparent was living in a dump instead of soaking up sunshine and umbrella drinks in some fancy resort. Best guess—she was playing it smart in case anyone bothered to track her down. While she hadn't advertised her plans, she'd made no real effort to cover her tracks.

He hadn't expected to get his foot in the door so quickly, but when he'd gone to check out the house and seen the for rent sign, a plan had started coming together. The handyman gig was a bonus, although he'd have to come up with a few answers when the guy she'd been expecting showed up. With any luck he'd see him coming in time to head him off.

This time he entered the house through the back door and called out to let her know he was back.

"Oh, good," she said, hurrying down the short hall with a wad of paper towels in her hand. Her version of work clothes reminded him of a fashion spread he'd seen recently in the Sunday supplement. "I was afraid you'd changed your mind. Before you get started, could I get you to help me pull out the refrigerator?"

She'd been grubby enough when he'd left to go buy tools—duplicates, for the most part, of tools he'd left back in Mystic. Now she was flat-out filthy. When his glance moved to her hair, she reached up and brushed it back from her face. The thick, shaggy braid was coming unraveled, a few stray tendrils curling around her high cheekbones.

"The fridge? Sure. After that, I'll get started on your shower." He wasn't exactly implying that she needed a bath, but it was about as close as he cared to venture. She should have smelled of dirt, sweat and stale grease. Instead he caught a whiff of something fresh and spicy that reminded him of warm nights in the tropics.

He walked the refrigerator out from the wall, something that obviously hadn't been done for the past few decades. Leaning past him to peer behind it, she shuddered. Then she said, "The phone man came while you were gone. That is, if you need to make any calls. Of course, long distance…''

''Cell phone,'' he said, and smiled. He'd wanted her a bit off balance, but damned if she wasn't teetering like a one-legged tightrope walker. If he didn't watch it, he might even start feeling sorry for her.

''Yours works?'' she said plaintively. ''I have to take mine nearly out to the road to get a signal, and even then it's iffy.''

Leaving her placing calls, giving out her newly acquired phone number, he headed toward the back of the house, whistling tunelessly under his breath.

Four

From the waist down, he was scrumptious, Val mused, gazing up at the man on the ladder, his upper torso disappearing through the trap door. And if that was a sexist observation, he could sue her. Not that she would dare voice the sentiment aloud, but a woman would have to be both blind and neutered not to notice. They'd been working together for a day and a half now. Actually, not always together, but in the same small house there was no way she could ignore the man. For one thing, he was usually tapping, hammering or scraping. Not only that, but he whistled while he worked. Did he have any idea how far off-key he was? Either he was truly tone deaf or he was going out of his way to get under her skin. But why would he do that?

As a plumber and a carpenter, he admitted to being adequate. When it came to inspecting the house wiring, he'd advised her to hire a licensed electrician. He had, however, checked the small heaters and the kitchen appliances, assuring her that the mice hadn't done any serious damage.

She'd asked him to check the attic for mice because of the scratching noises she still heard at night, and for leaks because of the suspicious circles on the upstairs ceiling. Only because it was rickety and she didn't want him breaking his neck and then blaming her faulty equipment had she insisted on steadying the ladder. The last thing she needed was a lawsuit.

As it turned out, there were squirrels in the attic, not mice. ''I'll get some hardware cloth and nail it over the places where they've chewed through,'' he called down.

Hardware *cloth?* She hardly thought cloth would suffice, but she was already learning to trust his judgment. He'd been here what—two days? A day and a half? With no particular routine and no appointments, it was easy to lose track.

An hour ago she'd stepped out onto the porch to turn down her empty scrub bucket to drain just as he was crawling out from under the house, where he'd gone to see if the floor had rotted through behind her leaky washing machine.

''Defies all common sense,'' he'd said, backing out and dusting off his hands and knees. She'd swallowed hard and tried to erase the vision of that trim, muscular behind emerging from under her house.

''It does?''

''These days beach houses have to be anchored against wind, tides and all other acts of God. Law requires it. This place was obviously built before building codes were invented. It's been sitting on top of a few skinny piers for how long—sixty or a hundred years?''

''Who knows? But then, it's not on the beach,'' she said, pleased that the man took his work so seriously.

''Doesn't matter, inspectors are real persnickety about things like tie-downs and distance above sea-level.''

''Persnickety. Is that a technical term?''

Grinning, he'd wiped his hands on a red bandana. ''About as technical as we professional handymen get. Did you know a couple of your girders came from a shipwreck? I'd make it mid-nineteenth century.''

Oh, great. She wasn't entirely sure what a girder was, but the last thing she needed was to have some historical group tying her up in legal knots so that she couldn't even rent out a room without an act of congress. ''My great-grandmother probably inherited the house from her husband. Or maybe her father, I don't know.''

''Pretty common practice in places like this, making do with whatever materials wash ashore.'' Wintery sunlight had highlighted his features. She'd stared, distracted, until he'd said, ''No signs of termites so far as I can tell, but you might want to call in an expert. Floor under the washer's in trouble, though.''

''A new floor *and* an exterminator?'' Worried about the escalating costs, she'd asked how much of the floor needed replacing.

''No more than a square yard, probably. Let me look around in your shed, might be something there I can use, since it won't show. Or we could check out the beach if you'd rather.'' He had a quick grin that came more frequently now, but never lasted more than a few seconds. All day she'd found herself watching for it, deliberately trying to tempt it into the open again.

''Check the shed first,'' she said, wondering what replacing part of a floor would cost if she had to buy new material. That had been when he'd found the ladder. He had also found several pieces of scrap lumber and crawled back under the house again with a folding rule.

Lord, he was something, she thought now. With the weight of all she had yet to do resting squarely on her shoulders, she could still admire a splendid specimen of masculinity. Just went to show what a powerful force survival of the species could be.

Not that there was anything like that at play here, she assured herself, watching him descend the shaky ladder. She might need to buy a new one before he went up onto the roof.

''I'm just glad you managed to fix my water heater so I can soak my bones in a deep, hot bath tonight instead of making do with four inches of lukewarm water,'' she said as he folded up the ladder.

It occurred to her that after crawling around under her house and in her attic, he might have a few aching muscles of his own. Should she offer him a soak in her bathtub?

Get a grip, Bonnard, you don't have time to play Lady Chatterly even if your gamekeeper happens to be willing.

''Looks pretty sound up there,'' he said, nodding to the trap door. ''I spotted a few possible leaks, mostly around the chimney. Probably needs new flashing. I can give it a go if you'd like, or you can call in an expert.''

''No, you.''

He nodded. He was still working for room and, as it turned out, board. Late yesterday afternoon they'd shopped for groceries together and split the bill. Mac had done the cooking and she'd cleaned up afterward. It was the perfect solution, so far as she was concerned. She had to eat, and her culinary talents began and ended with making toast and brewing a perfect pot of tea. At the moment she had to settle for tea bags, as she didn't even own a teapot.

Last night's dinner had been an enormous chopped steak doused with soy sauce and salsa, along with a plain boiled potato and bagged salad. Hardly gourmet fare, but she couldn't remember enjoying a meal more in ages. If that was an example of what she had to look forward to, she would definitely keep him.

Mac had mentioned buying a microwave and she'd told him if he wanted one, to feel free, but she wasn't yet ready to invest in any kitchen appliances. Her already meager budget was shrinking at an alarming rate—not that she'd bothered to tell him that. Probably didn't have to.

She'd checked the two regional newspapers for jobs, and even looked over the post office bulletin board. Jazzercise classes, a missing Jack Russell terrier and tax service. No help wanted ads. If nothing better turned up by the end of the week, she might have to take Marian up on her joking offer of a job cleaning cottages. By then, she should be well qualified.

Mac called the hardware store on her newly installed phone and discussed flashing material while she washed up for a late lunch. How much, she wondered, did flashing cost? She wasn't even sure what it was. Something copper? Copper was flashy. She suspected it was also expensive. The roof on her father's house was slate, the gutters solid copper, the best money could buy, Charlie had once boasted.

Amazing, the things she'd taken for granted. Leak-free roofs. Limitless hot water. Warmth.

"I'll replace the bulb in the front-porch fixture and clean out the gutters before I put the ladder away," Mac said, hanging up the phone.

"Can't it wait?" If he started in on another project, she would feel obligated to tackle one, too. She still had two rooms upstairs to go, but there was no pressing hurry. One of them wasn't even furnished.

"Might as well do it while I'm thinking about it. Or if there's something else you'd rather I start on, the gutters can wait until I do the flashing."

Distracted, she tried to think of her to-do list while her gaze moved over his backside. He was washing his hands at the sink, his sleeves shoved up over his tanned, muscular forearms. So far as she could tell, he wore a single layer of clothing above the belt. She was wearing three. Her layers concealed a bosom hardly worthy of the name, while his stretched to accommodate a pair of magnificent shoulders. Just from watching what he'd done so far, she was beginning to understand how a handyman might develop a set of muscles that would make a professional athlete envious.

"I don't suppose a few more days will matter," she said.

"No rain in the immediate forecast, I checked. Chilly, though. Lows in the high twenties, highs in the low forties."

It occurred to her that back home, forties wouldn't even be considered cold this time of year. Either the cold down here was different or she was growing more sensitive.

While he dried his hands on the fluffy, white-on-white monogrammed towel, she put on a kettle to heat for tea. The water had a slightly brownish tint, but no discernible taste. If it had been unsafe, Marian would have warned her.

She jotted down bottled water on her shopping list, then crossed it off. She seriously doubted if Grax had made her iced tea with Evian. Determined not to be distracted, either by the drafts leaking in around the windows or her moderately attractive handyman, she got out the box of Earl Grey teabags and two cups.

Moderately. Right. Like a blowtorch was moderately hot.

Lunch was sandwiches. She spread her own. Mac raised his eyebrows when she set the cup of tea before him. She should have asked what he wanted to drink instead of assuming.

''Here's sugar if you want it,'' she said, indicating the old-fashioned sugar bowl she'd found on a top shelf, which she'd like to think had belonged to her great-grandmother.

''No, it's fine as is, thanks.'' His expression said otherwise.

Her ex-fiancé, whom she was determined to forget, had thought nothing of sending a bottle of wine back if it didn't quite meet his expectations. She'd seen more than one sommelier roll his eyes when Tripp had held up an imperious finger.

What on earth had she ever seen in the man? Other than his George Clooney looks, his killer backhand, his low golf handicap and his flawless social skills?

Although not so flawless, as it turned out. Not in her book, at least.

Reaching for the last half of her sandwich, she caught sight of the square, capable hand that was resting on the table and wondered idly if Mac ever played tennis. Actually, she wondered a lot more than that.

Which reminded her that she'd never gotten around to asking for references. Marian would never have sent him around if he weren't to be trusted—still, she wondered about his background. The sweatshirt he wore said WOOD'S HOLE, not OD'S HO. But then, anyone could buy a sweatshirt. Felicity had one that said Souvenir of Folsom Prison.

"You planning on living here permanently?" he asked.

She blinked at the question. Had he read her mind?

She hadn't thought beyond the immediate future, which included doing the detective work the investigators weren't doing because they were convinced they'd already caught their man, even if they hadn't yet recovered the missing funds.

"I'm not sure..." Glancing around at the drafty old kitchen, she remembered the first time she'd ever seen it. From a child's point of view, it had all been an adventure. The island, the old house—the ship model and decoys that Grax had said her husband had made. My great-grandfather, Val thought now, marveling that she'd never even been curious about her ancestors. Grandparents were family, but great-grandparents qualified as ancestors. She had never really known any of her extended family.

Centered on the mantel she remembered the brass Seth Thomas clock that struck ship's bells instead of the hour. Grax had been explaining to Val why it struck eight times in the middle of the afternoon when her mother had insisted they really must leave if they were to catch the ferry to Ocracoke in time to catch the ferry to Cedar Island in time to reach Hilton Head in time to claim their reservations.

"I think I mentioned that my great-grandmother left me this house," she said now. Hesitating, she added, "I only visited it once, and now..."

He nodded, almost as if he knew what she was trying to say.

She didn't even know what she'd been trying to say. That she was grateful for a place to go after losing her home? That she was ashamed of neglecting one of her few relatives?

She was, painfully so. But she wasn't about to admit it, much less explain her initial reason for coming here. Not that he'd even be interested.

Watching him sip his tea, which had grown cold, Val wondered again what he was doing here. His accent wasn't local. At least it wasn't native. Perhaps he had relatives on the island—relatives who might even have known her own.

Or not. One of the benefits she had recently discovered was anonymity. At least now when a stranger spoke to her, it was usually to ask if she weren't Miss Achsah's granddaughter, not to ask if she was Frank Bonnard's daughter, and if so, how soon could they expect to be reimbursed for their lost savings.

"I heard you'd moved down," several people had said. People who'd known Grax. Friendly people, not prying—simply trying to place her in their context.

"That's right. She left me her house, so I'm living there now," she always replied, increasingly proud of her legitimate link to the island. Roots might not have mattered to her mother, but Val was more than ready to reconnect. Her father had been an only son whose parents had been killed in an embassy bombing back in the eighties. There was nothing for her back in Greenwich, but here? Time would tell.

Mac finished his thick ham, cheese, lettuce, onion and salsa on rye and shoved his chair back. Slinging one leg across the other, he picked up his cup, stared blandly at the tepid brew and set it down again.

''More tea? I could heat more water.'' She half rose from her freshly scrubbed white-enameled chair.

''Thanks, I'm fine.'' He frowned. She had a feeling he had something on his mind and was searching for the best way to phrase it.

Please tell me you're not backing out of our deal, she thought anxiously. There was still the flashing and the floor under the washer. The washer itself, for that matter. The thing leaked, and she certainly couldn't afford to replace it.

Had he noticed the way she'd looked at him when he was on the ladder or backing out from under the house? Was he uncomfortable sharing a house with her? There was no way they could avoid close contact in such a small house. The least thing—reaching into the same kitchen cabinet at the same time so that their hands brushed, or playing dodge as they passed in the hallway, one carrying a basket of laundry, the other a handful of tools—took on added intimacy.

Once in the middle of the night, unable to sleep,

she'd padded into the kitchen for a glass of milk and he'd been there. In a chair that had been turned toward the window, he'd been seated with his back to her, yet he'd known she was there. He couldn't have heard her, yet he hadn't even had to turn around. Barefoot and bare-chested, he'd been wearing only a pair of sweatpants. ''Can't sleep?'' he'd asked, his voice edged with middle-of-the-night roughness.

''Thirsty,'' she'd mumbled, and that had been the end of it. She'd poured her milk, taken it back to the bedroom with her and forgotten to drink it. At least the focus of her worries shifted to something more pleasurable, if no more productive, than how to get to the bottom of what had happened back in Greenwich.

Neither of them had mentioned it the next day. He had to know women found him attractive. Thank goodness they were both sensible adults and not impressionable, impulsive, hormone-driven kids.

''Why don't we go in where it's warm before we tackle the next job?'' he said. She'd mentioned being constantly cold, and the drafty kitchen was on the northeast side of the house, directly facing the wind.

Darn it, if he was going to be nice to her, all bets were off. Sex rarely tempted her, it was just something a man expected from any woman he dated more than once, especially if he gave her a ring. Personally, she could take it or leave it. Mostly, she'd rather leave it. Tripp had suggested she talk to her physician about hormone supplements before they were married.

There was definitely nothing wrong with her hormones—if nothing else she had learned that much over the past few days. Actually, what tempted her even more than the aura of sexuality Mac wore as casually as a favorite pair of faded jeans was the sense of strength he radiated. Not the macho-aggressive kind of strength, but the warm, benign kind. She found herself wanting to lean on him, to curl up in those powerful arms and forget everything but the moment.

Of course, if her hormones wanted to get in on the act, who was she to argue with nature?

Suddenly the small house felt entirely too intimate, almost as if it hummed with an energy all its own. "Can we get to the washing machine sometime today?" she asked abruptly. "I really do need it, but not if it's going to flood again and fall through the floor."

"I'll check out the hoses." To add to an already potent mix, he had one of those deep, quiet voices that registered in her nethermost regions.

"Thanks." Feeling a restless need to do something physical, she wandered into the living room, averting her face from the box of file folders that still awaited her attention.

He followed, lingering in the open doorway. It was toasty warm in the small room. If there'd been an open fire, she'd have avoided it like the plague, but there was nothing romantic about a smelly old oil stove.

She said, "I suppose now that the useable parts of

the house are as clean as they're likely to get anytime soon, I might as well finish unpacking.'' Two boxes remained, one of odds and ends, the other containing files. She'd already dipped into the latter several times, coming away after each session more frustrated, none the wiser.

''Need any help?''

''Oh—no, thanks. It's just...'' She needed help, but she doubted if his talents ran to bookkeeping or accounting. Hers certainly fell lamentably short. From what she'd seen so far, most of the files should have been shredded months, even years ago. Old bank statements for people she'd never heard of. Other papers, none of which appeared to be related to BFC. Sooner or later she was going to have to wade through every single item in search of something she probably wouldn't recognize if she saw it.

Why, she kept asking herself, had her father asked her to remove these particular files from his study? Following his instructions, she had gathered up only the unlabeled ones, leaving the alphabetized ones in place.

Could she have got it wrong? She'd been frantic that day—she might have misunderstood.

God, she hated feeling so inadequate.

Sighing, she stared at the stove that had been finished to resemble wood grain, which suddenly struck her as absurd. Nerves tight as a bowstring, she snickered.

''Something funny?''

''The stove.'' She nodded toward the ugly metal

box that sat on a brown metal pad in front of the boarded-up fireplace. "Would you call that a pecan or a rosewood finish?"

Mac glanced at her, saw her blink away a film of moisture, but remained silent.

"These fumes," she grumbled. "What would it take to get rid of the stove and open up the fireplace again?"

"An adjustment in your insurance policy, for one thing," he said dryly. He sniffed. The fumes were barely noticeable. The lady was edgy. Too much pressure applied too fast, he cautioned himself, and she'd either clam up or break.

Somewhat to his surprise, he was no longer certain he wanted her to break. The more he was around her, the more unwelcome doubts were creeping in. Will had called late last night to ask if he'd learned anything yet.

"Look, you might as well know," his stepbrother had said. "Macy's left me. She said her lawyer would be in touch, so I guess it's official."

"Hey man, that's tough." What could he say? Congratulations?

"Yeah, like I really need another lawyer in my life."

Now Mac studied the woman who was backed up to the stove, toying with a place on her inner thumb where a blister had burst. "Don't pick at it," he warned. "Where's your first aid stuff? You need to put something on it."

"I forgot to bring any." A wistful smile flickered

past so quickly he thought he might've imagined it. She snagged her full lower lip between her teeth, shifting his attention away from her hands.

"Salt'll toughen your skin up, but it'll burn like the devil."

"No thanks, I'm healthy as a horse." This time the smile lingered long enough to knock the wind out of his sails.

"Why do you think there are veterinarians?"

She rolled her eyes. "I'd better get the rest of the plastic on the windows before I tackle the other rooms upstairs. I did my bedroom and the bathrooms first thing, but I keep the other rooms closed."

He could have told her that her makeshift storm windows wouldn't do her much good, with all the gaps she'd left between staples, but he didn't. Instead, he said, "Let me do the rest. I can reach without having to stand on anything." Meanwhile, the air leaks from those she'd already covered would serve to offset any fumes from the old stove.

Besides, he didn't want to see her balanced on one of those spindly kitchen chairs, her shapely little behind roughly at eye level. He remembered too well the legendary sirens that reportedly lured unwary seamen to their death.

"You never did say where you were from," Val ventured a few hours later as she dried the last dish and placed it in the cabinet. The dinnerware was mismatched, most of it cheap and ugly. There were only a few pieces of the delicate pattern she half remembered from her one and only visit.

''Hmm?'' He was peering out the window at the traffic rolling past, mostly SUVs with rod holders affixed to one or the other bumper like big snaggled teeth.

Forthcoming, he wasn't, but as long as they were sharing a house, it only made sense to know something about him. She was beginning to suspect that he was no ordinary handyman. In fact, he occasionally struck her as almost scholarly. Not that a handyman couldn't be educated, but still…

An out-of-work professor? One on sabbatical? One who couldn't get tenure, perhaps, and had quit in a huff?

Whatever else he was, MacBride wasn't the huffy type.

''New England,'' he said. ''Mostly coastal.''

It took her a moment to remember what she'd asked him. That explained the shirt. ''I'm from Connecticut, isn't that a coincidence? How long have you been here on Hatteras Island?'' *In other words, what's a splendid creature like you doing clanking around in a tool belt in exchange for room and board?*

Something didn't add up, and she wanted it to. She really, really wanted him to be exactly who and what he professed to be. The last thing she needed was one more mystery to deal with.

''Not long,'' he said in answer to her inquiry.

''Me, either. Actually, I believe I mentioned that

I'd barely moved in when you came along. Thank goodness Marian found you—she was afraid all the available help was tied up on all these cottages under construction.''

The odd look that came over his face was gone too quickly to interpret. He shrugged and said, ''Lucky I was between jobs.''

''Lucky for me.'' But the more she was around him, the more certain she was that there was more to MacBride than met the eye. Not that what met the eye wasn't distracting enough.

They chatted a few more minutes while she wiped off the table and counters, comparing the New England coast with the mid-Atlantic area. Val picked over his brief responses, searching for clues. When Mac switched topics and mentioned the weather, she said, ''It might be a good idea to check the oil in the tank if you know how. I'd hate to have to rely on those little space heaters.''

''I'll check next time I go outside.''

To think she had always taken heating and air-conditioning for granted. Considering how much her father had spent on her education, from boarding school through college, she couldn't help but think what a waste it had been. She could probably qualify as a candidate for one of those TV reality shows. Sheltered woman, loaded with social graces, falls out of the nest and gets smacked upside the head by real life.

Tripp used to talk about the ''little people,'' as if a lower tax bracket were indicative of an entirely different species. It had always irritated her, but she'd let it pass. Tripp had political aspirations. He was going to be the ''champion of the little people.''

No wonder he'd been so quick to dump her, she thought, more amused than hurt. A business scandal that included not only a loss of wealth and social position, but a father-in-law who'd died in jail waiting to be indicted for embezzlement from his own company, was hardly the kind of baggage an ambitious young politician needed.

On the other hand, she was now one of the ''little people'' he'd vowed to help. Could he help her to learn to use a washing machine without flooding half the house? Or show her how to wield a mop and a broom without raising trophy-sized blisters on thumb and forefinger? Or cook bacon without setting off the smoke alarms?

She became aware that Mac was studying her with a curious look on his face. ''What?'' she snapped.

He flipped his hands palm up in a gesture of surrender. ''You were looking pretty grim there for a minute.''

''I was thinking about—about my furniture.''

He nodded slowly, as if he might be evaluating her sanity.

''Well, you've got to admit it's ugly.''

''I've seen better.'' And before she could comment, he added, ''Seen worse, too. Hey, it's not so bad. At least it's comfortable...for the most part.''

''All the same, I intend to replace a few things in

the very near future, starting with the mattresses and bedsprings."

That is, if Marian still needed someone to clean cottages.

"Plywood's good enough for me. I'll do your bed, too, if you'd like. And by the way, you need new batteries in the smoke detectors. The one in the hall's started clicking."

"Put it on the list." She wiped up a damp spot on the counter with more energy than the task demanded. "I guess you'd better cook the bacon from now on. I probably wore it out. The smoke detector, not the bacon. Either that or stock up on batteries."

He smiled and finally she did, too. His smiles were contagious and she was far from immune. It occurred to her that Miss Mitty would have liked him, and Mitty Stoddard's people-instincts were infallible.

Later that afternoon Val went through a file full of receipts for landscape services, plumbing and a new set of tires, most of them dated between two and eleven years ago.

Her father had scribbled across most of them—meaningless words, initials and series of numbers that defied interpretation.

"I need an aspirin," she muttered. "Either that or a Rosetta Stone."

Five

Tired of the fruitless task of searching for a needle in a paper haystack, Val headed for the kitchen for something rich and sinfully decadent. Lacking anything better, peanut butter dipped in chocolate syrup would serve as an antidote to frustration, only she didn't have any chocolate syrup.

Speaking of sinfully decadent, Mac was on his knees under the kitchen sink, an array of tools and a section of drainpipe beside him. She paused in the doorway to admire the view.

"Hmm?" he said, glancing over his shoulder.

"Nothing. That is, I thought we might take a peanut—that is, a tea break between chores."

He backed out, bumped his head on the edge of

the sink and started to swear, but cut it off. "Are we between chores?"

"I am. I've just gone through a dozen years of worthless receipts for a house I don't even own. I had no idea plumbers charged so much. Are we sure I can afford you?"

Sitting cross-legged on the floor, he grinned up at her. "Depends. How good you are with a pipe wrench?"

"About as good as I am with a frying pan."

"That good, huh?" He chuckled, and in one fluid movement, came to his feet only inches from where she was standing.

She inhaled sharply, aware of the intoxicating aroma of clean male sweat and the laundry detergent she'd bought because it promised sunshine-fresh results. "Yes, well...we all have our talents."

His eyes sparkled like polished amber. "Any in particular you'd care to brag about?"

She stepped back and tripped on a chair. He caught her arm before she could fall. "Let me guess," he said, briefly steadying her against his body. "You're a ballet dancer, right?"

No, she was a blithering idiot. She'd heard the term *brain drain,* but she'd never before experienced it personally. She backed away and he let her go, watching her as if he knew to the exact heartbeat how his touch affected her.

"How'd you guess?" When poise deserts, play the clown. "Three years, starting at age five." She struck a pose. "I was the one whose tights were always twisted, the one who was forever relegated to the back row because I was always two steps out of synch with the rest of the chorus.''

He laughed as he was meant to do and the moment passed, leaving her breathless, but otherwise unharmed. Now that she knew how susceptible she was, she'd take care to avoid further touching. Consider him her personal poison ivy.

''How about you? You're musical, right?'' A little polite sarcasm couldn't hurt. ''I've heard you whistling.''

''Ouch,'' he said softly. ''That smarts. I'll have you know I played comb and tissue with a four-man band when I was in seventh grade. I wanted to be one of the Bee Gees. Never got the call, though.''

''So you reluctantly settled for being a repairman,'' she said, and this time they both laughed. What had happened, she wondered, in the years between comb-and-tissue player and pipe-wrench wielder?

''Among other things. But about your plumbing,'' he said, a hint of laughter lingering in his eyes, his voice.

She really didn't want to hear about her plumbing, it was those ''other things'' she was curious about. ''Let's go outside first, shall we? The front porch is sunny and out of the wind.'' And the kitchen was too darn small. The entire house was too small. For all she knew, the whole island might not be large enough for her to ignore his presence.

Avoiding the swing by mutual consent, they sat in

the weathered Adirondacs, feet propped on the rail. There was a small graveyard on the other side of the road, backed by acres of marsh and stunted maritime forest. Two white herons flapped lazily across the rushes to land on the pale branches of a bay tree.

The not-uncomfortable silence lasted several minutes. "I used to spend summer vacations at Mount Desert Island," she said thoughtfully. "For Thanksgiving we usually went to Hilton Head. Christmas was Captiva Island—occasionally, Bermuda."

She was usually good at this—putting people at ease, encouraging them to open up, to give her some idea of whether or not they were suited for whatever position they were applying for. Even among volunteers for charitable causes, there were troublemakers.

He nodded, but said nothing. She wondered where he usually vacationed…or if he did. Maybe this, for him, was a vacation. "My great-grandmother's buried over there," she said, indicating the small cemetery. "Probably more of my family, too." Aware of how that must sound, she said, "I mean, I never met either of my great-grandfathers. I wish I could have known them, but I didn't." Her gaze slid away, "For that matter, I never really knew my mother all that well," she admitted. Embarrassment washed over her. She *never* discussed personal matters with strangers. "Sorry. You were saying—? About my plumbing?"

Instead of rescuing her, he said thoughtfully, "I

don't know if it's possible for a child to know a parent—another family member. Not objectively, that is."

"Is that MacBride the psychologist speaking? Or MacBride the philosopher?" Before he could reply, she said, "Let's stick to plumbing, shall we?" Okay, so he knew how to dismember a drainpipe and she didn't. Big fat deal. That didn't mean she was inferior, it just meant that their talents lay in different areas. At least she could carry a tune. He couldn't find a C-sharp if he tripped over it. "You were about to tell me what's wrong with it."

So much for poise. Her face was on fire and she had no one to blame but herself. She couldn't remember feeling this embarrassed since she'd spilled a glass of wine in her date's lap and then tried to mop it up with a cocktail napkin.

"Well, for one thing," he said finally, "your septic tank needs pumping."

"My *what* needs pumping?" One of her feet slipped off the railing.

"For another, your pipes are old and probably about to start leaking, if they don't already. Acid water eats away copper piping."

It wasn't acid water that was eating holes in her composure. "Great. I'm afraid to ask if there's anything more."

"You'll probably need to replace them with PVC in a year or so."

She glanced at the sky. No help there. Then she frowned at the once-white, size-seven sneaker that was still propped on the rail beside his putty-colored size-twelve Docksiders. ‘‘I’ll make a note. Is that all?’’

‘‘You need a new well pump.’’

‘‘A new *well pump?*’’ Her other foot plopped to the floor and she sat up straight.

‘‘Hey, don’t panic. Thing’s probably good for another few months, at least. On the other hand, it could quit tomorrow. Leaky foot valve’d be my guess.’’

‘‘A leaky foot valve,’’ she echoed numbly, wondering how much it cost to replace foot valves. Feet valves? She started to suggest corn plasters, but then she might have erupted in a horrible cackle. She didn’t even know this woman she was becoming. It couldn’t be the salt air—she’d breathed plenty of that without ever losing her cool.

‘‘Can’t claim I haven’t been warned,’’ she said brightly, fighting depression. Mood swings were nothing new to her after the past few months, but the troughs seemed to be deepening and there were no corresponding highs.

Mac reached across the narrow space between the two chairs and covered her hand with his. Well…perhaps a few highs. His hands were warm. Hers were cold. He had square palms, long fingers, and despite the fact that he’d been grunging around under her sink, his nails were in far better shape than her own.

‘‘Hey, it’s no big deal,’’ he commiserated.

Maybe to him it wasn’t. To her, with no job, a

house that seemed to be falling apart around her ears—a project she was afraid to tackle but desperately needed to finish, and a man she could no more ignore than she could ignore a tsunami, *everything* was a big deal.

But then, he had no way of knowing that, and she wasn't about to tell him. Her problems were just that—her problems. Sliding her hand from under his, she rose and moved toward the door. "I'll be in the living room if you need a hand putting the sink drain back together," she said, and fled before she could embarrass herself further.

Once inside the door, she paused to draw a steadying breath. All right, so she'd brought up her marginally dysfunctional family. She'd heard far more personal matters discussed at cocktail parties. Whose spouse was cheating with whom—who had just had a vasectomy. Whose silicon was starting to slip.

The box of files was the first thing that caught her attention when she wandered into the living room. She could think of a hundred things she'd had to dispose of one way or another in order to make room for those, plus the barest essentials. The Venetian seascape that used to hang in the dining room. The chaise lounge in the morning room, where she used to curl up with one of Belinda's romance novels when she grew tired of reading sixteenth-century poets or essays on the creative traditions of folk cultures in Appalachia.

And the piano. Even if she'd hired a moving van or rented a trailer to bring it with her, there was no room for it here. Was there even a piano tuner on the island? Probably not. She remembered hearing her father pick out simple melodies, mostly old songs from the forties. She'd given him a CD collection of songs from that era for Christmas one year, but whether or not he'd ever played them, she didn't know. She'd been too busy doing her thing in Chicago and later, in New York.

Oh, darn it, she was *not* going to cry! Was there any emotion more worthless than self-pity?

Her standard antidote was to think about all the women who, faced with overwhelming odds, attacked life with both hands and came out on top, Miss Mitty being a prime example. She had never married; her only family was the niece in Georgia whom she hadn't seen in years, yet she'd managed to build a satisfying and productive life for herself.

And there was Grax, a widow whose only son had died young, whose only granddaughter had ignored her existence. According to everyone Val had met since she'd been here, practically the whole island—certainly the entire village of Buxton—had claimed Achsah Dozier as a friend. She'd gardened and gone to church and even taken a driver's course for seniors at the Fessenden Center the year before she'd died, though she'd no longer owned a car. There'd always been someone to drive her wherever she wanted to go. She might have lived alone, but she hadn't been alone.

Val could do worse than emulate two women who

had been independent long before women's independence became a *cause célèbre.*

On his way out the back door, Mac glanced at the empty boxes waiting to be taken to the recycling center by the dump. It wasn't the empties that interested him, it was the box of file folders she'd made no effort to hide, which might or might not mean there was nothing there to hide. So far he hadn't found anything incriminating in the ones he'd gone through. He wasn't comfortable doing it, but he'd skimmed through a few of the files while she was out, knowing even as he searched that the type of information he was looking for wouldn't be easy to recognize. Sixteenth-century shipwrecks were probably easier to trace than offshore bank accounts.

When it came to deciphering ancient shipping records and ships' logs he was in his element, but high finance was another matter. That took training in financial crimes or forensic auditing. When and if he found anything that looked like incriminating evidence he would have to turn it over to the proper authorities and hope it proved what he'd set out to prove.

The fact that he was increasingly attracted to his chief suspect didn't make him feel any better about sneaking around behind her back. He'd been forced to remind himself more than once that Val Bonnard wasn't the first crook who didn't look the part. Hell, if crooks always looked the part, fighting crime would be a cinch. So she was funny and sexy and a good sport about being so totally out of her element—that didn't necessarily mean she was innocent.

It also didn't mean she was guilty, he admitted reluctantly. The odds were slightly better than even, he told himself, that she'd holed up here waiting for the heat to die down. That once things cooled off, she would light out for the Caymans or wherever she'd stashed the money, and never look back.

Yeah, right. That's why she wore herself out scouring every square inch of her dilapidated old ruin. Great cover. It almost had him fooled. Almost.

Mac had talked to his stepbrother every night since he'd been on location. Last night he'd confessed that things weren't moving quite as fast as he'd hoped. "Look, we both know I came down here expecting to find our prime co-suspect living it up in a cozy twelve-bedroom beachfront cottage complete with swimming pool, maid service and personal chef," he'd admitted the night he'd moved in, after Val had gone upstairs. Just to be safe, he'd waited until she was asleep and then gone outside to place the call.

"I thought you said the place she inherited was a dump."

"Yeah, well...happens I was right about that, but dead wrong about everything else. According to local tax records, the property's worth around fifty grand, max. The house is a fixer-upper. I've got someone checking to see if there's any possible link between her and any of the developers operating in the area. So far, no hits."

"Stick with it, okay? She's the only hope I've got unless someone comes up pretty soon with a smoking gun."

Which they both knew was hardly likely, as the hunt had slowed to a crawl for lack of fresh evidence.

From his own professional experience, Mac knew better than to go into any project with a closed mind. If he'd been diving on what was supposed to be an eighteenth-century galleon and suddenly discovered sonar gear or a fiberglass hull, he'd have known immediately he was way off base. He'd come down here expecting to find a sharp little cookie who had socked away a fortune without even raising a blip on the radar screen. Instead, he'd found a gorgeous, sexy, likable woman with dirt on her face, cobwebs in her hair, wearing designer jeans and a Cartier tank watch to scrub floors. It had shaken him up some. He'd had to back off before he could confront her again with an open mind, using the excuse of collecting his tools. Since then things had gotten worse instead of better. For a guy whose profession demanded objectivity, he was having some pretty serious problems.

The woman he'd seen that day at the country club wearing a haughty look and a rock the size of an ice-cube on her third finger, left hand, was nowhere in evidence. The watch, maybe—and her clothes. Those carefully faded jeans she'd been crawling around in hadn't come from Target, no matter how you pronounced it.

The first time he'd ever seen her, he'd summed

her up as post-debutante, Junior League, the whole ball of wax. Now that he was getting to know her—up close and personal, as the saying went—his earlier impression was turning out to be a hundred-and-eighty degrees off course.

"If she's pulling a scam, she's damned good at it," he'd told his stepbrother two nights ago.

"Yeah, well…women can fool you," Will had replied.

Mac had tactfully refrained from mentioning Macy. Nor had he mentioned the woman he'd briefly been engaged to a dozen or so years ago, who had dropped him in favor of someone rich and good-looking. As he fit neither category, he'd wished her luck and headed to the Azores feeling freer than he had in months.

Val scowled at the files, then lifted the only other box yet to be unpacked onto the coffee table. Okay, so she was procrastinating. Every file she'd looked though so far had left her more puzzled than before. If there was anything significant to be found, it must have been written in invisible ink. On the backs and even on the face of old bills, personal bank statements and obsolete brokerage statements, she'd found the usual scribbled phone numbers, initials and obscure notations. Having served as fund manager for a few large charities, Val knew the value of keeping clean, meticulous records. Evidently, for all his business degrees, her father had missed that lesson.

With a sigh, she turned to the box on the coffee

table and lifted out a figurine he'd given her after her first ballet recital, before they'd realized that her talents, if any, lay in a different direction. She had a good ear for music, but it didn't extend to her feet. They'd laughed about it since.

Now she unwrapped the china ballerina and she set it on the mantel. Framed photographs carefully wrapped in a scarf she'd purchased in Scotland emerged next. She took a moment to study the pictures of her parents, taken in the late fifties, shortly after they'd been married. Val had always likened them in her mind to Sean Connery and Greta Garbo. Her mother's beauty still reminded her of Garbo's cool elegance. Val hadn't seen Lola Bonnard, or whatever her current name was, in several years. They'd met for lunch once when Lola had stopped over in New York on her way from London to San Francisco. Gazing at the photos now, she whispered, "Hi, Mom. Hi, Dad. You'd never guess where I am now."

Next she pulled out a miniature oil she'd always loved. The larger paintings had all been sold to a dealer, but this one she'd held back. It could go where last year's lighthouse calendar still hung, even though it would be lost on the twelve-foot wall space. She'd have to find a few more things to balance it. Prints, probably...if she could even afford good original prints. If not, reproductions would have to do.

It occurred to her fleetingly that she was beginning to think long-term rather than short-term. She didn't care to dwell on it.

For nearly an hour she unpacked and found places for the mementos she'd brought with her, putting her own stamp on the old house. Meanwhile she listened for sounds that might indicate what Mac was doing. Not that he was obligated to work eight hours a day, but she had come to enjoy knowing he was nearby working on some project or another. At close range he affected her in an entirely different way, but out of sight he was...comfortable. Companionable. Much as she imagined a husband might be.

Bite your tongue, woman!

She'd do better to concentrate on having her septic tank pumped, her pipes replaced and whatever needed doing to her foot valve done. By whom, a plumber or a chiropodist? Horribly expensive, no doubt, either way.

Mac appeared in the doorway just as she lifted the last item from the box. A tube of brand new tennis balls. Why on earth had she packed anything so useless? She'd forgotten her racquet—it was still at the club, not that it mattered. "Anyone for tennis?" she asked facetiously.

Grinning, he shook his head. "Not my sport, sport. Looks like the weather's closing in sooner than I expected. We've just got time for a sunset walk on the beach."

"You're joking, right?"

"No, I'm not. You need a break. You've been holed up in here long enough."

Not long enough to regain her perspective, obviously. No sooner had he appeared in the doorway than she'd lost track of what she was supposed to be doing. Come to think of it, a brisk walk—maybe even a fast run—might be just what the doctor ordered, never mind that sharing a sunset walk with a man who could send her hormones into a wild tango with no more than a single glance might do more harm than good.

''Bundle up, it's colder than it looks.''

Immediately, her thoughts flew to the old Yankee courtship custom of bundling. ''Five minutes,'' she said, wondering if a few more layers of clothing would serve to insulate her against the man.

Hardly. He hadn't done a single thing to encourage her, it was her own wayward imagination that needed insulating.

Instead of driving his four-wheel-drive vehicle onto the beach, Mac turned off the highway, drove past the small airstrip, deserted but for a single red-and-white Cessna, and parked near a chained-off entrance to a National Park Service campground. The place was obviously closed for the season. ''You can warm up by stepping over the chain,'' he said.

''I thought you said a beach walk. Is this legal? I mean, are we trespassing or anything?''

''I understand the locals walk here year-around. There's a couple of boardwalks to the beach. We'll take one over, walk the beach and take the other one back. Suit you?''

He pocketed the car key and nodded toward the chained entrance. The deserted campground was situated among a series of high wooded dunes and deep, jungle-like valleys. "This way," Mac said, steering her right when she would have turned left and headed up a steep incline.

He set a rapid pace and neither of them spoke for several minutes. She wore a white mohair stocking cap, but the wind found ways inside her anorak. "There's nobody here," she said, panting only slightly. "I thought you said the locals walked here."

"Way the weather's closing in, I guess any walkers have already given up and gone home."

"Sensible people," she panted. He was making no allowance for her shorter legs.

"Might be a few fishermen on the beach," he offered.

"Freezing their bait off." She cast an uneasy glance at the rapidly darkening sky. When they came to a boardwalk, he touched her arm and gestured with a nod. "Leads to the beach," he said, "Come on, we'll be out of the wind for a few minutes."

Walking single file, they traversed the narrow boardwalk between scrubby pines and stunted, vine-covered oaks. Deer tracks were plentiful. The place was growing on her. Whatever else it was—an eclectic mixture, neither ticky-tacky nor self-consciously quaint—she rather liked it.

Before they were halfway there, the spray was visible above the wind-sculpted dunes with their dark mantle of hardy vegetation. Mac led the way and Val trudged behind him, determined not to complain of the pace he'd set. Housework, she was discovering, was no substitute for regular aerobic exercise.

When the boardwalk ended, she puffed up the last steep stretch of slippery white sand. And there it was, wild as any New England seacoast, only different. Without the rocks, the surf lunged up onto the flat, sandy shore, leaving behind trails of creamy foam and dark seaweed. "Oh, my mercy," she whispered. "It's...magnificent."

And it was. Winslow Homer water beneath a darkening sky that was streaked with all the colors of a Turner palate. Overhead, so close she could see the yellow on their heads, a trio of pelicans followed the row of dunes, taking advantage of the air currents.

There wasn't a living soul in sight. No fishermen, not so much as a solitary beach walker. As if by magic, she could feel months of anxiety slide from her shoulders, leaving her oddly weightless. Lifting her face to the wind, she closed her eyes and inhaled deeply.

Mac remained silent but she could feel his presence. He was a part of it all, even though he was standing several feet below on the seaward side of the dunes. They might have been the only two people in the world. Feeling the cold, damp spray on her face, she licked her lips, savoring the bite of salt. Then, sensing his nearness, she opened her eyes.

Standing with his back to the wind, he captured one of her hands between his. Hers were gloved. His were bare. It struck her as funny—Lord knows why—and she laughed. He smiled. Moving closer so that his body shielded hers, he shifted his hand to her shoulder and laid a finger across her lips. Overhead, hundreds of birds streamed across the sky in chevron formation, like tiny black ants traversing a gray marble counter.

Mac tugged off her stocking cap and pointed skyward. *Listen,* he mouthed.

She listened.

And then she heard it, the whisper of hundreds of pairs of wings, audible even over the roar of the sea. The kind of awareness that came over her was like the chill she'd experienced once when she'd been touring abroad and she'd happened to find herself alone in the ruined chapel of an ancient monastery. Voices—echoes, whispering through time.

His face crinkled into a smile as they shared the brief magic moment. Sea oats whipped around her legs. Raw wind rocked her physically, bringing tears to her eyes. "I should have worn sunglasses," she murmured, embarrassed by the flood of unexpected emotions.

"Valerie?"

"What kind of birds were they? Not geese, I didn't hear a single honk. Ducks?"

"Cormorants," he said. And before she could think of something witty, or even appropriate to say, he kissed her.

Wrapped in the wind, surrounded by the mingled scent of salt and millions of tiny dead organisms washed ashore with the mounds of Sargasso weed, he rocked his mouth over hers, pressing gently until she opened for him. Nothing in her entire life had ever felt so inevitable. His arms, strong, warm and anything but safe, pressed her against him so tightly that layers of clothing seemed to fall away. She felt *him.* His essence—his heartbeat.

His erection.

From far away, a voice whispered, *You don't even know this man!*

Another voice, stronger, far more assured, whispered back, *Oh, yes I do. I've known him all my life, I just never knew where to find him.*

The kiss ended far too quickly. They were both breathing heavily when he finally lifted his head. He swallowed hard, shook his head as if dazed, and she waited for him to speak. To say something trivial, anything to anchor her in her shaky world again.

A drop of rain struck her face. In a gravelly voice, he said, "Come on, let's head back."

Six

They were less than halfway along the boardwalk when the rain struck in earnest. Mac might have grabbed her hand to pull her along, but there was no room on the narrow pathway, so he let her go ahead. When they were nearly at the end, he pointed to a park service facility nearby. Val didn't ask questions. By now she was breathless, laughing and freezing, her shoes and jeans soaked through.

The small facility was locked, but there was a covered porch separating the men's side from the women's. Leaning against the back wall she laughed until her sides ached.

"What's so funny?" Mac asked.

"I don't know. Nothing." He shot her a quizzical

look, and she said, "Didn't you ever laugh at nothing?"

"Not in the past twenty-odd years. Not while I was sober."

Her laughter died and she bit her lip, picturing a much younger John MacBride, a little bit drunk, a little bit vulnerable—not nearly so sure of himself. The stabbing pain she felt in the region of her heart had nothing to do with having run a fast quarter of a mile in the driving rain.

Who are you? she wondered.

"You're freezing," he said gruffly, and before she could protest he gathered her in his arms and stood with his back to the blowing rain, offering her what shelter he could provide.

It wasn't the cold that bothered her. Cold she could handle. What bothered her—frightened her—was the fact that she was wildly off balance, deeply in lust and trying hard to ignore the whisper of common sense that urged her to back off, to run—to forget everything except for the reason she had come here to the island. Her personal needs weren't important.

Her obligations were. "I'm not freezing," she said, inhaling the healthy male scent of his skin. "I'm—I'm hungry."

"Me, too." There was no mistaking his meaning. Not even the layers of clothing that separated them could disguise the fact that he was seriously aroused. Instead of remarking on it, or acting on it—not that there was any way they could under the circumstances, he said, "Tell you what. Once it slacks enough to get to the car, I'll drive you up the beach for a sub. There's a place in Avon."

She didn't say a word. Instead, she burrowed her face in the warmth of his throat, clasped her hands around his back and savored the moment, knowing it wouldn't be repeated. She couldn't afford the distraction.

The rain ended as suddenly as it had begun. When he stepped back, she could have cried. Instead, she brushed past him and clambered down the steps. Once she got her directions straight, she marched out in front, setting a faster pace than was comfortable in clinging denim and soggy sneakers. With his longer legs, he had no trouble keeping up with her, even when she broke into a jog.

Wordlessly, Mac unlocked the Land Cruiser and she grabbed a handhold and swung herself up unaided. Neither of them spoke when he passed the turnoff onto Back Road and followed Highway 12 to the village of Avon, some six miles to the north.

Not a word, the entire six miles.

By the time Mac pulled up under the long-limbed live oak tree in the side yard and shut off the engine, he had more or less put things into perspective.

Okay, so he'd kissed her. He was thirty-seven years old. He'd lost track of the women he'd kissed, including the woman he'd nearly married. So what the hell difference did one more kiss make? It was no big deal.

She'd kissed him back, too. Sweet, hot and wet,

with cold noses pressed against cold cheeks. Sand whipping around their legs, rain blowing in on their backs while he tried to come up with some excuse to shed a few layers of clothing.

He needed his brain examined for even touching her. Ever since yesterday, or maybe the day before, when he'd walked into the kitchen and seen her with her head in the oven, her shapely little behind wriggling in harmony with her shoulders as she chipped away layers of volcanic ash, he'd been semi-hard. Not a comfortable condition for any man, especially one on a mission of entrapment.

If that weren't bad enough, he'd held the back door open a few minutes later when she'd headed outside with a box full of trash. After she'd sidled past him, her firm little butt pressing briefly against his groin, he'd had to go outside and whack weeds with a rusty scythe for half an hour before he was fit to come inside again.

At this rate he might need to invest in a suit of pikeman's armor, with the hinged steel apron.

"I ordered two twelve-inchers," he told her as he unlocked the front door. She'd opted to wait for him in the car when he'd gone inside to place their order. "You can have six inches tonight, and six tomorrow."

Ah, jeez, MacBride, cut it out!

"Onions?" It was the first time she'd spoken since he'd asked her what kind of sub she wanted.

She'd said, "Anything's fine."

Now he said, "Onions," and she said, "Cool."

The last thing he felt was cool, despite wet clothes, wet shoes and falling temperatures. He cut her a sidelong glance and caught a glint of something like amusement flashing across her face, which he interpreted as a good sign. Any expression at all was a good sign, even if it meant only, Might as well forget that damned kiss, buster. It never happened and it's sure as hell not going to happen again.

Of course, being a lady, she might not put it in exactly those terms, but the meaning was pretty clear.

"You want a beer?" he asked once they got inside.

She was peeling off layers, one by one. Gloves, anorak, soggy stocking cap, sweater. He wondered if she was deliberately trying to be provocative. If she stripped all the way down to a G-string and a pair of pasties, he might take that as a sign of encouragement. Anything short of that, no way.

"House feels toasty, doesn't it?" she observed brightly.

The thermometer read sixty-two. "It won't for long," he said glumly. He switched on the heater.

She said, "Thank you," and offered to make tea.

He said, "No, thank you." They were rappelling off each other, neither of them willing to admit that their relationship, whatever it had been before, had undergone a change. "I bought a six-pack earlier today. Want one?"

She shook her head. He shrugged and opened a bottle for himself. Given a choice between Corona, one-percent milk or hot tea, he'd take beer every time. In moderation.

They ate in the living room, avoiding by mutual consent the closer confines of the kitchen. She settled in the middle of the sofa, ensuring that there wasn't quite enough room on either end for another passenger.

He dragged the heavy, fake-leather recliner over to the coffee table and sat across from her. While he unwrapped his meatball-with-all-the-extras, his peripheral vision took in her flushed cheeks and the way she avoided looking at him. The flush might be weather-related, but not the avoidance of eye contact.

Back to square one. Employer versus employee. Tenant versus landlady.

Hunter versus hunted.

They ate in silence until halfway through the meal when she asked how much she owed him for her supper. He started to swear but cut it off. "My treat," he said. "Next time you can pick up the check."

"Then thank you. It's very good."

He was tempted to laugh, damned if he wasn't. Whether or not she was ready to admit it, she'd been as turned on by that hot, sweet-salty kiss as he was, otherwise she wouldn't be sitting there like Lady Whatsername at a tea party. It occurred to him that he might have set his mission back a few days.

Or maybe not. Maybe now that he'd defused this crazy physical attraction he could concentrate on doing what he'd come down here to do.

Okay, so there was still some electricity sizzling between them. Roughly enough to light up Shea Stadium. It might help if he could take her to bed and make love until he was cross-eyed, but that wasn't going to happen.

It might also help if he could find whatever he was looking for and get the hell out—put a few hundred miles between them—but somewhere along the line, the idea had lost its appeal.

The rain droned on, accompanied by loud claps of thunder and brilliant flashes of lightning as the storm swept out to sea. Mac awoke with a throbbing head, signaling that a front had passed through during the night. Great, he thought, disgusted. Just what he needed to help him concentrate.

He switched on the shower, adjusted it to a few degrees below parboil and allowed it to beat down on the back of his neck. By the time he dried off and pulled on a pair of jeans and an old Columbia U. sweatshirt, the pain had settled like a ground-hugging fog. He could function, but by no means at peak efficiency.

After a pint of coffee and a bagel smeared with peanut butter, he headed upstairs to take apart and clean the trap under the upstairs lavatory. Val had mentioned that it took forever to drain.

She was nowhere in evidence. Her car was missing, too. Not that he expected her to check with him before leaving the house, but she might have done him the courtesy of leaving him a note.

He bumped his head on the porcelain bowl, swore and reached for a bucket to catch the sludge. From the looks of it, the thing hadn't been cleaned out since the Carter administration.

Where the devil was she, anyway? It was too early for the mail. So far as he knew, they weren't out of anything.

Once he'd reconnected the drain, he cleaned up the site and went in search of a screwdriver, a bit of sandpaper and a tube of graphite. The front-door lock was getting almost too stiff to key. Might as well finish up as many small jobs as possible in case he needed to take off in a hurry.

Her car was still missing when he glanced outside. It occurred to him that instead of cleaning the lock, he should be going through those damned files. He was half tempted to tell her the truth and ask for complete access, including whatever was on the laptop she had yet to unpack. Just because the captain had gone down with the ship, he could argue, there was no reason to take his second in command down with him.

It was that kiss that had messed up his mind, he told himself as he wiped graphite from his hands. Major mistake, in more ways than one. There'd been a growing tension between them even before that—sexual awareness didn't wait for an invitation—but at least before he'd kissed her she'd trusted him not to take advantage of the situation.

Now she was wary for all the wrong reasons. He didn't know which was worse: feeling guilty because she trusted him when, once he found what he was looking for, it might lead to her being arrested for concealing evidence, or feeling guilty because he was tempted to walk away and let Will handle his own case. Let his lawyer earn his pay for a change.

It was eating on him. Last night he'd had to take a couple of antacid tablets before he could get to sleep. Could've been the meatball sub, but chances were it was this growing conflict between his brain and his libido, between what he'd come down here to do and what he really wanted to do.

He was out in the kitchen trying to scrub the gray film off his hands when she pulled into the front yard. A minute later she stuck her head in the doorway and said, "Hi. Did I get any calls while I was out?"

Okay, so they were back to the old footing. Cheerful, but casual housemates. He could live with that. "No calls, sorry."

She sighed, and he wondered whom she'd been hoping to hear from. Unless it was a Swiss banker or a big development outfit it was none of his business.

By the time he put away his tools and reheated the coffee, which by now was roughly the consistency of crude oil, just the way he liked it, she was curled up in the recliner, rattling papers and humming something slow and bluesy. Hell, even her hum was sexy.

He'd give his new Viking drysuit to know what she'd found that put her in such a good mood. He had a feeling that if it was good for Bonnard, it was probably bad for Will.

* * *

Across the hall in the living room, Val unfolded the Home Depot flyer, scanned it quickly and laid it aside. Maybe later she could afford to get into remodeling. She had a few ideas, but neither the time nor the money to carry them out. Besides, she had too many things on her mind.

What on earth was she going to do about MacBride?

She knew what she wanted to do, but it wasn't going to happen. Even if he happened to be interested, she didn't have time for an affair. Not even a single session of mind-boggling sex. And she had a feeling it would definitely be that. She was hardly inexperienced, but mind-boggling didn't come close to describing her relationship with Tripp. Or even with the tennis pro she had briefly fallen in love with the year she'd graduated from college.

One thing about it—before she indulged in any sex at all, mind-boggling or otherwise, she would have to do something about that mattress. Which meant she was thinking about it.

Which also meant she needed to find out if Marian had been serious about that job offer. She'd gone out early this morning to ask about it only to find a sign on the door of Seaview Realty saying, "Back at 1:00 p.m."

Disappointed, she'd driven on to Conner's and picked up another can of oven cleaner and some industrial-strength hand lotion. From there she'd gone to the post office to mail the last of her change-of-address cards. Shoving them through the out-of-town slot, she'd wondered who among her closest friends—if any—would be the first to attempt a bit of fence-mending.

Hopeful, but not really expecting a letter, she'd opened her mailbox and found it crammed full of catalogs and flyers. Disappointed that that's all there was, she'd stopped short of dropping them into the recycling barrel. Even junk mail was better than no mail at all.

Only half her mind was on the colorful catalogs, the other half on the man in the kitchen who was opening and shutting cabinet doors and whistling something that sounded like a dispute between a mocking bird and a tea kettle.

By the time she'd gone to bed last night they'd barely been speaking. Mac had made a few valiant attempts at conversation, but she'd been afraid to let down her guard, afraid he might try to kiss her again.

Afraid he might not.

Well, this couldn't go on, not as long as they were sharing a house. They were both sensible adults, after all. She needed to keep reminding herself of that fact.

At least, one of them was. "Mac? Did you know you can actually buy wheelchairs by mail?"

He called through the hall from the kitchen. "Never given it much thought. Why, you in the market for one?"

When he appeared in the doorway behind her, she flashed him a grin over her shoulder. "No, but I was just thinking—with mail order and the Internet, there's no real reason why a woman couldn't live here for the rest of her life without ever having to leave the island.''

There, that hadn't been so hard. At least they were conversing comfortably again.

Sending her a curious look, he came on inside the room. ''You planning on it?''

She shrugged. ''I don't know. Maybe.''

''Here? I mean, in this particular house?''

''Why not? It's mine. Marian called it a fixer-upper, but why bother to fix it up if I'm not going to live here?''

''You could rent it. The whole house, I mean, not just the back part.''

''Then I'd have to find another place to live. It would probably end up costing me all the rent I received, so what's the advantage?''

Wearing baggy cargo pants that still managed to hug his narrow hips, he lowered himself onto the sofa, leaned forward and rested his arms on his knees. She could feel her face flushing as she wondered if he was thinking about that kiss.

Obviously, he wasn't. ''What would you do?'' he asked.

''With my time, you mean? Well, first of all I'd have to find a job. As for leisure time, I don't surf, I don't fish, but there're all sorts of opportunities for volunteers. I might even paint my house, maybe a pale shade of yellow with black shutters. Or maybe classic white again, with dark green. I'll have to think about it. And landscaping. I have some definite ideas there.''

He looked at her as if he were trying to picture her as a permanent resident, or maybe a house painter. Actually, she couldn't quite bring it into focus yet either, but the more she thought about it, the more she liked the idea of living here. Roots had to count for something.

''Okay, the painting can wait another year, but maybe I can get started planting a few things. Seeds don't cost much.''

He looked at her and said nothing. ''Well, everyone has to live somewhere,'' she reasoned. ''I'm already here and settled in.''

He toyed with a screwdriver, twirling the business end against the palm of his hand. One curt nod, and then, ''What kind of job?''

''Cleaning cottages,'' she said, hoping he wouldn't laugh.

He didn't have to. The look he sent her spoke volumes, none of it particularly flattering. Lines from an old musical popped into her mind. ''Anything you can do, I can do better.'' She couldn't remember who the singer had been—Ethel Merman? Debbie Reynolds?—but the rebuttal had been, ''No, you can't,'' followed promptly by, ''Yes, I can.''

My sentiments exactly, Val thought, feeling oddly let down when he got up and left without a word.

By the time she'd finished going through her junk mail, the sun was sparkling like diamonds on the whole outside world. Stiff from sitting in one place too long, she rose, stretched and wandered to the door for a better look. The outside air had been cool earlier. Now it felt almost balmy. She considered opening a few windows to let the warm breeze blow through the house, and then thought of all the work of taking down and stapling up the plastic again.

Back to the drawing board. Or in this case, the coffee table. Once she finished with the flyers and catalogs she turned back to the files. The first one she picked up was filled with property-tax-related correspondence, most of it bearing her father's enigmatic notations. Oddly enough, in the middle of his personal medical records she came across several insurance-related letters addressed to Ms. Mitty Stoddard, dated over a period of four years. Why would her father have had access to those? As an employee, she'd been eligible for the standard company benefits package.

There were several more items pertaining to Mitty L. Stoddard, most of them form letters that should have been thrown away. Instead, they'd been squeezed into the middle of other folders. Mitty L. Stoddard. Matilda Lyford? That name had shown up on several documents. Could they possibly be one and the same?

Val was astonished at how much she had taken for granted about people she'd known half her life. Her father might have intended to start a Miss Mitty file like the ones he'd kept for Charlie and Belinda—although why he should, she couldn't imagine. Even

Charlie and Belinda were insured under the company's umbrella.

Whatever his intent had been, she only hoped Miss Mitty had taken her full retirement package with her when she'd left. Back in August of last year that shouldn't have been a problem, as the trouble hadn't even shown up until a few months later.

More confused than ever, Val tossed the file she'd been examining back in the box, flexed her shoulders and yawned. She needed an oxygen break. Briefly she considered seeing if Mac needed a hand with whatever he was doing, then thought better of it. She'd missed Marian this morning, but it was now after one. If nothing else, it was a valid excuse to enjoy a midwinter spring day while it lasted.

She was still wearing thc ivory suede slacks she'd put on this morning. They were creased, but she decided against changing. Instead of the thick, Peruvian knit sweater though, she changed into a peasant top that was fresh off the catwalk, but casual enough to have come from a discount store. Amused, she wondered if there was such a thing as a reverse snob.

On her way out, she found Mac up on the ladder, poking gobs of rotted leaves out of the gutter with a stick. "I'm going out. Do you need anything?"

"Dozen eggs," he said, looking down from his shaky Mount Olympus. His feet were braced on either side of the rung. The view from where she stood was spectacular, to put it mildly.

"They'll ruin your heart."

"I'll drink an extra beer to make up for it."

"Fine, Dr. MacBride, you just do that." They'd both read the article in a recent *Virginian Pilot* on drinking and its relationship to heart health.

He grinned down at her. She flipped him a wave and crossed the soggy lawn to her car, thankful that they were back on the old standing. Something more, perhaps, than before, but still within safe limitations. Nothing she couldn't handle.

Marian was in, and so was her daughter Tracy, a five-year-old with her mother's beautiful smile, minus a few teeth.

"I came about that job," Val said after greetings and introductions. "If it's still available, I'll take it, but you'll have to tell me what's expected. Believe it or not, I'm pretty good at following written instructions."

"I believe it. I meant to stop in a time or two to see how you were getting along, but now that we're into February things are starting to heat up, reservation-wise. So...how've you been doing?"

"Great. Much better since you sent me my handyman. He's a genius."

Without looking away from Val, Marian handed Tracy a yellow crayon. "What handyman?"

Seven

Twenty-five minutes later Val wheeled in off the highway, skidded on the wet grass and parked under the live oak tree. The ladder was gone. There was no sign of MacBride.

Damn him, who *was* he? Why had he lied to her? His car was still here. She'd half expected him to have fled.

Drumming on the steering wheel, she rehearsed the questions she intended to ask—no, to demand answers to. It didn't help when she noticed that her last two unbroken fingernails had been nibbled to the quick.

She *hated* this! They had just been getting to know each other. Talking, exploring—feeling their way. As for the kiss, she dismissed it as an impulse. Tried to, anyway.

All right, so maybe talking wasn't all she was interested in, but he'd lied to her, and that she could not forgive. Social lies—small lies intended to spare someone's feelings—those were occasionally necessary, but the intent of MacBride's lie had clearly been to deceive. There was never an excuse for that.

Feeling raw and shaky, she got out, closed the car door quietly behind her and strode toward the house, chin held high, back stiff as a palace guard. This was *her* house, she reminded herself. She could kick him out first, or she could demand an explanation and then kick him out.

Just as she swung the front door wide, Mac came in through the back, holding a length of black hose in one hand. "Notice how easy the door is to open?" The stubble on his lower face did nothing to minimize the effect of his smile.

She glared at him.

His smile faded. He lifted one eyebrow. Nodding to the hose he still held, he said, "Found your culprit." His eyes narrowed as he took in her frozen expression. "Hey, I was just kidding about the beer, you didn't have to make a special trip just for that."

She wasn't carrying any beer. It was a wonder she'd even remembered to retrieve her purse from Marian's desk. "Would you mind telling me who the devil you are and what you're doing in my house?" She tried for cool composure and missed by a country mile.

He took a step back, eyeing her the way he might some exotic reptile he'd found coiled in his bed. "John Leo MacBride? Checking out your leaky washer?" He turned both statements into questions, as if wondering how much of his story she would buy.

She'd already bought far more than she could afford. "Marian at Seaview never heard of you. She didn't send you. How did you know I needed a handyman?"

"You told me."

Her mouth fell open. "*I* told you. And just when did I do that?"

"Six days—maybe a week ago? You took down the calendar, how'm I supposed to keep up with what day it is?"

Nice try, but she wasn't buying it. He had a perfectly good watch that told him everything he needed to know, probably including the Dow Jones futures. Besides, the actual date had nothing to do with the big, fat lie he'd told her. "It was last year's calendar. Try again."

Without even glancing at the hose that appeared to have been mended with tape on the curved end, he hung it over the doorknob. "When I saw your sign and came to the door to inquire about the room for rent."

Her brain did a quick double take. Damn, damn, damn! The sign she'd meant to take down and had never gotten around to. She hated being caught in the wrong, especially when she was certain she was right. Basically right, anyway.

Desperately, she tried to recall everything she'd said that first day, as well as what his responses had been, but too much time had elapsed. It seemed more like weeks, or even months than mere days.

She narrowed a look at the man who had settled so comfortably into her house, carving out a place for himself in her life. At the rate they'd been progressing, she was lucky he hadn't already claimed a place in her bed. She'd like to think she had better sense, but the way she'd been acting lately, all bets were off.

What now? Miss Manners didn't cover this kind of situation. Taking a slow, calming breath, she said, "You're claiming it was a simple misunderstanding?"

He shrugged. "What else? I happened to be in the area, I needed a place to stay, I saw your sign."

It was just barely plausible. "And decided to apply for a job as handyman?" The need for one was certainly obvious enough, even if she hadn't launched on a list of all that needed doing.

"You needed help. I happened to be available."

She gnawed her lip, uncertain where to go from here. No matter what he claimed, he was no simple handyman. A reporter would have asked more questions. He hadn't mentioned Greenwich, much less BFC, which was hardly worth a journalist's time anyway at this point.

He stood patiently while she looked him over from

the tips of his top-quality, but well-worn deck shoes to the crown of his shaggy, sun-bleached hair. A federal agent? Hardly. Every government agent she'd ever met wore dark, nondescript suits and bad ties. Besides, why bother? ''All right,'' she said finally, trying to sound as if she had everything under control.

She had nothing under control. Not long ago she had cleaned out her bank account, signed dozens of documents, left the keys to her father's house with her personal banker and headed south in a secondhand car filled with impractical clothes, sentimental trinkets and stolen files. She'd had the misguided notion that getting away from the scene of so many painful memories would give her the objectivity she needed to get to the bottom of the mystery and restore her father's reputation.

So far, she hadn't found one blasted thing relating to BFC and the supposedly missing money. She couldn't even swear the money was missing, although if not, someone had an awful lot to answer for.

For all she knew, some minor accountant in the throes of a mid-life crisis had dreamed up the whole thing. Or maybe a computer virus was responsible. If viruses could make everything on a computer disappear, hiding millions of dollars should be easy. Either that or Robin Hood had cleaned out the coffers and donated everything to the United Fund.

Oh, Lord, she was no longer certain of anything

except that Mac was waiting for some sort of a response and her brain had turned to vichyssoise.

"Valerie?"

"All right," she said firmly in an effort to regain the upper hand. "Honesty compels me to accept part of the blame. I should never have hired you without asking for references, I just wasn't thinking clearly that day."

"Next time, ask for references and a deposit."

"You're *lecturing* me?"

"Only offering a suggestion. Now...do you want a brief biography? Character references? I think we're square on the deposit for now. A week's work in exchange for a week's rent."

He knew exactly how long it had been, which was more than she did.

She moved into the kitchen and he followed her there. She pulled out a chair and sat. He remained standing. She said, "The other day when you were sharpening the weed whacker—I asked you about your sweatshirt, remember?"

He nodded warily.

"Instead of answering a simple question we ended up talking about history, of all things." She should have known then that he was something more than he appeared to be, although what he appeared to be was impressive enough.

"Here? Right here? But what about the Pilgrims?" she remembered asking.

"Not that batch, the ones that came before."

She'd pointed to the ground beside her sheepskin-lined boots. ''You're telling me they landed right where we're standing right now?'' History happened to be one of her weaker subjects, but at that point, if he'd wanted to discuss Martian invaders, she probably would have listened avidly as long as she could watch the muscles in his bared forearms tense and relax with each stroke of the sharpening tool.

''Close. Advance guard stopped off a few miles up the beach to ask directions of a few friendly natives. Ended up settling a few miles northwest of here on Roanoke Island. Hand me that hatchet, will you? Might as well sharpen that, too, while I'm at it.''

''But I thought—what about the Pilgrims? The *Mayflower*?''

He'd grinned that slow-burner grin of his and said, ''Sorry to disillusion you, but we Yankees wrote the textbooks, so we got to slant history our way. Doesn't necessarily mean it happened that way.''

''You're saying truth is relative?''

''Now you're getting into philosophy,'' he'd dismissed with another contagious grin. ''That was never my strong suit. I guess what I'm saying is that truth is what actually takes place. How you interpret it depends on where you happen to be standing.''

Was it her imagination, or had he studied her face intently at that point, almost as if he were waiting for a particular reaction? A few moments later he'd shrugged and gone on sharpening the rusty old tools he'd found under layers of junk in her cluttered shed, leaving her wondering more than ever what he was doing working as a handyman.

All right, she thought now, so the truth was relative. She'd settle for a single particle of truth about John Leo MacBride, just one. Up until today he'd been simply a fascinating, increasingly tempting, surprisingly complex man who seemed informed on a number of topics. One who could kiss like a dream and then back away, leaving a woman hungry for more, she reminded herself. What was it they always labeled boxes of dynamite with—XXX? Or was that sugar?

He was triple-X doubled, on both counts.

Leaning against a counter, he grinned. "Know what this reminds me of? Remember that old movie, *Showdown at the O.K. Coral?*"

She purposefully kept her expression blank. She'd happened to mention enjoying old movies one night recently when he'd brought up the absence of a TV.

"You know the one," he prompted, as cheerfully as if his employment weren't hanging by a thread. "Couple of gunfighters facing off in the middle of the main drag while the townspeople huddle behind saloon doors?"

"It was *Gunfight,* not *Showdown,*" she said tightly.

He didn't crack a smile, but his eyes sparkled like wet amber.

Outside the kitchen window a flock of cedar waxwings swarmed into a yaupon tree, then took flight again. Momentarily distracted, she followed their movement before looking back. He was still leaning against the counter, arms crossed over his chest, one foot propped over the other, as if this were just another casual conversation.

"Yes, well," she said. "To get back to what we were discussing, I might have jumped to the wrong conclusion, but you didn't do one thing to set me straight." Had she even given him time to explain who he was before launching into a litany of what needed doing first? Probably not—she'd been tired, desperate and totally out of her depth at the time.

"I can leave now if you'd like," he said quietly.

She was half tempted to take him up on it. Probably be better off if she did. "Give me a minute, let me think about it."

For all the good thinking did. There was simply no rational way to explain the effect he had on her. This one man among all the other men she'd ever met, including the one she had almost married.

In desperation, she latched onto the least important part of their relationship. One more day and he would have started paying rent. Aside from everything else, she needed that money. Even if she threw him out and advertised for another tenant, who was to say the next one would be any better?

Well...he could hardly be better. The trouble was, the next tenant might be a whole lot worse.

"I can be out of here in five minutes," he repeated when the silence stretched to the breaking point. "Ten, if you want me to make a list of what still needs doing."

"I thought we were pretty well caught up."

"There's still those boards under your washer that

need replacing, and I haven't done the flashing yet, remember? Dare Building had to order stuff.''

''I guess I owe you for materials,'' she said reluctantly. And for last night's supper and for all the hours of fascinating conversations that had enabled her to justify putting off what she'd come here to do.

''No problem. I opened an account at Dare and charged everything to you. They knew your great-grandmother.''

She gnawed on a ragged nail, then caught herself and slid her hand guiltily under her thigh. She'd like to blame the rapidly changing weather for her inability to focus, but she knew better.

''You need a new hose for your washer, by the way, but the patch should hold until you can order one. I cleaned out the filter while I was at it. Thing was pretty well clogged with sand. You might want to do that from time to time. I can show you where it's located.''

Dammit, why did you kiss me? Did I look like I needed kissing? Like I was desperate for affection? For sex?

She flung out her hands in surrender. ''Oh, for heaven's sake, stay! It was my mistake after all, not yours.''

He waited so long she was afraid he was going to insist on leaving. She couldn't blame him after she'd insulted his integrity...or whatever it was she'd insulted. Certainly not his masculinity, that had never been in question.

''Speaking of mistakes,'' he said in that deep,

calm voice that shivered over her skin like the stroke of an ostrich plume, ''Next time you rent your rooms, be sure to ask for a deposit up front in case your tenant trashes the place or walks out owing you money.''

''I knew that,'' she snapped. ''You already reminded me.''

''Then I'll pay you a deposit now. We never got around to discussing how much rent you're asking.''

''We never got around to discussing your hourly rate.''

He nodded, but said nothing. Val lacked the patience to deal with another stalemate. ''A thousand?''

He whistled quietly. ''A month? A year? With or without kitchen privileges?''

She visualized the cramped, poorly furnished room and the barely adequate bath. ''Let me ask my friend at the agency. This place was one of her listings until I moved in. She'll know the local rates.''

Marian had been surprised and more than a little uneasy when Val had told her about her handy tenant and the agreement they'd struck. By the time they'd finished discussing the matter, Val had been furious, frightened and embarrassed. Not to mention disappointed. ''I don't think he's a—a beach bum, if that's what you mean,'' she'd said.

''What about a dangerous escaped convict?'' Marian had been joking, but Val had to admit that MacBride was dangerous, if not the kind of threat Marian had had in mind.

''If a personal check will do, I'll give you a deposit now,'' Mac repeated.

''You have a bank account?'' That indicated a certain degree of stability, didn't it? Even if the check bounced.

''Not here—in Mystic. Will that do?''

Mystic. He'd told her only that he was from New England. She wanted to know everything there was to know about him, but that could wait.

He was still standing; she was still seated. She wasn't sure which, in this case, was the dominant position, but she evened the odds by standing. ''I'll let you know what the rent is as soon as I find out. If you'd like to pay a deposit, then I think we should do it properly. References, lease—that sort of thing. I'll have to get a copy of a lease form from Marian.''

''Short term lease,'' he stipulated.

''Of course,'' she said quickly.

With a few added clauses: from now on, we'll stick strictly to business. No more cozy chats by the fireside, no more beach walks in the rain. Definitely no more kisses and accidental-on-purpose touches.

He nodded. ''It might take a few days to get written references from my last residence.''

''Fine. In the meantime, you know what needs doing.'' She turned to go, then added, ''Oh, and by the way, I'll be working, starting tomorrow.''

''Working. Outside the house, you mean?''

''I told you I was considering it. I'll be cleaning cottages on weekends between check-out and check-in. Mostly Saturday and Sunday mornings. So,'' she said airily—once again captain of her own ship, CEO of her own affairs. ''If you don't mind hooking up that hose thingy, I'd like to do a load of laundry.''

Eight

Later that night Mac, arms crossed under his head, stretched out on the hard bed. It no longer sagged, thanks to a sheet of plywood between mattress and springs. An unseasonably warm wind whistled through the window, rippling the light spread over his boxer-clad body. All that ladder work, not to mention crawling around under the house, hadn't helped his knee.

But a stiff knee was the least of his problems. What the devil was he going to do now? Admit that he was here on a mission that had nothing to do with leaky washing machines and clogged drains? That she had something he wanted, and one way or another, he was determined to get it?

Unfortunately, what he wanted most of all was the

woman herself, and that wasn't going to happen. His conscience alone would prevent it as long as he kept reminding himself that any evidence he might find to clear his stepbrother was bound to condemn her late father.

Hell, she had to know Bonnard was guilty, even if she didn't want to believe it. Loyalty was an admirable trait, but occasionally, it was misplaced.

Probably misplaced, he amended.

Restlessly, he got out of bed and stood at the window, staring out at the million or so stars that twinkled through a ghostly stand of dead pines, lingering victims of Hurricane Emily, or so he'd been told.

Recalling his very first dive off Cozumel back in the early seventies, he had to admit that even the evidence of his own eyes could sometimes be misleading. He'd seen what had appeared to be a five-gallon Coke bottle under some fifty feet of crystal-clear water and gone down after it. Green kid, first dive, rented equipment that would probably never have passed inspection. A few minutes later he'd surfaced holding an ordinary six-ounce Coke bottle. Layers of glass-like water had acted as a lens, magnifying its size. That's when he'd first learned that what you see is not necessarily what you get.

What if Frank Bonnard hadn't been guilty, after all? The man had barely had time to profess his innocence, much less to prove it, before he'd died. And without a paying client, his lawyer wasn't shaking any trees. So far as Mac knew, Val Bonnard was the only one who believed in her father's innocence.

Rumor was that he'd died on her thirtieth birthday. If so, that made it doubly rough. Losing a father was never easy, but losing him like that had to have been a staggering blow. According to Will, in only a matter of weeks she'd lost not only her father, but her home, her wealth and her family's reputation.

Mac had to admit that under the circumstances, she was doing a pretty fine job of rolling with the punches.

It wasn't the sun streaming into the room that awakened her, it was the sound of thumping and hammering. Val glanced at her watch and groaned. She'd meant to get an early start today, so as to go through a few more files before she had to leave for her first day as a cottage-cleaner.

Still groggy from a restless night, she felt her way downstairs to find that Mac had shoved the washer aside and was already at work ripping out the floor. Before she went to bed last night she'd used the machine. Thanks to the mended hose, it hadn't overflowed again.

Even so she was half tempted to send him packing for the simple reason that every time she looked at him her hormones overruled the few grains of common sense she'd managed to hang on to.

''Sorry. Did I wake you?'' Down on one knee, he was leaning over a hole in the floor, baring a band of tanned flesh between sweatshirt and jeans.

She stared, blinked, mumbled ''G'morning'' and backed out of the small utility room, which was actually little more than a shallow closet off the hallway.

There was a frying pan on the stove, used dishes stacked neatly in the sink, and two pieces of cold bacon on a paper towel. She nibbled on one while she made toast. Not bothering to make tea, she poured herself a cup of coffee from the carafe on the warming plate, added half-and-half and two spoonfuls of sugar, and took the lot into the living room.

Reluctantly, she lifted three files from the right side of the box—ones she hadn't yet searched, as she'd been working from left to right. It had seemed logical for reasons that now escaped her.

Why not start in the middle and work in both directions? With such a total lack of organizational skills, how on earth had her father managed to pull together a company that, while it hadn't been among the Fortune 500, might eventually have rated a listing among someone's top ten thousand?

It wasn't enough that he misfiled everything from old brokerage statements to veterinarian's bills for a cat that had died of old age the year she had moved from Chicago to New York—he had scribbled across the face of half the papers in the file. Sums, initials, odd things like, Check yesterday, and Call Tv. Agnt.

Television agent? Travel agent? But why? Her father hadn't taken a vacation in years, which was probably one of the reasons he'd died. The first bit of stress and he'd keeled over.

''Dammit, dammit,'' she muttered. She would not cry, she would not!

"You say something?" Mac called from the back hallway.

"No, go back to what you were doing."

Her untouched coffee had grown cold by the time she'd gone through each file twice. In the last few she'd examined there'd been several references to BFC, none of which she'd understood and all of which bore those enigmatic notations.

Dad, I know you didn't deliberately do anything wrong, but how do you expect me to prove it with the mess I've got here? Maybe if you'd done a better job of keeping records....

Or maybe if she'd turned the lot over to the experts....

"Or to a fortuneteller," she said, shaking her head. "Oh, darn." One glance at her watch and she realized she would have to choose between an early lunch and an early start.

As this was her first day on the job she chose the early start. Dashing upstairs, she dressed quickly in a Save the Whales sweatshirt, a pair of Diesel jeans that now bagged a full inch around her waistline, and her most comfortable tennis shoes. Chances were fairly good she wouldn't be playing tennis anytime soon.

Mac was in the kitchen when she went downstairs. He'd evidently finished the floor, as he'd shoved the washer back in place. "Lunch is ready," he called out just as she reached for her anorak.

"Don't have time."

"Take time. You'll work better with a little energy food."

Her stomach reminded her that a slice of toast, a strip of cold bacon and half a cup of coffee were only memories, and not altogether pleasant ones, at that. "Oh, all right. I guess I can spare ten minutes."

Lunch was canned ravioli and bagged salad. One whiff of tomato sauce and she was suddenly ravenous. She slid into a chair while Mac set out the plates and handed her a canister of grated cheese.

"You need any help?" he inquired.

"Why should I need help? It's only housecleaning. You think I don't know how?" Belligerence didn't come naturally to her, she had to work at it.

"Just offering," he said calmly.

She doused her salad with olive oil and dribbled on balsamic vinegar. "Thanks for lunch," she said grudgingly.

"I'll check the attic again while you're gone. Any leaks should show up after yesterday's rain."

Oh, great. What next, a new roof? She sighed and stared at the pattern of tomato sauce on her plate, then scratched through it with her fork. "I wonder if ravioli sauce is as accurate as tea leaves."

Looking thoughtful, he said, "What counts, I suspect, is the eye of the beholder, not the beheld."

Why was it so impossible to hold a grudge against the man, even when a grudge was justified? Her immune system must be seriously compromised. "My dad used to quote this guy who was famous back in his college days for saying the medium was the message."

Mac nodded gravely. "At that age, ambiguous phrases often pass for wisdom."

"I think I prefer something more concrete, such as, 'Unless otherwise indicated, start at the top, work toward the bottom, lock the door on your way out.'

"Your orders of the day?"

She nodded, wondering for the first time what that "unless otherwise indicated" involved. "Speaking of orders of the day, could you possibly take that air conditioner out of my bedroom window? On days like this, I'd love to be able to open it and get some fresh air inside."

"Will do. Want me to take down the plastic on the other window?"

She drummed her fingers on the table, then shook her head. "Decisions, decisions. Would you mind making that one for me? I can't worry about too many things at once, and right now I'm thinking about what Marian said about things people leave behind in cottages."

He chuckled and said, "Pass the salt."

They were both making an effort to patch up their relationship, but it wasn't easy. Not when her gaze kept straying to his mouth, with its full lower lip and its carved upper. She couldn't forget how those lips had felt moving over hers—over her throat, her eyes. Couldn't help wondering what would have happened if they hadn't been bundled up in layers of clothing, with a cold rain blowing in on them.

She raked back her chair abruptly. ''I need to leave.''

''You're really serious about this?''

She paused in the act of rinsing her plate. ''Did you think I wasn't?''

''How long is this job of yours supposed to last?''

''As long as I want it to last. Although if Marian's regular cleaner comes back from maternity leave, I'll have to look for something else.'' She quickly ran hot water in the sink and squirted lemon-scented liquid detergent. He handed her his plate and cutlery, but held back his cup.

''I might even apply at another rental agency if I like the work,'' she said, making short work of the wash-up.

''What's not to like about scrubbing and vacuuming?'' He pursed his lips, and she really wished he wouldn't. ''Good luck, then,'' he said. ''I'll finish a few odd jobs around here and then catch up on my reading. Handyman's day off. I brought along a few books I haven't even unpacked yet.''

Setting the rinsed dishes in the drainer, she thought about what it would be like to curl up before an open fire—or even an ugly oil heater—and spend a rainy afternoon together. Reading, talking, listening to music—maybe even napping.

Except that it wasn't raining and she had too much to do, not to mention having better sense than to put herself in jeopardy deliberately.

After a quick dash upstairs to grab her purse and the instructions Marian had given her, she was ready to leave. Time was critical during the season, but this time of year most of the cottages weren't even booked, according to the agent, who'd said, "I'd better warn you, a couple of the places haven't been cleaned since the last renters checked out two weeks ago. You might want to check the refrigerator first thing. Throw out everything, whether or not it's got moss on it."

Calculating quickly as she pulled out onto Back Road, Val figured that if she got through today's list she would have earned just over a hundred dollars. Not long ago, before the collapse of BFC, the death of her father and the collapse of all she'd held dear, that would have been pocket change. Now it meant that after this weekend she might be able to pay for her roofing material. Next weekend's work should probably go toward property taxes. After that she could start saving toward having her septic tank pumped.

If she'd come down here hoping to gain fresh perspective, she'd succeeded beyond her wildest dreams. Now all she had to do was put that perspective to use on those messy, mysterious files, instead of dreaming about yellow clapboards and Cape jasmine bushes, hand-detailed furniture and hand-hooked rugs.

Mac considered starting on the files again after Val drove off. So far he'd made a cursory search through nearly a dozen, reaching the conclusion that Bonnard had been in desperate need of clerical help. Maybe if they were to tackle the job together, bounce ideas off one another, they might make more headway. She knew her father's handwriting and would probably recognize most, if not all of the references.

At least he wouldn't feel quite so guilty. She'd caught him fair on the handyman thing, but she still didn't know the worst. He had put his life on hold until he'd cleared Will. Why hadn't she asked him why he was here? He might even have told her.

Dammit, he wasn't cut out to be a double agent, not even in a worthy cause. For a marine archeologist, he was a pretty good plumber, and not a bad carpenter. When and if he ever had to quit diving, instead of trying for a teaching position he just might open his own handyman business.

Meanwhile, he might check out that maritime museum down in Hatteras village. He'd been intending to all week, but he had an idea that once inside, he might not surface anytime soon. Right now, though, he had a more pressing agenda.

The question was, did he still consider her a suspect? *Remember that five-gallon Coke bottle,* he reminded himself.

The moment he opened her bedroom door, every male hormone in his body went on standby alert. Her scent was a subtle echo, reminding him of a patch of white flowers he'd noticed once when he'd gone down to the University of Miami for a conference. Struck by their fragrance, he'd asked what they were.

Ginger lilies. She smelled of ginger lilies and something else, something intensely personal.

Glancing around, he saw the figurine he'd noticed on the mantel downstairs a few days ago—a china ballerina with one foot propped on a stool, holding the laces of a red shoe in both hands. He remembered thinking at the time that there was something disarming about the tiny painted face.

Great. The last thing he needed at this point was to be disarmed.

He unplugged the air-conditioner unit, lifted it out and eased it onto a chair. She'd told him to store the unit in one of the unused rooms for now, so he crossed the hall and shoved open the door of the room at the head of the stairs. The room had two double-hung windows, both with what was probably the original glass. He lingered a moment in the musty room, looking out through the wavery glass to a marsh, a narrow creek and a steep, wooded ridge. The archeologist in him wondered what was underneath the dunes and ridges. While his ever-curious romantic side imagined a grounded shipwreck collecting sand over the centuries, the realist in him admitted it was far more likely to be a fallen tree, or even a clump of grass. It didn't take a geologist to know that barrier islands were constantly moving.

Closing the door behind him, he returned to her bedroom to close the window, making a mental note to look for a screen. A flash of color caught his attention when he turned to leave. Her closet door hung open. Another project for him to tackle, although, short of leveling the whole house, there wasn't much he could do. Maybe reset the hinges.

His gaze strayed to the colorful array of clothing crammed inside the narrow space. He was no fashion expert, but he figured most of the stuff, while it might be suitable for the country club set she had moved in, wasn't going to do her much good down here. Maybe the blue jeans. The pair she'd been wearing when she'd left could have cost anywhere from ten bucks to a couple of hundred, he was no expert when it came to ladies' clothing. A few months ago they'd probably fit her like a coat of primer, but not anymore. She'd lost weight. Too much worry. Too much physical labor on top of too little sleep.

At least he was seeing that she ate three squares a day now. Before he'd showed up she'd evidently been subsisting on peanut butter and tea.

Her bedroom was directly over his. Instead of claiming the front room with its eastern exposure, she'd chosen one where the sun wouldn't wake her until mid-morning. He could hear her up here at night, rolling and tossing. More than once he'd been tempted to offer his own insomnia cure. Fortunately, his survival instincts had kicked in before he could make a major mistake.

Still, he lingered in the room that smelled of her subtle perfume, staring at the pillow that bore a faint impression of her head. She hadn't made her bed. Probably used to having someone do it for her.

Restlessly, he shifted his stance. Now what? Go through the damned files, or go out and whack some more weeds?

Downstairs, he opened a beer and settled down in

the recliner, determined to discover why she'd brought these particular folders with her. He figured he had a minimum of two hours before she got back. After some forty-five minutes of scanning documents, most of which should long since have been consigned to the shredder, he stood and stretched, wondering how a man with the organizational skills of a three-toed sloth could have managed to rip off his own company without leaving a whisper of evidence. BFC's computers had immediately been impounded. Bonnard's personal secretary had been questioned repeatedly, to no avail. According to Will, the executive offices were still off-limits to all but authorized police personnel.

And here he was, more than five hundred miles away, searching through obsolete dental records and unpaid traffic tickets. One entire folder had been devoted to statements from a department store where, according to Will, Macy regularly maxed out her accounts. Somehow, he couldn't see Val Bonnard letting overdue accounts pile up. Not the way she'd tackled the stalagmites inside that oven.

On the other hand, he couldn't see Frank Bonnard running up bills at a place that catered mostly to women—unless he'd been keeping a mistress on the side, and there'd been no evidence of that. No evidence of any women in his life other than the daughter and a few close friends, most of whom weren't exactly arm-candy material.

Damn it, he liked nothing better than a challenge, but so far, this one had him buffaloed.

He closed the last folder and laid it aside. When it came to thinking like an accountant he was at a disadvantage. His brain simply wasn't wired that way. It didn't help when his thoughts kept straying off the reservation.

He kicked the recliner back another notch and tried not to think about the way her bed had looked, with its rumpled sheets and the thick duvet. Tried not to think about the way it smelled—the lingering scent of white flowers.

Finishing off his beer, he set the bottle on the floor, closed his eyes and made an effort to view the overall situation through the lens of a maritime archeologist faced with the task of locating a well-documented wreck. With Will's help, he'd done the preliminaries before he'd ever left Greenwich, both of them reaching the same obvious conclusion. Trouble was, their conclusion no longer held water. Their damned conclusion had begun to crumble the minute he'd seen her—seen the way she was living.

At first he'd rationalized that she was smarter than he'd given her credit for being, but even that hadn't held up. Too many times he'd seen her face after she'd been holed up in here with the damned files—a mixture of sadness, frustration...even irritation. He'd been tempted more than once to tell her he felt the same way himself. Not the sadness, but the rest of it.

But if he told her that, he'd have to admit he'd been lying to her from the first, by omission if not commission. Whatever her opinion of him was now, it would sink even lower. And dammit, it mattered to him. More than it should. Torn loyalties were the pits.

So ease off on the testosterone and jump-start your brain, jerk!

Even a disinterested spectator would be forced to concede that Bonnard hadn't dug a hole under his cabbage patch and buried his plunder. Nor had he shoveled a ton of gold bullion down a coal chute to his basement. The question remained—how the devil had he pulled it off? If he'd been skimming profits over a matter of years, why hadn't anyone noticed? These were professional number-crunchers whose sole purpose was to invest money for maximum profits, see that it was properly allocated and that none of it, other than legitimately earned commissions, went astray. If any money had followed her here, she'd been damned clever at hiding it.

Granted, there was that closet full of fancy clothes upstairs. And her watch—the only jewelry she wore—was a good one. Even so, it had probably cost less than his old stainless-steel Submariner. From what he knew of Val Bonnard—and he was getting to know her far better than he'd ever intended—material things weren't that important to her. Not if she was thinking about keeping this old relic of a house and making the kind of improvements she'd been talking about recently. Cape jasmine bushes on each side of the porch and a fresh paint job?

The most telling of all, though, was the fact that she was cleaning cottages. Hell, he didn't even want her cleaning this one. Her hands were a mess—she had blisters on top of blisters. Some of that stuff she was breathing, she probably needed a mask for.

He had started out wondering how far a guilty woman would go to cover her tracks. At this point he was all but convinced that not only wasn't she a part of the scam, she honestly believed in her father's innocence.

Which meant that, in her own way, she was as much a victim as Will.

Nine

Mac stood and glared at the white satin ballet slippers half hidden under the sofa. What in God's name, he wondered, had made him offer to play detective? He didn't have the right mindset, much less the right skills. Not in this century. Not when real, live people were involved, people he cared about. People who wore ballet slippers and muttered ladylike curses at a dirty oven.

Flipping the last file into the box, he thought about getting himself another beer, but he'd already had two. He was having enough trouble keeping his mind on track without blurring the edges with alcohol. He'd never been much of a drinker, mindful of the familiar warning that drinking and diving don't mix.

"Okay, MacBride, put it in perspective. Small

company, fewer than half a dozen employees in a position to cook the books."

The most likely candidate, CFO Sam Hutchinson, had been turned inside out and given a clean bill of health. Next most likely was in no condition to testify, at least not in any earthly court. If Bonnard had hoped to escape paying taxes, he'd succeeded...the hard way.

For the first time Mac wondered if Will could have pulled it off. Opportunity wouldn't have been a problem. As for motivation, one had to look no further than Macy, who had left him as soon as she'd realized that any accountant whose name was even whispered in context with a financial scandal might as well look for a job bagging groceries.

Will had started out as an accountant shortly before he and Macy were married, then had worked his way through law school with Macy cracking the whip. A small-town beauty queen, she'd been working as a paralegal when they'd met. Macy had always been more ambitious than her husband.

Will had practiced law for less than two years and had hated every hour of it. So when the opening at BFC had come along with its promise of advancement, she'd relented and let him off the hook, lawwise.

So yeah—Will had to be seen as a candidate. Trouble was, he couldn't lie. Even as a kid he'd turned red-faced and glassy-eyed whenever he'd tried to lie his way out of some minor indiscretion.

Back to Bonnard, then. Which meant back to Val.

And dammit, he didn't want her involved. He wanted her free to build a new life for herself with no messy ties to the past. With room somewhere in that new life for a freelance diver, a marine archeologist who was motivated more by intellectual curiosity than ambition.

Okay, he'd passed that hurdle—he'd admitted it, to himself, at least.

Closing his eyes, Mac allowed himself to consider various possibilities and probabilities, keeping in mind that six-ounce pop bottle that had been magnified out of all proportion. He was almost asleep when Val burst through the front door.

"Did you know it's raining again? I can't believe this crazy weather! Mac?" She was staring at the folders that had slipped off his lap, scattering papers across the floor. "What's that? What are you doing?"

Oh, hell. Crunch time. He could lie and tell her the tooth fairy left them on his lap while he was napping or he could give his conscience a break and tell her the truth.

"Mac?" She was standing just inside the door looking pale, grimy and exhausted, her dark braid half unraveled, damp tendrils clinging to her face.

"You're wet." Caught off guard, he took the easy way out and stated the obvious.

"My car wouldn't start. I had to flag down a jumper. Mac, what are you doing with my private papers?"

"Would you believe I was trying to figure out how to build you a file drawer?"

"No."

"I didn't think so. Look, there's no easy way to say this—"

"Try the truth for a change." She kicked off her sand-caked shoes and came inside the room. Sinking down onto the sofa, she folded the ends of the duvet over her lap. The temperature was probably up into the high fifties outside, but she was wet and shivering.

"Truth, whole truth, nothing but the truth. Okay, my name really is MacBride. But my stepbrother's name is Will Jordan." He waited for the implication to sink in. She'd been pale before. Now her face lost the last vestige of color. "Would you have given me a chance if I'd told you up front who I was?"

Spanish-moss-gray eyes darkened visibly. "I'd have—" She took a deep, shuddering breath and started over. "I might have. No, I probably wouldn't. But why?" she begged plaintively. "I mean, why are you even here? You're obviously not a handyman looking for work."

He felt like the lowest form of life. There was no excuse for what he'd done. Or rather, there was, but somewhere along the way he'd become entangled in his own motivation. Now, like the tentacles of a Portuguese man o' war, those motives were threatening to do him serious harm.

"Why were you going through my personal papers?'' she repeated when long moments ticked by in silence. Her voice was too quiet, too controlled.

''Because Will's not an embezzler.'' He waited for her reaction. Wouldn't blame her if she kicked his ass out the door and threw his gear out after him. From the way she was looking at him, she was seriously considering it.

''You don't know that,'' she said finally. ''Nobody wants to believe their relative could do anything dishonest.''

''Yeah, I do know it. Val, whoever ripped off your father's company, it wasn't Will. For one thing, money doesn't mean that much to him, even though maximizing profits is probably part of his job description. Was, I should say. Career-wise, he's pretty well washed up.''

Her searching eyes never left his face. She took another deep breath and said, ''My father was not a thief. I don't care what they're saying about him, I knew him better than anyone else, and one thing he was incapable of doing was lying. He never stole so much as a—a book of matches. Money was never what motivated him—not for himself, at least.''

Mac wondered if she realized what that admission implied. ''I'll have to take your word for it. I never met the man.''

Other than the fact that he'd lived in a pretty ritzy part of town and drove a classic Bentley, Frank Bonnard hadn't struck him as a conspicuous consumer. Not like some men who earned considerably less, Will included. But that was Macy's doing.

She sneezed, sniffed, and stood. "I need a tissue."

"You need a hot bath and something to eat."

"Hot tea."

He grimaced. "Go get clean—put on something warm and dry. I'll have the kettle boiling when you come down again. We'll talk."

"We're going to talk, all right," she said grimly. "Don't think you're getting off this easy."

Easy? There was little she could do to him that his own conscience hadn't already done.

He watched her leave, her damp socks leaving small cloudy footprints on the dark varnished floor. *Oh, lady, why couldn't you have been what I started out believing you were? Shallow, spoiled, greedy—crooked as a corkscrew?*

Before heading upstairs, Val tossed her muddy sneakers on top of the washing machine. If she'd been alone in the house she'd have peeled down to the skin, cold or not, and left everything there. What a rotten stinker this whole day had turned out to be. Her first day on the job...and now this.

It wasn't enough that she'd had to deal with some unidentifiable substance left in the sink to grow mold and attract bugs. It wasn't enough that some creep had spilled a sticky drink on an upholstered chair that had run down onto the floor, and in cleaning it up, she'd crawled through the gunk and backed halfway across the floor, leaving a trail of sticky knee prints.

And after all that, to come home to this. Damn him! Damn him all to hell and back, how *dare* he do this to her! Not once, but twice. What was that old saying—fool me once, shame on you; fool me twice, shame on me.

She should have known. Whenever a man went out of his way to be charming, it usually meant he wanted something. Not that Mac had gone out of his way to be charming—he hadn't had to. She'd been easy prey, she admitted reluctantly as she collected a change of clothes from her bedroom.

How had he charmed her? Let me count the ways, she thought bitterly. By drinking the hot tea he despised with barely a grimace. By fascinating her with tales of historic shipping lanes and early colonial settlements, making her forget that she was so tired every bone in her body ached. By making her listen to the whispery flight of the cormorants. By making her laugh when laughing was the last thing she felt like doing. Wasn't it enough that he'd crawled up in her attic and under her house, doing all the grungy things she'd never even had to think of before in exchange for a rust-stained shower and a sagging bed?

Damn him for being so tempting—and herself for being so gullible.

She ran the tub full of tea-colored water that was steamy hot, thanks to her handy-dandy, double-dealing tenant. She dumped in a handful of bath salts, and then another one, just because she needed to make a gesture. Probably slip and break her neck getting out.

Serve her right.

She sank into the welcome warmth, lifted her face and closed her eyes as clouds of fragrant steam rose around her. *Stress, be gone,* she willed silently. Felicity would have had her chanting mantras. Felicity was into the latest version of New Age. Sandy, already a borderline alcoholic, would have poured her a stiff drink and reminded her that life was too short—she might as well enjoy what she could, while she could.

Lacking such help from her friends, Val slipped down until her hair floated around her shoulders. She had barely enough energy to manage a bath. A separate shampoo, complete with conditioner, roller drying and all the rest of her old routine, was out of the question.

Downstairs, Mac waited until he heard the water gurgling down the drain to fill the kettle and switch on a burner. Then he rummaged in the refrigerator for sandwich makings. She needed energy food. Carbohydrates were supposed to be calming, weren't they? Hadn't he read that somewhere?

Setting out store-bought chocolate cookies, bread, pastrami, cheese and a variety of condiments, he noticed the note he'd left for her, anchored with the salt shaker. He'd taken the call shortly after she'd driven off, promising the caller to give her the message as soon as she returned.

Not surprisingly, it had slipped his mind. On first hearing the name *Mitty Stoddard* he'd had a sinking feeling that things were about to go from bad to worse. Although from Val's point of view—his, too, come to think of it—they probably couldn't get much worse.

He smelled her before he heard her. Not that her scent was blatant, it was more a case of his being sensitized. *Susceptible* might be a better term.

"Come sit, drink some tea, eat a bite and then you might want to return the call that came just after you left."

She was wearing a fuzzy pink outfit that didn't deserve to be called sweats, but probably was. He waited for her to read the message.

She scanned it, caught her breath and lifted a pair of gleaming moss-colored eyes. "You talked to her? Was she—did she sound all right? I've been so worried."

"Briefly," he said. "She wanted to know where you were, and I told her you'd gone out for a couple of hours. Then she wanted to know who I was, and I told her—"

"You told her what? That you were Will Jordan's brother?"

"Stepbrother." He shook his head. "I told her I was doing some house repairs for you."

"That's all?"

He jerked a chair from under the table and straddled it. "Look, whether you believe me or not, I'm not in the habit of deceiving people. But neither am I in the habit of broadcasting my private business to strangers."

"Miss Mitty's not a stranger. You knew I'd been trying to get in touch with her."

"I knew you'd called several times. I suspected you were worried, and yes, I knew she used to work for your father." According to Will, Mitty Stoddard was an over-the-hill busybody who'd guarded Frank Bonnard like a junkyard dog with a juicy bone. Also according to Will, Bonnard's secretary might even have had a hand in the lady's early retirement, if being figuratively shoved out the door at the age of seventy-two could be called early retirement. Will didn't know quite how, and Mac considered the whole topic irrelevant.

Leaving a half-made sandwich and taking her tea with her, Val hurried into the next room. Mac could hear her punching in numbers and muttering under her breath. Then he heard, "Miss Mitty? Oh, thank goodness! I can't tell you how worried I've been."

He stepped out onto the back porch to give her some privacy. Eavesdropping was a cut below what even he would stoop to. He'd already stooped pretty low, but he'd like to think he was too honorable to dance this particular version of the limbo.

The rain had slowed to a drizzle so he went and padlocked the shed he'd left open earlier. No reason why—there was nothing of value inside—it was just something to do. Then he stopped by her car, ran a visual check on her tire pressure and did the same to his Land Cruiser. There was just enough light left to see by. When he figured he'd given her enough time, he went back inside, noisily shutting the back door. He was damp, disgruntled and curious.

She met him in the kitchen. "Is your friend all right?" he asked.

Her cheeks were flushed, the blotches of color standing out against her pallor. "She is now. Well, not really—at her age…" She shook her head, dislodging the towel she'd been wearing like a turban.

Unwilling to press her, he switched on the burner to heat more water for tea. The sandwich makings were still on the table. He waited, sensing that she needed to talk, and, as his were the only available ears, chances were he wouldn't even need to prime the pump.

"She broke her hip. That's why I couldn't get in touch with her for so long, she was in this rehabilitation center after she got out of the hospital, and didn't want to worry me with everything else that was going on. Her niece could've called me. I forgot to ask why she hadn't, but then, being practically without a phone for almost a week…"

"Make your sandwich, you need food. Or I'll make it for you."

While she was smearing bread with mustard and horseradish, he pulled up a chair across the table. "Did she know about your father? Will said she retired before the—that is, a while back."

Between big hungry bites, Val told him about Miss Mitty, her father's all-around assistant and adviser, who had been almost as much a part of her life as had Belinda, the housekeeper who'd had a big hand in getting her through puberty and adolescence.

"You know, I never realized it before," she said thoughtfully, "but I don't think they particularly liked each other—Belinda and Miss Mitty. They both loved us, though—my father and me—so they never let it show."

He nodded. When the kettle began to simmer, he got up, retrieved a fresh tea bag and filled her cup.

"I was afraid Miss Mitty hadn't heard about Dad, and I'd have to be the one to tell her, but she reads all the news online. She's better with a computer than I ever was, isn't that amazing? I mean, everyone knows how babies are practically born hooked up to the Internet, but women Miss Mitty's age..." She diluted her tea with milk and spooned in sugar. "It's just a shame her bones aren't as flexible as her mind."

They talked some more, but it was obvious that she was exhausted. "Leave everything," he told her. "I'll wash up and put away. Either go to bed or go relax in the living room."

"Oh, no," she said, and stifled a yawn. "You're not getting rid of me that easily. We still need to talk about why you were snooping through my files."

"Ouch. Could we retract the term *snooping?*"

She crossed her arms and leaned against the counter. He said, "Okay, here goes. Chances are I was looking for the same thing you've been looking for. That is, some evidence that might lead to whoever cooked the books at your father's company."

"My father didn't do it," she said flatly.

"Neither did Will."

They eyed each other warily. When Mac found his thoughts straying in another direction, he turned and stacked the few dishes in the drainer and ran water over them. "If we're going to talk, you need to sit down. Lying down would be even better, because whether or not you want to admit it, lady, you're bushed."

This time she couldn't stifle her yawn. Still yawning, she wandered away, and moments later he heard her sigh as she settled onto the sofa. He was tempted to join her, to fold the duvet around her, massage her shoulders and finish up by rubbing lotion into those red, rough hands.

After drying his own hands, he rolled down his sleeves and joined her. "All right, start talking," she said before he could frame his first question.

Sergeant Valerie. Make that General.

"Like I said, I'm looking for the same thing you are. Makes sense to me to pool our resources." He waited for a reaction. While he watched, she closed her eyes and grimaced.

"What?" he said.

"Cramp." The word came through clenched teeth. She started to stand, but he was up before she could get both feet on the floor.

"Where? Your calf? Right or left?"

"Foot. Right one."

By the time he'd slipped off her shoe and bent her toes toward her body, then worked the sole of her foot between his hands, she was lying back on the sofa, eyes closed, groaning in either pleasure or pain, he couldn't be certain which.

"I think that's got it," she whispered.

"Anything else?" He held his hands up as if he were a surgeon scrubbed for an operation.

She looked at his raised hands and almost smiled. Almost, but not quite. "I shouldn't," she said. "We really do need to talk."

"We can talk tomorrow, tell me what else hurts."

"I have to go to work tomorrow."

"Valerie, what's hurting? You can't tackle another cleaning job if your muscles freeze up on you."

Instead of answering, she rolled over onto her stomach and twitched one shoulder. It was all the invitation he needed.

Eventually she said lethargically, "I still have a bone to pick with you. Ahh…right there."

It was weakness on her part, sheer self-indulgence, but Val let him work his magic on her aching shoulders. When his hands moved to her lower back, she couldn't find the energy to protest. By morning, that would probably have stiffened up, too. Crawling around on her knees, dragging junk out from under furniture. A single wading shoe. Two used paper plates. A kid's snorkel.

She sighed again. They had come to some sort of an agreement…hadn't they? And honestly, she rationalized, it made sense. What one person saw as insignificant, another pair of eyes might see as vitally important.

''Two brains are better than one,'' she murmured sleepily.

His hands slowed, circled her shoulders, his thumbs now working at the rigid deltoids. Where had it all come from—the tension? It couldn't be simply the result of cleaning one filthy cottage and two fairly clean ones. Red hands and sore knees, sure, but tension?

He leaned over and inhaled. She could feel his breath on her cheek, her neck. ''Your hair smells like ginger lilies. I think.''

Without opening her eyes, she smiled. ''You think?''

''White flowers. Grow in Florida. Smell sweet, not at all like ginger?''

''Close enough,'' she managed to whisper just before she felt his lips on her nape. *Oh, please don't do that. I don't have the strength to resist....*

He backed away, bumped against the coffee table and one of the files slid to the floor. Neither of them noticed. When he scooped her up in his arms, Val made a weak protest, but both of them knew they were past that point. Logical or not—timely or not, he was going to do what she had dreamed about ever since that kiss on the beach. Ever since they had huddled out of the rain in a deserted shelter, his body pressing hers against the wall, her arms around his waist, her hands cupping his lean buttocks.

Nothing else in her life made any sense—why should this?

Ten

Mac wanted to carry her upstairs, but Val insisted on being set on her feet. As the steps were too narrow, they jostled their way to the top, arms around waists, hips nudging hips, hearts pounding as one.

At least, hers was. As she wasn't wearing a bra—didn't really need one—her feather-soft sweatshirt moved against her sensitized nipples until all she could think of was tearing off her clothes and feeling his hands on her body, his lips—

It's going to happen, a voice inside her whispered. *Don't fight it.*

Another voice answered, *Who's fighting?* Something told her it was now or never, and never wasn't even a faint possibility.

Her bed was a double and her mattress was in

somewhat better condition than his, but he could have taken her on any floor in the house, sandy or not, and she wouldn't have complained as long as he joined her there.

She felt for the overhead light switch just inside the door, but he stayed her hand. Instead, he turned on the hall light and left the door ajar. Just as well. She was hardly a centerfold candidate.

And while she was not without experience, she suddenly felt awkward. Unlike the polished sophisticate she'd nearly married, and the tennis club gigolo she'd briefly fallen for, Mac was a real man in every sense of the word. What if he was disappointed? She would die if he looked at her flat chest and said something like, "Where's the beef?"

Tripp had said that once, then laughed as if he'd been only teasing. Looking back, she realized that Tripp's brand of teasing had almost always held a hidden barb.

"Val? It's not too late," Mac said, but of course it was. It had been too late the first time she'd seen him standing in the middle of her front yard like a conquering hero looking over the spoils of war.

"I know that," she snapped. So much for lifelong lessons in deportment. She couldn't even manage a simple seduction scene with any style.

Reaching for the drawstring at her waist, she looked at him as if to say, *I will if you will.*

Stepping out of his shoes, Mac's gaze never left her face. He unbuttoned his fly—he wasn't wearing a belt. *You first,* those whiskey-brown eyes dared.

Boldly, she stepped out of her pants, then quickly tugged the bottom of the pink sweatshirt down over her hips. If he liked big-bosomed women, he was flat out of luck, *flat* being the operative word.

Judging from the way he stepped out of his pants, tossed them onto a chair and pulled his Columbia U sweatshirt over his head, self-consciousness wasn't even in his vocabulary. If briefs came in cup sizes, his would be a double-D.

He caught her staring. "Val? If you've changed your mind, just say so. But don't wait too long...please?"

Frantically, she shook her head. Oh, for goodness sake—thirty years old and you'd think she'd never done it before.

But standing there in his navy briefs, his thick, sunstreaked hair awry, he looked so heartbreakingly beautiful she wanted to weep. Instead, she tugged off her shirt, stepped out of her panties and confronted him, daring him to back out.

When he closed his eyes her heart sank. Then he stepped out of his briefs and stood there, fully aroused, but still not touching her. Her mouth was dry. Other parts were embarrassingly wet. "Well, are we going to do this or not?" she demanded belligerently.

At least it broke the tension. He laughed unsteadily and reached for her. If she didn't know better, she might even believe he was as nervous as she was. Together they made it onto the bed, and Val told herself it would be all right. This was Mac—she trusted him.

Don't think about tomorrow. Don't think, just live the moment.

"I don't want to hurt you," he said.

"I'm hardly fragile." When his flattened palms made small circles on her nipples, she caught her breath.

"Yeah, you are. Lucky for you, I'm good at handling beautiful, priceless, fragile treasures."

It was the last word either of them spoke for a while. He kissed her then, a gentle exploration that quickly escalated to a carnal assault. As if the taste of him weren't intoxicating enough, the feel of his arousal pulsing against her drove her out of her mind with need.

"Please," she managed to whisper. "Now?"

He murmured something that she was beyond hearing, much less understanding, and left her briefly. Moments later he returned. He kissed her eyes, her nose, her chin, and then moved down her throat and beyond, his hands leading the way, his lips following. She could feel her small breasts swell under the gentle assault from his tongue as he sucked her nipples, then gently grazed them with his teeth. All the while his hands were moving on her body, tracing erotic patterns on her most sensitive flesh.

Digging into his shoulders with her fingertips, she twisted her head on the pillow, whimpering as he carried her to new heights, leading her to the very brink and back again and again. Stunned with sheer sensation, she was barely able to breathe. By the time he settled himself between her parted thighs, her fists were gripping the sheets to keep her from soaring into orbit.

He entered her slowly. Impatiently, she thrust her hips to meet him, urging him to hurry. Braced on his elbows, he was trembling, his face the face of a stranger.

A stranger…

Before second thoughts could wedge their way between them he slipped his hand down her body and touched her in a way that jolted her into final orbit. ‘‘Shh, easy,’’ he whispered, but his voice was unsteady.

Slowly, he moved deeply inside her. Clenching her thighs around his waist, she moved frantically to meet his thrusts. They were wildly out of synch, but it didn't seem to matter—didn't matter at all, as wave after wave of pulsating pleasure washed over her.

She shuddered, caught her breath and released it in a soft scream. Never…*ever*…had she flown this high! Not until the last sweet, heavy ring of sensation faded, leaving behind a deep, mellow ache, did it occur to her that she still couldn't breathe.

She must have made some sound because Mac shifted his weight and rolled onto his side, taking her with him. ‘‘Sorry,’’ he muttered. ‘‘I died for a few minutes.’’

Petit mort. The small death…

As reluctant as she was to move, Val felt her defenses click into place. She felt a desperate need to prove that what just happened meant no more to her than it had to him.

Simple sex, she reasoned. People did it all the time.

Simple? Pompeii had been simple. The San Francisco earthquake had been simple. Sex with MacBride was anything *but* simple.

He was stirring against her again...down there. She was tempted just for a moment, but then common sense prevailed. "This is all very well, but I need to get some sleep," she said shrewishly. "I have to go to work tomorrow."

He stared at her as if not believing what he'd just heard.

She couldn't believe she'd said it. Oh, God, how utterly awful. It was no less than the truth, but far from the whole truth. If they did it again, he might fall asleep in her bed, and if they spent an entire night together, nuzzling, nestling, making love again and again, she might never allow him to escape. Too weak to make it down to the kitchen, they would eventually starve. Sometime in the distant future Marian would send someone to check on her, and there they'd be—two naked skeletons, bones entwined on a rumpled bed.

Carefully, she disentangled herself, then pretended to be asleep. The moment she felt him ease out of bed, she opened one eye. God, he was gorgeous!

"Want me to bring up an alarm clock?" he asked. Obviously he hadn't bought her pretense of sleep.

Nor was he the least bit self-conscious about his nudity.

"No thanks," she said coolly, watching as he casually scooped up his clothes and left. When he was halfway to the stairs, she called after him. "Yes—would you mind? Just set it on the dresser."

Mac let the cold shower drill down on him for several minutes. He was deep in uncharted waters without a tank, without so much as a snorkel. His left brain had shut down completely—he couldn't have reasoned his way out of a coat closet. As for his right brain, it kept creating these crazy images of big, soft beds and a certain slender, soft woman. A woman he'd come down here to entrap, only nothing was turning out the way he'd expected. He could no longer even pretend to be objective. Peel off the surface patina and Valerie Bonnard, heiress and socialite, was as real as any woman shoving a basket through the supermarket with two kids hanging onto her skirt. Same basic hopes, same basic fears—maybe even dreams, although she hadn't shared those with him.

Instead, she had shared her body.

And now he found himself picturing a half-grown boy with dark hair and eyes the color of damp Spanish moss diving beside him, while just offstage a little girl in a white tutu and red ballerina shoes tried out a few classic moves.

Shutting off the water, he stepped out of the shower and toweled off, still picturing those long legs. She had a slight tendency to knock knees that probably bothered her, but it sure as hell didn't bother him. Her hips flared nicely—that much he'd noticed in those jeans she wore under all the layers on top. Her breasts were barely a palmful, the nipples dark and proud, as if begging for his attention.

Jeez, at this rate he'd need another cold shower, Mac told himself, reaching for the boxers he slept in.

There was an alarm clock in the kitchen. It was set for seven. He left it that way and headed back upstairs. She was feigning sleep when he let himself into her bedroom, Baby Ben in hand. He let her get away with it. Morning would come soon enough, and by then he needed his mind to be completely clear.

Or at least marginally functional.

Downstairs again, he glanced at his watch. It was barely ten o'clock. He had plenty of time to tackle a few more of those frustrating files, knowing she wouldn't come downstairs again before morning.

But that would be cheating, and suddenly, he couldn't do that any longer. "Hell of a position you put yourself in, MacBride."

He swore softly, checked the front door and then headed toward the back of the house. If you can sleep, lady, then so can I, he thought grimly. But the first time he heard her bed so much as squeak overhead, he'd be out of there and up those stairs so fast his feet would strike sparks on the worn old treads.

In other words, fellow, you're down for the count.

Val opened her eyes moments before the clock went off and lay awake, thinking of those enigmatic scribbles she'd found on so many of the papers in her father's files. Initials, single numbers, sums—random, seemingly meaningless words. If it was a code of some kind, he should have given her the key.

She showered, thinking of Mac's enclosed stall downstairs. She pictured him standing there, his naked body with its generous dusting of dark hair gleaming wetly.

''Stop it. Just stop that!'' she muttered, roughly toweling her hair before snatching up her blow-dryer.

She had two more cottages to clean before she could get started on the files again. One had to be done this morning, the other could wait, as it wasn't booked, but she might as well do it anyway. She needed the money, and besides, she hated having anything hanging over her head. Anything more than she already had.

Over breakfast, which Mac had waiting for her some twenty minutes later, he announced his intention of helping her clean.

''Last night we agreed to tackle the files together,'' he reminded her. ''Same thing applies to the cleaning. We'll get it done faster and then we can come back here and concentrate on those files.''

Last night she would have agreed to jump through a ring of fire. Today she was back in control. ''I can do it and be back here in two hours. In the meanwhile, you might want to—to—'' She couldn't think of another chore that needed doing at the moment. At least none he was capable of that she could afford.

She said, ''My showerhead. It drizzles. I prefer a needle spray.''

''Hard-water deposits. I'll soak it out while we're cleaning your cottages.''

She slanted him a skeptical look. ''You're not going to give up, are you?'' She'd counted on spending a few hours away in hopes that she might be able to restore a few of her defenses.

''A handyman does what a handyman has to do.'' He had the nerve to grin at her.

''Fine,'' she snapped. ''I'll pay you half of what I get paid.''

But nothing was fine, she thought. Her whole orderly life had been turned into a gigantic roller coaster. All she could do was hang on and hope it would eventually come to rest.

He insisted on driving, so she got out the map Marian had given her and directed him to the road that ended in two soundside cottages. Traffic was light. They'd passed a car and two trucks, one of them towing a boat bigger than it was before Mac said, ''Look, about last night. I want you to know—''

''I don't want to talk about it. It happened, it's finished, just forget it. That one with the white trim—that's one of them.''

They finished well under the allotted time. Mac insisted on doing the vacuuming and mopping floors while she cleaned the bathrooms. Four of them, with only three bedrooms. If she'd learned one thing in the brief time she'd been living in her great-grandmother's house it was that the quality of life had little to do with the standard of living.

"Can you think of a single reason why someone would go off and leave a vegetable drawer full of cosmetics and a kitchen garbage can half full of dead oysters?" she asked as they pulled up before her house less a few hours later. "Should I get the address from Marian and mail the woman her cosmetics?"

"Toss the cosmetics and mail her the oysters."

She bit back a snort of laughter and opened the door.

"Go sit," Mac ordered once they were inside. The house smelled slightly of vinegar. "I'll rinse out your showerhead and reinstall it, then I'll fix us something to eat."

"Don't spoil me," she said, dropping wearily onto a chair.

"Don't tempt me." He flashed her a quick grin as he poured the bowl of white vinegar down the drain and ran fresh water through the showerhead.

A few minutes later he made them both sandwiches. She sat and watched him layer on cheese and pastrami while he told her about the concretions he'd left in Will's garage, some soaked free and carefully pried apart, others still in their natural state.

She followed him into the living room feeling spoiled and just a wee bit decadent, being waited on by a man like MacBride. He carried the tray. She carried the paper napkins.

''Got an idea,'' he said after consuming half his sandwich in three bites.

''What, more mustard? You used half a jar.''

''About your dad's hieroglyphics. I don't think it's stock symbols, I think it's someone's initials. Who do you know whose initials are M.L.?''

''Nobody. I've thought and thought about it, but that doesn't necessarily mean anything. I didn't know half the people who worked at BFC.''

Mac had watched her eat. For a lady who probably knew her way around a six-fork table setting, she had a healthy appetite. In more respects than one, he thought, feeling his heart kick into a higher gear. She left the pickle till last. When she started nibbling on the tip, he stood and snatched up her plate. ''I'll just, uh—go put the food away. You want to wash up before we get started?''

She avoided his eyes, and it occurred to Mac that she might even be thinking about the same thing he was remembering in intricate detail. To get them both back on track, he repeated his suspicions as soon as he rejoined her in the living room with coffee for him, hot tea for her. ''M stands for Mitty?''

''M. L., not M. S. Miss Mitty's name is Matilda, but her last name is Stoddard. And anyway, she couldn't possibly be involved because we knew her forever. At least since the middle eighties when BFC was incorporated.''

''Everybody knows somebody.'' For a woman he knew to be highly intelligent, she was incredibly naive. "This accountant who left, what are his initials?"

"Hers. P. T. I thought about her, too, but I don't remember seeing those initials."

They went through the names of everyone on the executive floor and a few of the lower echelon, only three of whom had been there since the beginning. Of the three, Mitty Stoddard, was gone. Frank Bonnard was dead, and that left—

"You're sure about Hutchinson? I know he was questioned and finally cleared, but someone ripped off all those people, and it wasn't Will Jordan, I'd stake my life on it."

"It wasn't my father, either. I've known him all my life." She shook her head, muttered, "Duh," and then said, "Look, integrity is something a person either has or he doesn't. It's not a—a situational thing. If my father picked up a dime on the sidewalk, he'd ook around to see if he could find who might have dropped it."

A dime, maybe, but several million dollars?

Mac sighed. "Back to square one. M. L. shows up more than any other set of initials, right? So let's see what else we can find, and this time check out the context. Remember, it doesn't have to be someone who's been there from the beginning, it could easily be a new hire…only not too new."

"Like your brother."

Ignoring the comment, he lifted three files from he box and placed them on the coffee table. "By the way, where did you say this friend of yours moved to when she left Greenwich?''

''Miss Mitty? Monroe, Georgia. She has a niece there.'' Val's eyes held a warning glint, but she didn't argue.

''You happen to know the niece's name?''

''It's Brown—Rebecca Brown. I have the phone number.''

She could have refused to cooperate. By now she had to know that someone was going to get roughed up before they were finished. He said, ''Look, if you're determined to clear your father's name, it's a case of no holds barred.''

''Holes?''

''Holds. Don't you ever watch wrestling?''

She rolled her eyes, and it served as well as anything could to break the tension. She picked up a folder, spread the papers on the table and pointed to the distinctive turquoise-colored ink. ''M. L. again. And there's a date.''

For the next few hours they went over page after page, noting context as much as what had been written across the face of the various documents. By the time Val had yawned half a dozen times, Mac was pretty sure he knew where the trail was going to end. Now all he had to do was figure out the best way to follow it, because suspicions alone weren't enough.

''Come on, let's call it a night.''

Eleven

Neither of them bothered to pretend they weren't going to end up in bed together. In matters concerning BFC they might be skating on thin ice over moving water, but when it came to personal matters, Val couldn't even pretend to hold back. What had happened before—spontaneous combustion described it best—might have been ill-conceived, but she'd be lying if she said she didn't want it to happen again…and again.

"Shower's all ready to go," Mac told her. "If you need any help, just yell." He stopped at the bathroom door, leaned back against the wall and drew her into his arms. It was a long time before she reluctantly stepped away.

"You might smooth the bed. I don't think I ever got around to making it today."

"Yes, ma'am. Anything else, Miss B.?" The devil lurked in his clear brown eyes. She loved it when he teased her this way.

"Wait for me on the left side of the bed. I always sleep on the right."

"Who said anything about sleeping?" He leaned in for one last kiss, then opened the bathroom door.

Laughing, she said, "Five minutes. Oh, and Mac…be naked."

It took her four. One minute to splash off, one to dry, one to smooth on a layer of body lotion, and one to hurry across the cool bare floors to the bedroom. By the time she opened the door she was scarcely breathing. *Am I stark, raving mad?* she wondered, staring at the dim pink-lit room. He had found her peach-and-black Hermés scarf and draped it over the lamp on the dresser. Lying on his back in the center of the bed, arms crossed under his head, he was grinning like a drunken satyr.

"Last one in's a rotten egg," he jeered softly. She dropped the towel, darted across the floor and dived onto the bed. He caught her, laughing, and pulled her on top of him.

Not until much later, when she collapsed in a damp heap, every nerve ending in her body still tingling, did she manage to speak. "Mine's the superior position, you'll notice."

"I noticed." The sleepy look he sent her could

asily be described as a leer. "Just try it without me
nd see how superior you feel."

"Mmm, now that you mention it, I believe further
esearch might be called for."

Between sessions of serious research they man-
ged to sleep for a few hours. Eventually Mac got
p and turned off the light, saying something about
fire hazard.

Any fire hazard, Val remembered thinking, was
ere in bed, not across the room on the dresser. She
woke sometime in the middle of the night with her
ead on Mac's shoulder, one knee curled up over his
high and her hand dangerously near ground zero.

Carefully, she eased it away. She needed to go to
he bathroom, and if she'd learned anything at all last
ight it was that Mac had a low threshold of arousal.
lmost as low as her own.

Another thing she'd learned, with decidedly mixed
motions, was that she was deeply, irredeemably in
ove, and it felt nothing at all like the few other times
he'd thought she was in love.

Not that love was going to prevent her from doing
what she'd come down here to do. Today they were
oing to go over those damned files with a magni-
ying glass, if necessary. Mac was determined to find
omething he could interpret as proof of his step-
rother's innocence, never mind that it might seal her
ather's guilt for all time. That done, he would leave.
Iission accomplished. Damn the torpedoes, full
peed ahead as an Annapolis cadet she'd once dated

used to quote whenever he downed one drink too many.

Okay, he was a lover and leaver. She could handle it. "What the dickens does a marine archeologis know about criminology, anyway? Or accounting, for that matter?"

The belligerent face in the bathroom mirror issued a reply. "About as much as an art history major with a minor in English lit."

Mac waited until he heard the shower running be fore collecting his clothes and heading downstairs He had a feeling he was in deeper water than he was rated for. Decompression was going to be a problem if it was even possible. One place to start was with a phone call to his hacker friend Shirley, and anothe one was to an old diving buddy who was currently working with the Atlanta PD Special Crimes Unit.

He showered, dressed, placed both calls and wa frying bacon when Val made the scene. The firs thing he noticed was that she was wearing makeup and one of those fancy outfits that was probably sup posed to look casual. White chamois pants, several loose layers of cashmere and silk, with shirttails dan gling. Her hair was twisted up in a knot and she'd taken time to put on makeup.

He could have commented, but he chose not to in case she happened to be feeling as vulnerable as he was. He could afford to allow her whatever armo she thought she needed. Hell, he might even have joined in the masquerade, only he'd left his forma vear back in Mystic. Three ties, a navy blazer and a ›air of khakis that still held a crease.

''Scrambled or fried?''

She shuddered. ''Tea and toast,'' she said, and as ;oon as he set the food on the table, proceeded to ilch bacon off his plate until he got up and handed ıer a plate and a fork. ''Help me out here, I scram- ›led enough eggs for a platoon.''

They finished breakfast, mostly in silence, and hen he said, ''Leave the dishes. Come on in the iving room, I think we're on the verge of a break- hrough.''

Three-quarters of an hour and half a pot of coffee ater, the second of the corroborating phone calls :ame through. Mac had also talked to Will while Val ıad been showering. Now, surrounded by open files, he documents sorted in chronological order, he took he second call, allowing Val to hear his sparse re- ponses. Her lipstick had been chewed off, and the ›lush on her cheeks stood out against her pallor.

''Uh-huh,'' he said. ''Gotcha.''

Damn, he hated this. If there was any way he could ıave spared her, he'd have done it, even at Will's ·xpense. That was a sign of just how deep these par- icular waters were.

But the evidence was damning. The trail had been arefully followed and just as carefully concealed by man who'd been clever, but far too softhearted until t was too late. Bonnard would've soon turned over the evidence, Mac was certain of it, only there hadn't been time.

There was no way to make this any easier for her. It never even occurred to him that she might not believe him without proof. As unlikely as it was, especially under the circumstances, a deep level of trust had grown between them. She was as aware of it as he was, even when they bickered over details.

He pressed the off button, laid his phone aside and stared out the window, stroking his chin between thumb and forefinger. She had to know what he'd been leading up to. The only thing that had been lacking was the identity of M. L., the initials that had turned up on more than half her father's papers.

Finally, she said, "What?"

"Honey, you're not going to like this."

"Mac, you're scaring me."

He eased her over on the sofa and sat down beside her. "Matilda Lyford. Did your friend ever tell you she'd been married?"

She stopped breathing, shaking her head slowly. "Miss Mitty, you mean," she whispered.

"In eighty-seven, Matilda Stoddard married Vernon Lyford. The marriage took place in Morganton, West Virginia, and lasted approximately three weeks. Lyford was jailed on a check-kiting scam. Meanwhile, the bride moved gradually northeast, spending eighteen months working with a mortgage bank in Cumberland, Maryland, and another few months as a receptionist with a medical insurance firm in Philadelphia. Both times she left under—I guess you night say under a cloud. By the time she arrived in Greenwich, she'd reverted to her maiden name, although there's no record of her ever having it legally changed. For that matter, there's no record of a divorce.''

''Mitty Stoddard,'' Val whispered.

Mac nodded. ''Honey, I'm afraid your Miss Mitty wasn't all she pretended to be. She'd be how old when she married, late fifties?''

Val nodded, her eyes suspiciously bright. ''You never met her, but Mac, she was everyone's idea of the perfect grandmother. Gray hair, lace-up shoes, plastic-rimmed bifocals. Back when everyone else was wearing granny glasses, I remember hearing her say that they were fine for the young, but not for any woman past middle age. She went to church. She—she—'' Swallowing hard, she shook her head and whispered, ''I can't believe it.''

Mac drew her head down on his shoulder and covered her hands with his. His were tanned and callused. Hers were rough, with the beginning of a rash. God, he loved this woman, dishpan hands, smeared mascara and all.

''Your father knew.'' Even though Bonnard had not been the embezzler, he'd been Stoddard's employer, and as such, a target for liability suits. No point in bringing that up now, though. ''He probably hated to confront her, but he'd have done it, Val. That's why he was collecting evidence.''

She laughed brokenly. ''Evidence? If that was supposed to be evidence, then why did he hide it? Why not just tell someone about his suspicions?''

''Because suspicions alone aren't enough. Before he accused an old friend, he had to be dead certain. Sooner or later he'd have gone to the authorities.''

''Only later never happened,'' she whispered.

''Best I can figure, Matilda Stoddard, or whatever she called herself, had been inventing retirees, settling up accounts and shifting the money to another account for at least a couple of years. Some of the initials could represent different banks, or maybe fictitious accounts. As for the sums, add a couple of zeros and that probably represents a pretty accurate figure for each phony account.''

Once they knew what to look for it became all too clear. Matilda Lyford, complete with at least two different social security numbers—possibly others, as well, had set up four separate bank accounts, careful to keep each transaction under the limit of ten thousand dollars, which would have automatically flagged the transaction.

''And nobody ever figured out what was going on,'' Val murmured.

''Because no one was looking for it. A few thousand a month here, a few thousand there—after a while it adds up to a pretty nice package. Especially once she started scooping up real money.''

''Just before she retired, you mean.''

''Couple of months. Probably figured by the time anyone caught on she'd be out of there.''

''She was right,'' Val said with a shuddering sigh.

lmost a sigh of relief. "Mac, it hurts. No one likes o be wrong about people, but..."

"On the other hand, sometimes being wrong is ust fine." His look said it all. He leaned over and ipped her face up for a quick kiss. Quick only because they still had some ground to cover before he eaded north with the collected evidence to turn it ver to the authorities.

"I take it you know where she is now," Val said, bviously determined to get every painful detail over efore the anesthesia wore off.

"Florida. One of the better retirement communies. Fancy apartment, water aerobics, weekly conerts, trips to Disneyland and Sea World. At a minnum rate of about eight grand a month she'd be set or a long, comfortable retirement. Instead..."

"Do you mind if we don't talk about it any nore?"

"Nope. I think we both pretty well accomplished ur missions. Will's in the clear. Your dad's reputation is restored. In fact, he'll wind up being someing of a hero for having figured out what was going n. If he'd lived, he'd have taken his evidence to the uthorities, and you and I would never have met. Vill's wife would never have left him—yeah, well, aybe she would, at that."

"Go back." She was rubbing his knuckles, then etting her fingers trace the length of each finger.

"To Greenwich? To Mystic?"

Then she came up on her knees beside him and

shoved her face close to his. ''Back to where you said we wouldn't have met. Betcha you're wrong.''

He caught on pretty fast when it came to shipwrecks and women he loved. ''Betcha you're right.''

She said, ''Prove it.''

And he did.

Epilogue

She knew he was there, but refused to turn around. She'd heard him drive up. The old Land Cruiser was going to need a new muffler before long. Beach driving was rough on vehicles.

Imagine my knowing that, Val thought, amused. She turned slightly and aimed the stream of water on the other Cape jasmine. It got a tad more sun now that Mac had trimmed a few branches. Both of them were coming along nicely.

She felt his breath on her nape a second before she felt his lips. "You shouldn't be out here in this heat," he scolded.

Dropping the hose, she turned and let herself be folded into her husband's embrace—which wasn't as easy as it had been only a few weeks ago.

"Any luck?" she asked after being thoroughly kissed.

"Not yet." In his free time her husband and a local historian were trying to get a lead on a schooner that had gone down more than a hundred years ago in the mouth of Hatteras Inlet. Neither of them seriously expected to find anything, but Mac enjoyed a challenge.

"Ever the optimist," she teased.

"You bet. Look what optimism got me."

When he went over to shut off the hose, Val thought dreamily—she spent a lot of time these days in that state—about the fact that neither of their worst fears had been realized.

Which reminded her— "Will called," she said. "He insisted he doesn't want to impose, but I insisted right back. He can have the back rooms." Along with the rest of the house, those had been refinished and refurbished. "How good is he at painting ceilings?"

Mac laughed. They were finishing up the nursery. Marian Kuvarky had brought over a sack of baby clothes and offered to help with the trim. He had a feeling his stepbrother might be in for a surprise if Val's machinations bore fruit. He liked the real estate agent just fine, but he didn't know if poor Will was ready for any matchmaking.

"You hungry?" he asked, leading his bride of nine months inside the yellow house with the neat black shutters.

"Always," she answered with a ladylike version

of a leer. "One more month, and then six more weeks after that."

He chuckled. "Six inches or twelve?"

"Twelve. I'm starved."

They always had subs on Wednesdays. On Mondays and Fridays, Mac grilled fish. Val had discovered several new talents, but cooking wasn't among them.

"I joined another group today," she told him with a sly grin.

"That makes one for every day of the week. What's this one, Mothers Against Toe-dancing?"

She elbowed him in the ribs and adjusted the thermometer. The heat pump had been one of her wedding gifts from her bridegroom. "Genealogy, smartmouth. This baby of ours has cousins out the wazoo."

"I keep warning you, you're going to have to clean up your act, honey. Ladies don't use vulgar terms like *wazoo.*"

"Guess what else ladies don't do," she teased.

"Afraid to ask." Already grinning in anticipation, Mac tossed his baseball cap onto the coat tree she had found at the local thrift shop.

"Come on upstairs and I'll show you."

Besotted, he followed her swaying backside up the narrow stairway, thinking vague thoughts of sea sirens and tiny ballerinas.

Supper could wait....

* * * * *

0804/51a

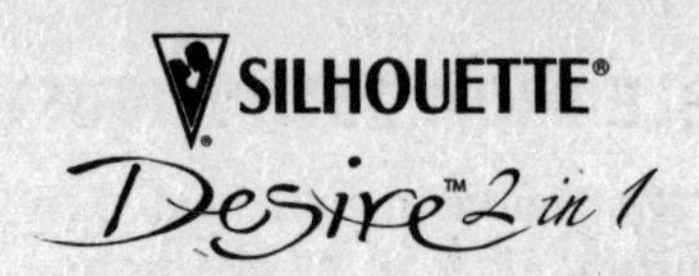

AVAILABLE FROM 20TH AUGUST 2004

EXPECTING THE SHEIKH'S BABY Kristi Gold

Dynasties: The Barones

Sheikh Ashraf and long-lost Barone cousin Karen Rawlins knew the marriage was only for the benefit of the child they both craved. But after one Arabian night she'd fallen in love with her husband.

BORN TO BE WILD Anne Marie Winston

Dynasties: The Barones

It had been thirteen years since black sheep Reese Barone had abandoned the woman he loved, and the last thing Celia Papaleo wanted was a reunion now. But one night in his arms and her passi was rekindled—until he told her his one little secret…

TAMING THE OUTLAW Cindy Gerard

When rugged Cutter Reno breezed back into town, his pride demanded he reclaim the one woman who had ever mattered. However, Peg Lathrop was now older and wiser and not going to allow her heart to be broken again.

TANGLED SHEETS, TANGLED LIES Julie Hogan

Settling in a small town with her adopted son Jem, Lauren Simpson thought she didn't need another man complicating her life. Posing a handyman, Cole Travis was searching for the son he'd never known—could this secret father find his son and a woman to love?

THE COWBOY CLAIMS HIS LADY Meagan McKinn

Montana

Bruce Everett was arrogant and wild, and his penetrating gaze had settled on visiting city girl Melynda Clay. Though Lyndie tried to deny the mutual attraction, Bruce was determined to possess her—body and soul.

SLEEPING WITH BEAUTY Laura Wright

Living alone in the mountains, Dan Mason couldn't resist a damsel distress—especially a violet-eyed 'Angel' suffering from amnesia. Angel may have forgotten her past, but she recognised Dan's loneliness and her own desire.

presents...

Cherokee Corners

by Carla Cassidy

Where one family fights crime with honour—and passion!

Last Seen...
(May 2004)

Dead Certain
(August 2004)

Trace Evidence
(November 2004)

0504/SH/LC85

are proud to introduce

DYNASTIES: THE BARONES

Meet the wealthy Barones—caught in a web of danger, deceit and...desire!

Twelve exciting stories in six 2-in-1 volumes:

January 2004	The Playboy & Plain Jane *by Leanne Banks* Sleeping Beauty's Billionaire *by Caroline Cross*
March 2004	Sleeping with Her Rival *by Sheri WhiteFeather* Taming the Beastly MD *by Elizabeth Bevarly*
May 2004	Where There's Smoke... *by Barbara McCauley* Beauty & the Blue Angel *by Maureen Child*
July 2004	Cinderella's Millionaire *by Katherine Garbera* The Librarian's Passionate Knight *by Cindy Gera*
September 2004	Expecting the Sheikh's Baby *by Kristi Gold* Born To Be Wild *by Anne Marie Winston*
November 2004	With Private Eyes *by Eileen Wilks* Passionately Ever After *by Metsy Hingle*

0104/SH/

SILHOUETTE

Sensation

Passionate and thrilling romantic adventures

NIGHT WATCH

Suzanne Brockmann